NICOLAS FREELING

SAND CASTLES

THE MYSTERIOUS PRESS

New York • Tokyo • Sweden • Milan

Published by Warner Books

Part One

Groningen

1

Van der Valk, police officer: middle-aged cop and more occasionally, gentleman. The proper euphemism is 'approaching
middle age'.

Used to be a big tall chap, and what is called rawboned.
These are two perplexing thoughts. He has the impression of
shrinking: also he had always thought that most people's bones
were raw. He has perhaps shrunk from too many years' cooking
in overheated offices.

There is, when one looks in the glass sideways, a waistline
too, no longer truly slenderform. Moral: don't look in mirrors,
even sideways; you're not a tailor.

The title in Dutch is Commissaris van Politie. People say
the Saris, as they do the Smeris which is a prison warder.
This word Kommissar has a bolshevik sound. In Holland it's
a senior civil-service official and there are different sorts. One
can be a Commissaris of the Queen, which is grand. Still, he
has an office, and a secretary; everything deserving of respect.
And he's quite well paid.

Right now, he was having trouble with his nasal cavities: a
tendency towards blockage. One could put that in police prose,
which is an administrative language bearing no resemblance to
the Dutch spoken in the street or in the bathroom. 'Adhesions,
of gelatinous, elastic and tenacious nature, hardening at point of
contact with air-passages and forming obstructions.' Brief, snot.
An April cold. Arlette, his wife (nastyminded woman) says
'You smoke too much.' Hm, there's nothing more hardheaded

and badmouth than the average Dutch woman. The French maybe are cattier?

I need a holiday. Haven't had one since uh, uh, since . . .

"Miss Groenendaal, would you look up, please, how much of my holiday entitlement I had last year."

You don't say 'Miss' in Holland but 'Juffrouw' which means unmarried-woman, irrespective of age or virtue.

Her name is Ria, short for Rita. The Dutch shorten this further to Rie. Since they then add diminutives to everything, they say Rietje, which means little-Rie. This is now longer than saying Rita. Back in the mists of time she might have been christened Margarita. Nigh on two metres high and never been anything but Rietje.

He has just thought of what he wants for his birthday. Looks out his notebook, in which is found condensed: criminal affairs – much personal autobiography – observations of socio-logical significance, etc. Writes down 'Shooting stick'.

The English have them. You open the top, insert the other (spiky) end into the ground, and rest your bum. You then watch racehorses, or people playing golf, or maybe criminals. He has a damaged hip, painful in wet weather, and in Holland it's forever wet weather.

"You've nearly three weeks." She never says 'sir'. The Dutch are democratic; when they say 'Meneer' they're being sarcastic. Like 'Meneer, would you kindly take the point of your shootingstick off my toe, please.'

Watching people shooting. One would wait a long time, since it is in Holland forbidden to shoot anything, especially birds. But there are too many people. One could always shoot them.

"Very well. I think I'm going to take a holiday, Rie."

"All right," kindly giving him permission. "Where you going?" The Dutch ask these abrupt personal questions.

"I don't know yet but being an experienced criminal inves-tigator am now going home to look into it."

The French wife is a little smaller, lighter, thinner than Rietje but still tall, blonde and noisy, passing thus unnoticed in Holland but for the nose, bony and high-bridged with an arch, sometimes called roman. Also the cooking which is not quite as heavy. One doesn't fart as often as in the real fatherlands-kitchen. But equally a hellhound; muscular, strident, given to personal remarks about her man's appearance, morals, and behaviour in bed.

"I'm not at all averse to this holiday idea."

Since getting stinking rich (which they do increasingly; a people gifted for commerce) the Dutch have become tremendous sun-worshippers. Freshly-boiled Holland-size lobsters are a commonplace hazard all over southern Europe. Arlette, being southerner, does not share this mania for sunburn. Indeed, like the Marseillais she will go double the distance, wearing a large hat, in order to stay on the shady side of the pavement. And van der Valk's nose flames; until cured like a kippered herring he comes out too in a rash, which he scratches, to the irritation of his consort.

There is still a long tedious argument. It's only April, but . . .

"Too hot, in Spain. Wouldn't say no to Dalmatia."

"Too windy."

"Sea too cold."

There will already be hordes of Dutch everywhere. Except of course in Holland. Now the north coast of Holland . . .

"Oh God. One might as well go to frigging Zandvoort."

A Dutch joke; this draughty seaside resort near Amsterdam (lots of sand) has the same reputation as Margate. Fat uncles wearing a handkerchief knotted at the four corners; fat tantes going for a paddle with skirt tucked into voluminous knickers; and vulgar postcards. It is no longer like this, since indeed the thirties, but then neither is Atlantic City. The Dutch when getting a bit jolly start to sing, banging the rhythm with beerglasses,

We're going to Zánd–voort, on the Zée! Rhymes with hay.

We're taking a Sánd–wich, and coffee Mée! Rhymes with bay. And the tempo is much the same as 'On the Bóard–walk'. And life will be peaches and cream.

"If it rains, you see, we're nicely close by and can whip home to dry our socks."

"Jesus, on a little pink bicycle."

"We'll go along the coast, you see. Hamburg! Lovely town. Or uh, uh, Denmark."

"I see. The sea, that is."

It doesn't occur much to the Dutch to go north. To the Amsterdam native (and he is one, born in the Pijp), this part of the world has as comic a reputation as Zandvoort and strikes a lot more terror. Unless you're interested in birds or something: there are lots of birds. Maybe seals. Bit early for seals.

You go up to the tip or *Kop* of the hollow-land, and from there over the big dyke, which shuts in the former Zuider Zee (south sea as opposed to North Sea: I hope you're following). The dyke is supposed to be turning this vast expanse into sweet water, and draining it eventually for farmland. The 'polder'; very flat but so is all the rest. Very fertile too, and farmers' eyes gleam when they think of all those cows.

Van der Valk says that there are far too many cows already. So are there far too many Dutch. It's not so much that we want less sex (which we quite like) as more discriminate. And stop wanking all those bulls off all day.

You then reach Friesland, also a great joke, where people have funny names and comic accents. Or so the Amsterdammers think.

Only one more problem and that is the Chief Commissaris, who when his attention is secured looks and listens, intermittently and with the deep suspicion all departmental heads entertain of everyone.

"Not ill, are you?"

"Bad nasal catarrh. Terrible constipation." It's only, really, that the old swine loathes the idea of anybody else ever going on holiday. One could see him trying to invent objections.

"What? Feel bound to say, a little consideration wouldn't come amiss." In reproof of all this brutal egoism. "Well, I suppose it's your funeral," as though it were his own.

There was the usual flinging into the back of the car of a great many things that one is convinced will be badly needed, and which stay there getting in the way while one searches for all the things which have been forgotten. It's at this moment too one's wife discovers the total impossibility of going on holiday because every stitch she wears isn't back yet from the cleaners.

Van der Valk is a potterer. The Chief Commissaris calls him 'unstructured'. Routines are unavoidable at work. Most of the policeman's day is spent doing the same thing over and over again. So off duty there's a wish to be untrammelled, and especially unregimented. You wouldn't have got him on to a tour bus or a cruise liner.

So if there's something he likes, he wants to sit and gaze; and if he's bored, there are peppery agitations. This makes voyaging in his company some fun and a lot of exasperation, because he will be wildly extravagant and then say suddenly 'We're spending far too much and we're going home tomorrow.'

Arlette, on the whole a sensible woman, has learned to cope with this: she leaves him alone a lot, and has her own interests. She is serious about Art, is a great consumer of maps and little guidebooks, and carts about in galleries and castles while he sprawls on café terraces, boozing rather a lot. Anchorage points are agreed upon. Very well then, I'll see you at that restaurant round about one, okay? At the risk of fury when, nonchalant again, she has gone off with both sets of car keys . . .

Details are lacking of the trip through Friesland. They'd be boring. There was a noisy, undignified squabble when both sets of car keys were lost. South Friesland, now best known for very big, very milky cows, was in the fifteenth and sixteenth centuries a place of great wealth and high civilisation, whose harbours traded all over the world. They are now silted up, like the Kentish Cinque Ports, sleepy little places with an alarming wish to be picturesque. Arlette roots about in museums. Beyond the dyke, the passage between the coast and the islands is called the Waddenzee. Now much polluted. He hears horror stories in pubs.

The islands with familiar names, Texel and Terschelling and Ameland, unseen but solid, reassuring places with houses and even roads, give way as one goes north to frightful sandbanks with uncouth names. One has no wish to go there. Nothing there anyhow but a few chaps looking after lights and buoys, other earnest chaps measuring the mercury levels in fish. An ichthyologist, mean to say, can be fascinating company over a beer, but somehow saturation level is fairly soon reached.

There is also the weather. As predicted it is cold, wet, and windy. It doesn't worry van der Valk; he rather likes weather. It will be much the same in summer, but the tourist is then deceived into belief that it might be warm tomorrow, sitting underclothed and blue and determined that deep down he's really enjoying himself. Wrapped in burberries and woollies van der Valk pokes with his stick at piles of weed and finds lovely sea-shaped pieces of wood while Arlette is being artistic in the museum in Leeuwarden.

They have turned the corner, and reached the town of Groningen, capital of the province of that name, northernmost corner of the kingdom of the Netherlands. Beyond is the Ems estuary, a fearful hole, and Germany. Oddly, he has never been in Groningen, and it's nice: a well-made solid town with some good buildings, an unriotous university, a comfortable feeling. There is an absence, here, of haste and greed.

"A sentimental remark," said the helpmeet, muffled by being nearly upside-down, which is what happens when you drop your lipstick in the car and it rolls under the seat.

"I am sentimental," remarked van der Valk, dallying with the thought that her bottom presented a tempting target.

"A police officer," reappearing, "shouldn't be."

"The word," he said in pedantic tones, "has become corrupted into a pejorative meaning. When Flaubert speaks of a sentimental education he means – "

"Yeah? Cut out the pig Latin," says Arlette. Unconscious quotation from Marlowe, who says as much to the Hollywood Indian, and adds 'I'm no school-marm at the snake dances', which is what van der Valk is saying, but less well.

"You don't mean sentimental then: you mean sentient. What you're being is sententious."

The trouble with women is that they have to have the last word.

Nightfall saw them back on the coast; a quiet, small seaside town with nothing of the resort about it. A place where people lived, in tranquil comfort. There was a smell of sea, a maritime smack to things, but only a vestige of harbour left: a creek, a little boat-repair yard shut for the winter, a few small yachts hauled on a slipway and sleeping on cradles until the summer weather comes to tempt out their owners. There would be a small increase in the population then – little notices outside boarding houses, saying 'Open at Easter'; wooden shacks where you could hire a boat or buy bait for fishing but shuttered up and lifeless: until Easter; until Pentecost. Right now, if you wish to – well, you can play golf. It was the English who discovered that these windy little places between mud and sand-dune are good for golf. See Deal or Sandwich.

There is thus a hotel, quite a biggish one, for the golfing weekenders, and it's open.

Van der Valk was delighted because it was an oldfashioned hotel of the kind he loved, with Biedermeier furniture. Heavy wooden chairs with over-ornate legs, massive tables with carpet-like oriental-patterned covers, little vases of flowers and big stainless-steel ashtrays; a smell of gin and of musty old gentlemen who sit reading the financial news in the papers provided on wooden racks. There was a glass of beer nicely served, sliced off at the top without cheating you with a glass that is half foam.

Their room overlooked the sea. Like all Dutch rooms it was overheated and a bit stuffy. He threw the window open and sniffed with enthusiasm. The wind had gone. It was still, mild, and fairly foggy: nothing to see but a coast light winking, far off: nothing to hear but an intermittent fog warning, further still. Tired from all the sightseeing, hungered from a faraway lunch, he felt a strenuous appetite. He had time indeed to work it up into a frenzy, because a man has nothing to do but pee and wash his hands. A woman wants to change from trousers to a frock. Fiddle with her stockings and redo her hair. Change her mind about her shoes; and again about her earrings. At the last minute, decide upon another pee. Her lipstick, which should be in her bag, was in her jacket pocket all the while. He contained his patience: one has to.

The diningroom made up for this. Starched white tablecloths and napkins in sharp conical peaks. Heavy pretty china with little flowers which he had to lift up (to look at the bottom to see where it was made). A quiet old waiter in a steward's jacket with gold-braided shoulderstraps: this is all very nice. And a really Dutch menu. Sighs of satisfaction; also from Arlette, who manages to keep her belly flat and the behind not too over-exuberant, but is always very good friends with the dindin.

Homely Dutch dishes. They have become difficult to get,

in public eating places. There has been a horrible tendency towards phony French food, such as the Dutch understand it (a national tendency to add little bits of pineapple to everything). They do not really understand food: the instinct is lacking which Belgians, marvellously, possess (when they can be persuaded to do their own dishes). The lunchtime special had been curly kale with sausage, but it's crossed out: none left.

"Kapucins!" said Arlette greedily. "With crispy bacon." It is a kind of bean seen nowhere but in Holland, though coming doubtless from Spain originally; like chick peas but much nicer. They are a dark brown (hence no doubt the name of 'capuchin' from the brown Franciscan robe), shiny from the hot bacon fat. With them come big sweet-sour gherkins, and finely chopped raw onions, and a lot of mild mustard: altogether yum.

Van der Valk is a fishy fellow, and there are Zeeland oysters, and there is halibut, and instead of the sauce called hollandaise which nobody in Holland can make, he'll settle for melted butter and lemonjuice and lots of parsley.

What is the purpose of these details? Only that they had a bearing on subsequent proceedings which turned out important. A day it had been – perfectly agreeable, nothing really to criticise. But pent-up with unseen frustrations and irritations. Have to admit, he overate.

He also got rather pissed. In the respectable sort of Dutch hotel one can get French wines and they'll often be very good. They are also extremely dear, and on the list he had found a German wine from the Palatinate at half the price, and it turned out so nice – perfectly dry while still pungently fruity; an odd, seductive flavour of grapefruit, strongly fancied – and of the two bottles gluttonously ingested he had certainly more than his fair share.

Arlette – my God, the woman's got hollow bones – has some sort of orange and chocolate confection on top of her beans, and moreover orders cognac for herself while saying he's had too much to drink. Awful cheek.

11

She also got into earnest conversation with a ghastly cultur-ally-minded German couple at the next table (in mid-week there were few people in the diningroom, and this is conducive to con-versation) who were telling her all about a wonderful prehistoric monument over there in Germany called the Something-Bride, which frankly he found very dull.

"I think I'm going to go for a walk."

"Do," said Arlette, one was bound to say pointedly. The Germans were strong too upon the merits and benefits of a digestive stroll while showing no sign whatever of heading that way themselves. He said something vague about exploring the environs; stumped off to get his leather jacket.

The fresh air made one feel slightly more pissed than one was in reality. But no denying, bit of brisk, bit of crisp, does positively no harm. It was quite cold. One should have put on a warmer coat. But how tiresome of women to shout after one 'Make sure you're warmly dressed.' There is no better way of ensuring that one only puts on a jacket.

So he hadn't gone more than maybe a kilometre and a half. Well, that is a mile. Along the sea front. And going back through inland streets it will be more. Say two and a half miles. Come, that is a respectable stroll for digestive purposes around ten at night.

It sounds so terribly boring. What could be drearier than the streets of a small town after nightfall, the raw wind reminding one that winter is not over yet? Anywhere else this would be the case. Enter two formidable elements in Dutch society.

First is their passion for electric light: the streets may be no better lit than in the remotest burg of central Texas, but inside a livingroom of twelve square metres it is a commonplace to find ten lamps burning. The Dutch don't call this wasteful; they call it cosy.

Second is the habit of not drawing the curtains, and living what anywhere else would be their private lives in an area lit like a stage set, and just as visible. You won't find here the tall

12

narrow window of France, occulted by heavy wooden shutters and not a chink of light to be seen. The Dutch like a whole wall of glass, kept shining clean, framed at the edge by curtain, so that from without one has the strange illusion of being able to lean right in and read a magazine over their shoulder, nibble their peanuts and share in their commentary upon the evening television programmes.

It is also a pleasant sight: the Dutch love flowers and exotic plants. Outside on the street may be nothing better than a shrivelled shrub or two, much discouraged by wind and small destructive children; but inside will very likely be an Amazonian jungle. There will not, you object, be monkeys, parrots, butterflies, jaguars, tapirs or anacondas. Very likely not but there will be the Dutch, instead.

Of no conceivable interest, you say, to someone like van der Valk, to whom this spectacle has no novelty? True, but he's the oldfashioned kind of cop; brought up to be nosy.

One has to keep this under control nowadays: was the time when cops went about lifting the lids of dustbins. The Dutch put up, through long habit, with a snuffling and rummaging into everyone's affairs that in any other European country would be thought monstrous. Cops seemed to have nothing to do but keep detailed diaries of every back-bedroom fornication. Commissariats worked cheerfully through long lists of dog licences, defective rear-lights on bicycles, and old men pissing against the wall on the way home from the pub. The State Police rode up and down the beach on horseback, to keep bathing costumes within the limits of permissible decency. All this has now changed. The Dutch have become liberal. Van der Valk, living through this revolution, took it easier than some of the elderly colleagues, clucking and tutting at thick dossiers of misdemeanour being dismissed out of hand by broadminded magistrates. There are places in the United States where you'll go to Fort Leavenworth for thirty years on account of a forgotten joint in your jacket pocket. In Holland you could be smoking three briar pipes full of opium at high noon and nobody will even turn round. But it caused frightful crises among the police – the old ones.

He wished he'd brought a thicker coat (this mist is chilly) when, turning a corner, he saw a row of windows showing an orangey light at street level behind *drawn* curtains! This meant a bar, and a place to get warm, and if there's a drink going too, he's on holiday, no?

Comfortable; this is relative. But warm yes. Not really pitch-dark; at least the barman could see what he was doing. There seemed to be an unusual number of whores for a little town this size: there was also the usual row of sad men escaped from their overpolished overdusted livingrooms, alone with their thoughts. As his eyes got accustomed to the lighting there was also a couple or two at the tables along the wall.

The cop look; it gets stamped upon one: around the eyes unmistakable, and what in the young is no more than arrogance and cynicism at the sight of so much greed and folly, becomes, once they pass thirty, etched in. It's an indifference, an unblinking watchfulness, and a patience. You wouldn't notice it in this lousy light, but whores and barmen are on the lookout for it. One of the girls leaned across the bar and whispered. The barman shrugged. He's not doing anything illegal.

Van der Valk wasn't interested either. He'd only come in for a warm. He undid his jacket, so as to get at least an imaginary benefit when he buttoned it up again going out. A glass of wine here will be plonk at a fancy price. So he'll have the sort of drink he only has when business or accident takes him into a place like this. Like a Jack Daniels. He'll still enjoy it. He just says 'No ice' and allows his eye to wander. It's a bar where business is done, quite a number of clever little traffics, because the business in drinks wouldn't pay the rent otherwise. These will be squalid, and fraudulent. But what does he care?

A man comes in to the bar. He is tall, well-dressed, confident. The whores look round with their 'Tu montes, chéri?' face and he gives them a disapproving, straitfaced look. "Just a cup of coffee," he says, and the barman repeats, "Just a cup of coffee," unnecessarily and rather loud. The newcomer glances round, and goes straight over to a table where a little man is sitting alone with a small glass of gin: the kind of little man who has always a small glass of gin. There'll be another, and another if somebody pays for it. Van der Valk wouldn't notice this little man, but for his being furtive when there's nothing to be furtive about. He sits roundshouldered, close in to the table, and hugged on his knees is a kind of briefcase. What's he doing this late at night with a briefcase? A man with a briefcase at ten in the morning is a traveller, planning his day's itinerary.

The barman brings the coffee, over-ostentatious. The tall man feels in his pocket to pay, asks perfunctorily whether the little man will have a drink. They are bare acquaintances; there was no warmth in their greeting. Well yes, says the little man, just a drop of fatherlands-comfort since you insist. So the tall man, who hasn't enough small change, feels in his breast-pocket for a notecase, extracts more paper than is needed for a gin and – yes – quickly and smoothly, while the barman drifts off with a ten-spot, there is a pass of larger money, and you wouldn't notice it but for the little man looking around. Being, again, unnecessarily furtive. It isn't the bland, trustworthy face of someone palming a card. It isn't crooked or weaselly. It's perfectly ordinary. But it does attract a cop's eye because it looks unstable.

Van der Valk couldn't see how many there were – two, three? – hundred-gulden notes. It's not a lot of money. He is wondering, idly, what one buys for it, while – still idly – thinking it's time he made a move.

What one buys is in the briefcase whose lip lies up against the edge of the table. Quite a large envelope, of that dreary beige colour one associates with forms-to-fill-in: income tax or a building permit. A cash-and-carry business, no cheques accepted. All rather amateur. It certainly wasn't drugs or the Russians. Quite openly, in a bar? Well, it could be an unimportant piece of industrial espionage. Not the highly secret new turbine design for the Dnieper dam, but quite possibly advance details of some local factory's new line. It couldn't be much, to be worth so little.

Yawning, he rebuttoned his coat. Outside, he stood for a moment, getting his bearings. Yes, the short way back to the hotel would be that way. The couple came out and passed him. The tall man went straight across the street to unlock the door of his car. The little man set off in front of van der Valk, going the same direction. Why not? It's just an ordinary street but plainly a main thoroughfare. There are two or three other pedestrians. Two women in fur coats with their heads together and a look of having spent an evening with the neighbours playing bridge. The street took a curve and there was a level-crossing over train tracks.

The Dutch are disciplined about level-crossings. No train was to be heard or seen, but the bars were down and a large yellow light blinked importantly, saying Wait. The little man with the briefcase, a rapid walker, stopped, waiting. The two women waited, van der Valk waited. All very Dutch. Nothing happened. The unseen train could be heard clanking slow and important, on its way into the station. Staring around while waiting, the little man caught sight of van der Valk standing there doing nothing, and looked, wondering where he'd seen him before.

A boy on a bicycle came pedalling up, dismounted and in the same movement pushed the bike past the gap in the barrier, himself after it and was through and across like a rabbit nipping into a hole.

"Hooligan," said one of the women loudly. And suddenly the little man tried to do the same thing. Goddamn, the train was ten metres away! The cop's hand, in a pure reaction of civic disapproval and no damn lifesaving involved, shot out and grabbed his raincoat.

"Dangerous!" said van der Valk, loudly because irritably, to an idiot.

The train passed, heavy and majestic, a sleepy face or two gawking at the windows. The light went off and the bars sighed upward. The little man walked fast. Van der Valk, chilled again by the wait, walked fast. The two biddies waddled on behind. 'Had to winkle out that ace of clubs' floated to his ear. The little man walked faster, and suddenly ducked into a side street of residential houses full of parked cars.

No, that is not good enough! Without either hesitating or thinking about it, instinctive as a dog, he turned to follow. There wasn't another soul in the street. Probably the television movie was not quite over, and in another ten minutes there would have been three yawning householders letting dogs out for a pee and checking their front-door locks.

The little man whipped around abruptly, swerved, and made to pass him on the pavement since the cars nose to tail stopped him stepping in the roadway. It was supposed to be sudden, and was both obvious and foreseeable.

He might well be middle-aged, not very solid on the gammy leg, a little out of breath from hurrying – even a tiny bit drunk again from fresh air on top of the Tennessee whisky – it was still too easy. The hard-swung kick in the crutch, telegraphed, became a shoe in mid-air which one catches hold of. When the foot goes up the cop gets his hand underneath and if feeling tough himself helps it further up, right up like a fancy footballer, a gesture which deposits the author in a heap; all right on a football field but on a concrete pavement might easily crack the skull. So he just caught the foot, held it, gave the chap a slight push, and over he went sprawling. And gave his head a bump, nothing bad but he must have seen a few bright winking yellow lights telling him not to rush because One Train Can Conceal Another.

"So now we'll see what all this is about." Van der Valk found a small gap between two cars, sat down on the pavement, looking to see there was no dogshit, and opened the briefcase. There was nothing but two more of the official beige envelopes, but these were quite fat. He put one in his pocket, got up, picked up his stick, which even if not a shootingstick could, if need had been, become a naughty weapon, and walked off back to the main road, leaving Tarzan sitting rubbing the back of his head. Why make any further fuss? He's on holiday. Above all he wants nothing to do with local cops, or robbers either.

Back on the main road there is a large school. Then there is a crossroad. Then there are two shopping streets: by a lucky hit he gets it right first time and two minutes later he's walking into that nice hotel, smelling stuffy and foody and of dusty carpets after the sharp misty sea air; feeling his pockets for his key and wouldn't you know it, there is Arlette still sitting chatting to that German couple, and what's more with brandy glasses in front of them.

"Did you have a nice walk?" brightly.

"Good grief," said the German gentleman (tall, grey, professorial) looking at his watch. "This is debauchery! Beddy-beddy, definitely." They were only up one flight; not worth buzzing the lift. Van der Valk walked up the stairs, studying Arlette's bottom on a level with his eye. He felt quite zestful. Was this the fresh air? The Jack Daniels? The bit of exercise? Certain is it, he gave no thought at all to the envelope in the pocket of his leather jacket.

"You didn't get cold?" asked Arlette politely, making rather a thing of getting the key in the lock – slightly pissed, it's undeniable.

"A bit, yes. But I'm nice and warm now." He closed the door behind him, turned round and found her standing there not quite sure whether on her knee or her elbow, and gave her a gentle push so that she flumped on the bed face down, in which position he had her skirt up and her knickers down inside a shake of a lamb's tail.

"Remember the Porter in *Macbeth*," she mumbled.

"Porter?" Mystified. What porter?

"Now stop these obscene games," struggling up dishevelled. "If you're going to undress me then do it without these loutish pleasantries." At home too she has one of the antique enamel plaques (stolen from the Netherlands State Railways) which say Please Adjust Your Dress Before Leaving. The Porter grumbling about the way whisky increases desire while taking away performance had got hopelessly mixed up with music-hall figures of fun; all those cocufied French station-masters, and Marie Lloyd. 'Oh Mr Porter whatever shall I do? I wanted to go to Birmingham and they've took me on to Crewe' . . . Small wonder that he had forgotten all about the envelope, and after delights achieved upon a proper level of concentration fell into virtuous sleep, peopled by dreams in which female figures absurdly costumed in the uniform of the Netherlands State Railways pursued him over level-crossings, with unmentionable designs in mind.

2

He hated breakfast in bed (Arlette liked it, on his days off) because of sharp crumbs getting under one's bottom and the coffeepot lurching about; but breakfast in a hotel room is one of the pleasures of a holiday. Needed is a table which will not wobble and two large comfortable chairs, found in expensive hotels. This wasn't expensive, being indeed quite shabby, but was oldfashioned. A comfortable, out of the way, easygoing little town. The chambermaid who brought the tray didn't look a bit like Brigitte Bardot but had a beaming smile and a warm goodmorning voice. There was a big coffeepot and plenty of butter. The coffee was strong and hot. Van der Valk was at peace with the world. There should, to be sure, have been a big sunny balcony overlooking the sea, but Holland is short on sunny balconies.

Arlette went to have a shower, promising she wouldn't be a minute which meant a good twenty. Sprawling, everything unwound, he poured out some more coffee and hunted for a cigarette. It is the best one of the day, though the next one, after shaving and brushing one's teeth, can be better still if there's no bus to catch; and he hadn't.

Where? . . . Oh yes, jacket pocket. Nestled in along with a largish thickish beige envelope. Ho.

The envelope didn't tell one much. As used by the administration. Income-tax forms, schoolchildren's reports. Perfectly plain. Nothing on it save in one corner an enigmatic scribble in pencil – *Ir Al. W'wg*. To be sure, if delivered by hand they needed no addressing. Anyhow, to a Dutch cop this is not enigmatic a bit. *Ir* is a title, like Dr. It means Engineer, and like Doctor can cover a lot of different professional activities. *Al.* is the start of a name. *W'wg* is easy because Wilhelmina is the name of the former Queen of Holland, and there is a Wilhelmina Street, Square or Avenue in every dorp in Holland, and this one was a Weg. No problem; he had information enough to deliver this envelope where it belonged. If so inclined.

Men turn sealed envelopes round and round in their hands, taking a deep interest in gum and postmarks. A woman says 'Open It.' He did so, carefully, with his knife, which isn't Swiss Army (too heavy for pockets, too clumsy, and absolutely useless for cutting one's toenails). Instantly he lost his peace of mind.

He made an instinctive movement of concealment, glancing nervously up towards the bathroom door because he didn't want Arlette to see this. Safe, still. He shuffled rapidly through twentyfive or thirty photographs, quarto size; carefully composed, brightly lit and of good clear technical quality. Clear they were; good they weren't. He whisked them back into the envelope, back into the pocket, picked up the forgotten cigarette, and sat back to think. To be fair, he didn't think 'That's spoilt my holiday.' He thought, as a pro does, point by point.

This stuff comes from Manila or Mexico City; anywhere you find children taking any expedient that might lead to a handful of rice or beans. This hadn't. These had the well-rounded, well-nourished figures and features, the straight fine hair of Dutch children. Which – quite a simple equation – doubles, triples – no, quadruples the problem. The children hadn't a clue; had the stunned blank look of children anywhere who have been manoeuvred – manipulated is the word – into this . . . There are few things in the world which make a cop's blood turn over after twenty years in the métier. This is one. Most cops if asked will say it is the first. And yes, van der Valk with his eyes shut is seeing red. The literal application of a wornout cliché.

"Eight is too late," he muttered viciously, coming out much louder than a mutter, because Arlette opened the bathroom door saying cheerfully, "Is that all it is?" Naked, hair pinned to keep it from getting soaked under the shower, she crossed cheerfully to the bedside, picked up her watch and said, "Yours has stopped, it's nearly nine." In front of van der Valk's eyes is passing a row of perhaps ten little girls and boys of between seven and eleven.

"An elementary school," he snapped at the for-once blank target of two nicely-shaped female buttocks, decidedly slim and tight for a woman of thirtyeight after two childbirths. And he'd never imagined that this sight would be downright repulsive to his eye. What after all is prettier than the sight of a naked woman wondering where she packed the clean bra?

"What? But I know I had three. Damn, now I'll have to pass by the launderette this morning." There you are: those are the domestic details you ought to be busied with.

"Now if you'll please see how you're fixed still for shirts – shit, hotels are always so mean with hangers. Some people will pinch anything. Tja, I can always find some at the Hema, I saw one in the High Street. Knickers one can always air on the radiator, it's these shirts of yours – what's the matter?" The matter is that he wants very badly to hurry on out of this. Get out of this country altogether. Get over to Germany. A long way. Next stop Hamburg. And he can't. Sex is for adult women.

"I've hit a horrible great snag." There's nothing for it; he has to show her. Reluctant, because this is not . . . He's oldfashioned. He does not believe that the eyes of an honest woman should be poisoned with – but women are a great deal tougher than men. She looked at the first two or three.

"That is enough," levelly. "Well, I can see a long story, both behind and in front, and I don't want to know. Or you'll tell me in good time. Just – why not turn it straight over to the local people? You are, after all, on holiday."

"Yes. The trouble is that this is a small town. This stuff was floating about rather openly, even if it was a coincidence that I – look, this sort of traffic is going on among the village bigwigs. There's protection involved. You understand – it might not be such a very clever idea to go to the local police commissariat."

"Are you meaning that they . . . ? Oh dear. But you could ring the inspectorate in the Hague, and explain that – no, I see, it wouldn't do. And might create even more delays. Am I right? – what you're telling me is to get myself out and away from underneath your feet and I'll see you tonight, and we'd better keep this room, and with any luck you might have some progress to report, is that it?"

"That is it."

"So I trot off and learn all about the local geology, and ethnology and uh – " failing to find a third and falling back upon, "Nice, I don't think."

"I have to learn too, and a lot more than I want to know," wondering why – not for the first time – the French like the Englishwoman has an impossibly high soprano in the speaking register. Arlette, it is true, possesses the deeper voice of a German woman, but when cross the squawk is that of a seagull.

She finished dressing, in a pettish style which decreased as she thought, until selfpity vanished. The hands putting in earrings framed a quietened face. She put on her coat, picked up her handbag, gave him a kiss and asked, "May I have the car?" like a good child.

"Of course," more decidedly than he felt.

"Then perhaps rendezvous at dinnertime this evening? Right here?"

"That will be best." She couldn't quite stop her heels tapping a sharp female tattoo down the passage, until her feet reached the stair carpet. Largish feet, but she's a tall woman. Aggressive in Italian walking shoes, hardly the thing for a day's sightseeing but he recalled that she had boots in the car. Her feet throw out a little at each step; she has a balanced, elegant walk. Shapely calf-muscles clenching and relaxing, bony knees and ankles, unusually long thigh-segments so that she's taller standing than she is sitting down. A good dancer; invariably gets angry because he hates to dance – unless very drunk.

The chambermaid put her head round the door and said, "Sorry, I thought I heard you going."

"Give me five minutes." To concentrate. He didn't like to carry those photographs about; they burned his pocket: but he had nowhere to leave them.

He had felt shocked, and disturbed. The shock is that he has children too: it is a blow in the diaphragm, paralysing and painful, but the effect is not long-lasting. A police officer, of necessity, has seen most of the world's dirt. Indeed it is a nasty job, with hands in the shit. You get used to it, just like a nurse, because you learn detachment. The senior officer becomes isolated, by his age and rank. He gets squeamish; he is not on the street enough.

How provincial of me, he thought, to be surprised. If shown those things in Los Angeles or Marseille . . . it's the happening here, in this dusty corner of a tight, righteous little land, which took me aback. But how absurd. As though battered wives were only to be found in Argentina, cocaine smuggled only in Colombia. Black beetles come out too upon scrubbed kitchen floors. One moment and get that right (his mind has gone back to police school: he has been well taught).

Chamfort had said, 'One runs the risk of disgust when observing the cooking process – of justice, of administration, or of food.' Had his finger on the spot, the old boy.

Porn is just porn, in still photos or eight-millimetre home movie. Comes in scruffy variations of sado-maso-scato, but is still a bread and margarine deal to any cop. In may come charging the business executive from Grand Rapids, demanding that you discover the whereabouts of his daughter. Well you know, Joe, she'll have been set to work, likely. We'll show you a few faces.

But child prostitution . . . All right, take it step by step. It has always existed, and that goes for Dutch provinces as for ancient Egypt.

Because there are always keen admirers. It is a wellknown and welldescribed pathological condition, and the modern attitude is sane; this is a matter for psychiatry and not of punishment.

If only it were that simple! Children have been lured and entrapped, and that meant abuse of confidence by people in responsible positions. That is a grave crime, under the criminal code. The cop looks for orphanages, institutes for backward or perturbed children; scouting movements. Highly respectable places.

It comes expensive and this means corruption: a lot of that money goes to grease palms.

It implies protection too, and often highly placed: because the fan club contains notables, people with important positions and high reputations, and around these people must be built a barrier. A barrier of silence. The world is full of noises unheard; among them what a journalist 'making a phrase' once called the steady susurrus of doffed knickers. His own first instinct had been the same as Arlette's: to dump the nasty packet on the local cops and tell them to get on with it. Wouldn't do. Not in as small a town as this.

The chambermaid was about forty. A kind gentle face. A housewife part-timing to help out the budget at the month's end She might well have two or three children.

"Where's the Wilhelminaweg, can you tell me?"

"Oh it's over – quite a distance – but if you've got the car – "

"M'wife's taken it, I'm afraid."

"Oh. Well, you go down to the bottom of the main street and turn left when you come to the canal and then you take the first bridge over, and it's not far then."

"Have a little street map then at the desk, would they?"

"They might," dubiously. Well well, he has cop feet and

25

they're made for walking. But closer at hand perhaps he has a little man, and that might be the place to begin.

For the little man was plainly the runner, the go-between or hinge of this sort of operation, where there has to be a link between the production and the consumers. It wasn't a big, practically world-wide affair like the trade in drugs or arms: there at the local, street-side level, it is quite easy to lay hands upon the smallscale distributors but very difficult to get further up the pipeline, because of the huge sums of money involved. Instead of the furtive little man shuffling about a dockside in Marseille you run your nose against the bland and impeccable façade of banks in the Bahamas and holding companies in Liechtenstein. This was a local black market, a cottage industry. Or so he supposed; so he hoped.

One didn't know for sure, because these things can run like dry rot behind a panelling or under a floor. There could be a sophisticated traffic reaching Germany – the border is only a few kilometres away – running down through tiny Holland into Belgium and France; up to Hamburg and Denmark . . . and if anything like that came to light he'd have to make a telex to the Inspectorate General in the Hague (Haguey as Arlette frivolously refers to the sober and pompous administrative capital) and then – and then Mr van der Valk's holiday is shot down for good and sure.

But if the dry rot has only reached the borders of this little town, and if this stuff is only distributed by hand, distrusting the mail – then the hinge is the weakest part of a door. You can lift it out. Or you can kick it in.

A small town; you could cover it on foot in a couple of hours. So you can be relatively optimistic. Twentyfour hours, or well – he has lost much of the morning, so say fortyeight. There is a temptation too to forget the whole thing and disappear.

No, that is no longer possible: Arlette knows. Nor can one shuffle it off with a written report about 'I have coincidentally uncovered a trace which might . . .' They'd come back at him very smartly with 'In that case why didn't you investigate it?' A lot they'd care about his leave! Unanswerable.

A distressing thought occurred; that once upon a time, some few years ago, an odd but unpleasant outbreak of anonymous letters had resulted in his being sent to a little town not much larger than this, some way to the south. And he'd been stuck there for months. And furthermore he'd uncovered more than either he or his superiors wanted. That was the way of these things. You find a loose thread, you pull it, and it runs like a handknitted sock!

That had been a gloomy little town, in the neighbouring but dissimilar province of Drenthe: a discouraging place because poor, a land of sour bog and heath, and people to match.

Whereas this is good farming land hereabouts. His spirits rose as he looked about him.

A nice little town, and nice because of trees, and trees spell civilisation anywhere. Up on the sandy dune which protected the village from the sea, there were of course no trees, unless you counted the few windwarped and scrubby conifers which could survive the salt blast. But the moment you were inland the street sloped down into a hollow, making a nest for the original settlement. Not a lot of shelter but enough: they'd planted trees and looked after them, and these were not the scraggly wizened oaks of the heath country, but noble trees, which had got their roots into honest soil and held on. His unpractised townbred eye (Amsterdam is woefully short of trees) looked at trunks a metre across. In their winter dress, bare of foliage, they did not allow him to make identification (oak yes, and ash, and thorn). Could this fine avenue, worthy of a far bigger town, be limes? Their bareness – it was the end of March and they were just waiting their chance to start – only added to their beauty.

27

The High Street made a T-junction with the coast road near to where his hotel stood, and ran inland, more or less straight for most of a kilometre. Wide! and in this lay its character and pleasure, for the houses, as always in this part of the world, lay low and humped like hedgehogs, crouched to the ground, wind- and rain-swept eaves hanging over them in curving bellshapes. There are, to be sure, some very ugly hard-edged modern houses too. But even the ugliest, the chain stores and banks and insurance companies – even the shinyfronted horrors respected the scale of the trees, which had been set well back from a road wide enough for modern traffic even when there had been nothing but carts: and inside the line of trees ran broad pavements, from which in turn the shopfronts sat well back. These restful proportions were not, naturally, repeated in the new streets to either side, which were as mean and cramped as anything one could find in Holland.

It was a blustery day, typical of the mad month, with large white clouds in full sail across the big horizon, their edges blown ragged by the relentless wind – but it was a westerly wind and not too cold, and large lumps of bright hard blue sky sent the cloud-shadows chasing in giddy patterns. Nobody of course will trust this for more than an hour; least of all van der Valk, much buttoned in to a trench coat and topped with a hat. The slightest veer into the northeast, and the cloudscape would go dark grey, the rain – certain by lunchtime – would change into wet sleet and bucket down. But for now, and one counts one's blessings from minute to minute, the sun shone, and everybody was in a bright and smiling frame of mind.

The town hall was halfway down; a simple square building painted white, a roof culminating in a bell-turret (to call the fire brigade in older days), and the ugly modern annexe tucked away behind, where it was less noticed.

A Dutch town hall is a little civil-service heaven. One must remember that they aren't servants: nor are they civil. Civilian if you like, in the sense opposed to military, but still an army,

ruled by regulation, hierarchy and caste. Not for Holland the
easygoing, gossipy, quite friendly atmosphere which in Latin
countries masks the iron determination to do nothing. Nor
is there the madhouse feel which comes of being lodged in
barracks built for the Hungarian navy, a Napoleonic military
hospital, or the erstwhile municipal lunatic asylum, before they
moved it outside the town and surrounded it with laurel bushes.
It's all very neat, smells of fresh paint and prissy righteousness,
and like so many computers creates an illusion of efficiency,
until you come to ask what it's all for.

Van der Valk is at home in such places. Here information, of
amazingly detailed kind, is to be had about the population, and
little maps too. The Wilhelminaweg is the good district, where
people who are not nouveau riche live in villa-type residences
with little gardens of their own and nice neighbours. Engineer
Albinga at number 25 is a considerable wheel in the administration known as the Rijkswaterstaat: dykes and canals and
drainage of the hollow land. He works at the provincial headquarters in Groningen, has a wife and three children between
teen and university ages, is a pillar of the community and active
upon committees of many a good-works nature. Scouting, did
you say? Orphans? What exactly is the nature of your interest,
Mr uh – ? Oh, of a purely statistical nature? Deprived or delin-
quent children? Not here actually, though we can of course put
you in touch with the relevant provincial authority.

You can be nosy about pretty near anything, but this encour-
ages their own nosiness, and while you can burble away about
confidential statistics and selective Ministry interest in social
studies, to maintain discretion you end up knowing a great
deal more about municipal civil defence precautions, in case
of the Russians coming or the nuclear power station blowing
up, than you wished.

Schools, yes, of course; now the evacuation plan in case of
an alert, graded to the nature of said alert, covers – oh, you just
want schools? Oh, I see. Well, the Protestant one, the Catholic

one, the non-denominational one (this is all very Dutch) – and then the secondary mixed-grade, and in the neighbouring commune the technical training-college, and let's see, in Groningen of course, the train and bus services are specially geared to – sure, sure, all on this map here.

Almost next door was a camera shop, and on an impulse . . . but alas there was only a tiresomely thickwitted girl and sorry, the owner, yes, but he won't be in before lunchtime and if it's the new Pentax then it'll be in today or tomorrow but what we have, look . . .

But further down, over the crossing with the flowerbeds and the war-memorial, he hit upon another, bigger camera-shop and here there was a helpful gentleman, so helpful that van der Valk had to invent a hideously lame tale of a man met on a train and a mislaid address. Let's see, a keen amateur technician? Yes indeed, he and the colleague up the hill did all the professional developing, wedding groups and – as for equipment he thought he could safely say that he himself – and yes there would be two or three keen fans, I wonder could it possibly be Mr Strijver, what did he look like, the gentleman in question? "My memory for faces . . ." said van der Valk cursing silently.

Well, not to say stout, but quite thick set? Of course, laughing heartily, sitting in a train across the paper cups of coffee one gets into these conversations, I know it well.

The over-helpful are more of a burden to the enquirer than the over-reticent.

"I wonder," risking the long shot, "I do seem to remember his saying he had something to do with schools." Oh yes, delighted, that will certainly be Mr Strijver. Darkish complexion, longish dark hair, he's the director of the Huizinga School. Keen nature study man, and what was the precise area of your interest, Mr uh – ? You see, we're very well equipped for fine-quality work, let me just show you . . .

And van der Valk, who knows as much about cameras as about civil-protection precautions (in fact a good deal less)

•

30

has an appalling job to extricate himself. But this is a commonplace. Shopkeepers are well used to their customers being
mentally deficient to startling levels.

He went into a pub to recover over a beer, and do some
homework on his map, and spy out too a place where a
lunchtime cup-of-soup is likely not to be too vile. Because
the morning has leaked away but there are bits and pieces
here that don't seem too unpromising.

Now where was he? Turning off the seafront, somewhere
round here . . . The railway line of course: that must all have
been open countryside when the railway was built, so that they
were stuck with a crossing over the main road – yes, there.
And there was a school at the next, I recall it distinctly. Yes,
Huizinga School. Good doggy then, you've found a scent.
Because when one thinks about that little man . . .

He had been afoot, the little man. The other joe in the bar
had a car parked opposite, one recalled distinctly his climbing
into it. But the little joe hadn't a car, nor a bike, and since
it wasn't likely that he'd gone out for a digestive stroll after
rather too much dinner, then it's heavy odds he lives there in
that quarter. Which is residential, those tight little streets of
semi-detacheds. And while alarmed at having been indiscreet
in the bar – hence the absurd effort at putting a train between
himself and a suspected follower (in a dangerous way showing
a pretty bad conscience) – not so alarmed he couldn't make a
little plan: so he knows those streets well: he'd worked out that
it would be deserted there at that time of night.

I should have run him in straight off, for an attempted
mugging which is common assault. Why didn't I? Would have
saved a lot of trouble.

Or would it? If I'd steered him along to the local police
bureau (which I noticed in passing, up the top of the High
Street) then they'd have gone through his pockets, and it would
have been a night-duty cop who found the envelopes, and then
it could have been a shower of shit hitting a high-speed fan,

because to prefer charges I'd have had to identify myself. No, it's better this way.

But I have as yet no evidence whatever against the no-doubt-intensely-respectable Mr Strijver. An amateur camera-hound keen on nature study. We have to link this gentleman up, and for that we need the little fellow. Let's go and look at this school. It's nigh on eleven-thirty, and school will shortly be out, and there might be something eye, ear, or nose can pick up. Come to that, I can always eat in the hotel. Though there ought to be a pub too, around there somewhere. Exercise and a beer are giving me an appetite.

Mr van der Valk sallied out, intent upon his spoor.

The children were streaming out, racing and twisting and jostling and shrieking in the high clear voices with which they greet release from constraint. The shrill echo bounced and clattered in the narrow bricky street. They formed up in a knot at the corner crossing. Two seniors, sturdy fairhaired boy and girl of eleven wearing the white crossbelt of traffic wardens, held the mob back on the pavements with their staves, waited till the traffic slackened, marched out to the centre of the road and held their staves out at arm's length, the red and white circular discs at the tip crossing: a barrier understood by all of Holland. No policemen are needed outside a school, no fussy ladies; the children themselves control and discipline the street.

Inside the yard the bicycle racks were emptying fast, the solid, high Dutch bikes that look too big for their small riders; the child standing on the pedals and thrusting to gain speed, turning on to the path that lines every Dutch street: no sight more typical and none more moving. The children are the gauge of our survival and nowhere does the message come with more impact. It may explain why van der Valk, a

32

wearied, bored and often cynical cop, had been so hideously shocked by the envelope found in his pocket.

Standing outside a school he is struck again and always by the immense gap separating us from the prewar years, for here too this is nowhere more apparent. He is not old – but he feels so old. Born as he was, in the nineteen twenties, he had gone to school in the depression years. He is tall, strongboned, even massive, but he had been one of the children of his time, thin and pale. He was the son of a small jobbing woodworker and joiner in Amsterdam's old-south district, who made most of his living repairing chairbacks and table legs, replacing shutters or rotting windowframes, and not always paid for it; a taciturn man, small and thin, proud of his son who was bright, going without to pay for the school extras for the boy. Holland, by an odd piece of fortune, was spared the war of fourteen–eighteen, but the men looked just like the soldiers one sees in old photographs, massacred by the hundred thousand on the Somme and the Chemin des Dames, the sharp scrawny little men, narrowfaced, sucking their bad teeth, average height five foot six, so that one wonders how they humped along on foot with those monstrous piles of equipment.

The soldiers of nineteen thirtynine looked and were no different. It doesn't do to imagine that they were like the tall brawny figures of guardsmen and the SS. They came out of the back courts of slum Berlin and London, Paris and Pittsburgh. But the generation which has grown to manhood since is twenty centimetres taller and muscled like Joe Louis. To us, pathetic old men shuffling about, they are frighteningly big. The girls are a metre eighty as often as not and would throw us over their shoulder as easily as they lift a school bag. We're not likely to go about raping *them*.

Two children belated in the gateway were squabbling because one had got his bike pedal entangled in the other's spokes, and noisy abuse was being freely exchanged. The janitor, a small man of van der Valk's age, darted out of his lodge to

33

yap at them in the voice of authority, looked up, and caught the cop's unwinking grey eye: level, unhostile, placid. Terror spread across his face the way a grey raincloud driven by a Dutch wind spreads over the sun. So extreme a terror that he stood there frozen in the unchanged attitude of wagging finger and bullying forearm, while the two boys mounted their bikes and rode off noticing nothing, and the two men stared at each other across the dusty entry where the concreted schoolyard met the unmortared earthbedded bricks of a smalltown street in Holland.

So there he is, the little cronky man – and found so surprisingly easily. It hits the cop with a gust of cold wind – that they should be so open, so confident.

Terrified because astonished at being caught, pinned down, so quickly? Not quite knowing – over halfway certain, but still in doubt whether this is a cop facing him or some street sharpie who has accidentally got into the act and sees profit in it? Having told nothing to the man who owns him? He had been too frightened and too prudent to admit his loss of that valuable envelope. All last night and all this morning he has been turning over in his mind how to go about that, hoping for the best perhaps, hoping that the man who opened that envelope would keep it for himself, saying nothing? Or, perhaps, feeling the wave of shock and repulsion, throw it away or destroy it, trying to blot it from his conscience?

But this was all speculation. Van der Valk need do nothing but stand there and look, and wait to see the reaction. Terror made for obstinacy. Standing there and shouting like a drill sergeant would only make him more rigid.

The cop stood loosely, hands in his pockets, produced a winning smile and said softly, "Come and have a drink."

The man looked irresolutely back at the lodge, and at the same second a shrill female voice called, "Jan-Gerrit. Jan-Gerrit!"

"Your dinner's ready. So tell her you've a bit of a job,

and she'll keep it warm. Little drop of fatherlands-comfort. I'm paying." A second's irresolution, before he darted back in. Van der Valk waited quietly, knowing he'd be out again in a moment.

He didn't have anywhere else to go.

3

There was a biggish café on the corner, very Dutch, with the glassed-in verandah and its clean tables, each with the carpet-patterned oriental runner, the stainless-steel ashtray, the four Heineken beermats, the little vase of flowers. Standing there the neat waitress with thick white socks under her shoes, hands clasped under her apron on the change-purse slung in front of her belly and giving her the pregnant look. Welcoming. But of course Jan-Gerrit wasn't going to sit out there where everyone could see him. He whipped in past the bar to the darkest corner, where a languid shirtsleeved waiter, the seat of his black trousers shiny even in that dimness, said "Moyng" languidly, made a pretence of flicking ash off the table, nodded vaguely at a vaguely-familiar face and said, "What'll it be?"

"A beer," said van der Valk cheerfully, "and yours is a small gin, am I right?"

"So now," settling himself to be comfortable, "you don't smoke, do you? Let's hear all about it. Your dinner won't spoil – what is it, meatballs? And if she's curious, bear in mind that I'm a lot more so. Commissaire, Criminal Police. So you're up shit creek you see, Jan-Gerrit, and your one chance is to come squeaky clean here and now." And the little man tried to bargain.

"What proves you're who you say? . . . Well, I did nothing," staring at an identity card. "I had to follow my orders."

"That's what Adolf Eichmann said. They hanged him just the same."

36

"Yes, but – look, suppose we make a bargain. I'll tell you what I know if you give me immunity. I can help you but I stay anonymous, all right? That's fair."

"You can help me, yes. You'll tell me, yes. And you'll tell it all again to the judge, and he'll decide about your immunity."

"But look, I'll lose my job."

"Your job, mate, is past tense. That was a position of trust. Children involved. You know that. Nothing for me to say yes or no to. Speak out now with no evasions and it might count to your credit later on. Any hindrances and I'll have you in the cell. And that before the local cops have finished their own cabbage, all right?"

Van der Valk just sits; dazedly. He has had two beers. The cronky-man has had two small gins. It is an hour later. The waiter has come asking if he wishes to eat. Yes but . . . He had better eat, though. A pompous menu has been brought, which he hasn't looked at.

It hadn't been like that when he went to school . . .

Came then, as usual, the self-indulgent reminiscence of what it had been like. Everyone can sentimentalise about the good old days. But if honest, would anyone really wish to be young again? Live through the bad moments a second time? A fine romance, van der Valk, and you are as cold as yesterday's mashed potatoes.

"The veal," he said to the waiter.

Wartime too. Freezing cold, in his memory, and never enough to eat. We wore our fathers' old clothes cut down to size, and our hair was cropped for lice. Schools were not inspiring places. The smell of little boys, of chalk, of pipi – come on, this is a bad prelude to eating lunch. The strongest memory was that left by the maths master who could draw perfect circles, freehand, on the blackboard.

While the schools today (whatever he'd been given to eat, he wasn't noticing it) . . . We hear nothing but complaints; that the children learn nothing save how to racket their juniors, and to traffic in every undesirable commodity.

Greatly exaggerated: the schools are sunny, relaxed places, and the children are happy there. No repeating of multiplication tables, every tot of eight equipped with a calculator. And they have drama classes, dance classes, nature-observation – it struck him: might they have a photo lab? Large numbers of extra-curricular activities, and he had better go back to school too, as well as doing his homework.

Heavens, his own primary-school director, an overbearing and rotund individual with unpleasant breath, known to the girls as Desiderius and to the boys as Beerbelly Bart; forever gassing on about 'respecting the scholastic programme'. And now this one, so appreciated by the doting parents for his imaginative enrichments of pedagogic method. Enrichments, you-said-it. Children staying on late, so handy for the working mums, or coming back in the evening for art-appreciation and the rehearsals for the concert.

He could understand how the fellow put the parents in his pocket. But how did he make so certain that the children would keep silence?

Well, of course (yes, he had time still for a cup of coffee) they might keep silence, but it was the *Flucht nach vorn*, the escape forwards. Keeping that knowledge locked inside them meant that the children would show – very probably were already showing – perturbation; psychological violence on a widespread scale. It would be quite certain that a parent, puzzled at fierce, incomprehensible destructions and savage sulks, would be running to the child psychiatrists. Who would already be eyeing rather keenly a Dad or two, suspected of incestuous affections.

All that he himself could do would be to precipitate matters – and once more the temptation rose up, to forget it, to mind his own business . . . But no. It wasn't just another-naughty-scoutmaster and a handful of corrupted children. What about Mr Engineer, licking his lips back there in the Wilhelminaweg? And who knows how many more? And the conniving. This is known to half the regiment. He sighed; drank his coffee; paid his bill.

He didn't know, and he didn't care, how the janitor had prepared for his coming. Probably again the 'fuite en avant' – Meester, there's a man at the desk, pedagogic materials, films and stuff, sounds pretty interesting, shall I send him up?

Jan-Gerrit met him at the lodge, greyfaced (he hadn't enjoyed his dinner but neither had van der Valk). You'll remember, won't you, that I was never any more than a go-between? Yes; I'll remember.

A nicely furnished scholastic office, brightly lit with sunlight; pretty vase of tulips. And of course a man of impeccable respectability. The English say of a sly child that butter wouldn't melt in its mouth. The French that 'you'd give them holy communion without looking'. So plainly too an able, charming, cultivated man. How on earth had he come to lock himself into . . .

"Do sit down, won't you. Tell me how I may be of service." Not a traveller in videotapes. Perhaps the parent-needing-reassurance had been the role cast for him. Little Johnny is a child needing special attention.

"Let me introduce myself; van der Valk, Commissaris, Criminal Investigations, the Hague." Pretty good: not an eyelid did he bat. "And let me come straight to the point. You are engaged, have been engaging, in the traffic in child pornography."

"Preposterous. Impossible. In the highest degree insulting. And a gross slander. For which, make no mistake, I shall not hesitate to call you to account."

"Your porter has been taken in flagrante delicto."

"Commissaris, you must see that the man is an unstable neurotic, trustworthy in the small matters that are the condition of his employment, but no further. He'll say anything, to exculpate himself."

"Doubtless. You're a keen camera addict, the shop in the High Street tells me."

"I won't tolerate this. I will not listen to it. I must ask you to leave on the instant, if you wish to retain dignity."

"Married man, Mr Schrijver? I should think you would be, in your position."

"I must warn you, Commissaris, if you are what you claim, that you are counting perhaps on my inability to call a police officer to have you put outside. You are mistaken. The local inspector is a close personal friend and he may be able to recall you to a sense of what is proper to your position."

"Yes, I was afraid of that. He'll feel the wind, you know."

"Not a further word will you get from me. Upon reflection," stretching a hand towards the telephone, "my legal adviser will be best placed to take note of whatever you are imprudent enough to repeat in the presence of a witness."

"Perhaps you'd prefer it if I repeated these imputations in front of your wife? You haven't a hope, you realise, and she may as well know now."

It happens in interrogations that suddenly, to quote Alfred Lord Tennyson (approved school author), the mirror cracks from side to side. The-curse-has-come-upon-me cried – I forget who, but always good for a laugh from the schoolgirls.

"How dare you?"

"More to the point, how dared you? A point for the psychiatric expert, whom no doubt the Officer of Justice will wish to call into consultation pretty well instantly. I had better tell you that I've quite enough authority to have you taken out of here in handcuffs. Or shall it be at your private address, in the Hortensiastraat, am I right? It will be better for all concerned if we do this discreetly, since I am naturally concerned to protect the children as far as may be possible. Make your mind up now." The mirror cracked, and the man burst into tears.

There's a lot of loose talk, about compassion. Mr van der Valk is wary about improper usages of the word. Etymologically a bit sloppy, like empathy, um? He feels sorry for people, and sometimes he feels hatred for people, or contempt, and it has all of it very little to do with the job. One has these long lists of people to be sorry for, from widows of those assassinated in Argentina to folk suffering from that wellknown disease of the computer multiplying their phone bill by ten.

Bloggs here blubbers about his lost honour more than did Katharina Blum. But we won't introduce loose factors like noble/ignoble. We'll just do our work.

"It's going to be painful," spreading photos in a row across the meticulously kept desk-top. "No anaesthetic. I have myself two boys and an adopted girl, a bit beyond this age group. You will be dealing with magistrates, family men as I am. And others, doubtless also family men, became your customers. Not only Mr Albinga from the Rijkswaterstaat, but since you were so confident, feeling so thoroughly protected, we might find a canton judge, or a commissaire of police? That will be for the Hague to worry about.

"Little Sandra here, sucking off a man whose head is hidden and whom you will identify for me – you're an able man, with training and experience. I think that you were pretty skilled at picking vulnerable subjects – both ways. Little Micky here, yes, it's called fellation in technical vocabulary, looks to be her brother.

"We're going to go back to how you came to start. Nature studies, mm? Trees and plants and heaths and the shadows on prehistoric megaliths. And naked children are very healthy, aren't they? Open and balanced, that's very Dutch. Shadows of rocks, highlights on flesh tones. Pedagogically valuable. You had the complete confidence of the parents. Healthy and innocent. Little Sandra on a summer's day, what could be nicer than to run around naked? – she's only eight. And little Micky, lovely child, natural athlete. Something so spontaneous about these unformed muscles, so plastic, yes?

"And here we have little Marlene. Innocent! One day in the gymnasium climbing those goddamn ropes, blabbing out that she enjoyed that, gave her such a nice feeling between her legs.

"Very nineteen-twenty, all this. There were lots of schools which encouraged the brats to take their clothes off. So good for them, such a healthy contrast to church schools which sewed up the boys' trouser pockets so that they couldn't fiddle with their dicky. Paralysed with inhibitions. But you never know, with a man, when you might hit a weak spot in him. And then modern parents – they get this idea too of freeing children. Walking about naked in their own house. One of the birthday presents that central heating has given us – thank you, Shell Mex. Children chatter at school, and make up these little rhymes. Daddy's got a wee wee, Mummy's got a cunt – obviously a skipping rhyme, that.

"But when I call at your house, Mr Meester, I have the idea I won't find anything at all like that. I think I'll find a very strongly inhibited woman who can hardly get her own clothes off even with a can-opener. That's our Dutch society for you, half of it busting to be modern and liberal and the other half still screwed tight into a calvinist nineteenth century; and it's a bad mix."

So that's it, is it? The job is done? Is it hell! That nasty part, yes: the breaking of a stiff wooden upright man. Van der Valk has talked his head off, feels flat as a filleted plaice. One of the Roosevelts, Theodore rather than Franklin, said to a journalist complaining about prolix politicians 'Jaw is better than War.' What was he supposed to have done? Put the man across his own desk and jump on him with both feet to break his spine? Big macho policeman.

"Time now to ring your friend, the inspector of police."

42

This gentleman was alarmed at finding himself faced with an official from the Hague. A Commissaire, to him, is a Kindly-call-me-God. In his own village he may be God-calls-me-God. But not in the Hague.

When he saw the photos on the desk, and the weeping man, he became (favourite word of Henry Kissinger's, another wellknown GCMG in his time) discombobulated.

"Oh dear Jesus." Van der Valk drew him tactfully aside.

"Take him out of here. Clap him in the cell. Make damn sure he doesn't hang himself. Put all this under sequestration. The home – he may have done darkroom work there too. All the lab material. The porter may have the sucker list. He was completely under the thumb of our friend here, dependent for his job. Look him up; he may have a criminal record. Subject to blackmail in any event – may have been touching up little boys himself. The wife you'll have to handle. Then you get on to the academy in Groningen, tell the rector to send a replacement, to sort out the senior staff here: they may not be entirely clear."

"Commissaire . . . try and believe I had nothing to do with this."

"I am trying," said van der Valk soberly.

"I can do what you tell me. But I realise what you realise. I have to ask to be suspended, pending an enquiry. I was friendly with . . . him here. I can't present him to the Officer of Justice."

"No." Another toad to be chewed up and swallowed. "I'll talk to the officer. I'll want one of your men to drive me; I've no car."

"Yes, of course."

It wasn't at all yes-of-course.

In the legal system of the Kingdom of the Netherlands,

the Officer of Justice is a key figure; an amalgam of a French judge of instruction and public prosecutor. He examines persons against whom the police believe they have a legal case, and decides upon the weight of the charges: his is the responsibility for putting them before a court.

He didn't say 'oh dear Jesus', though he plainly thought it because he jerked at a ballpoint pen so that it flew clear across his office and clanged against a radiator.

"When the press gets hold of this . . . Commissaire, plainly you have a case, and I do not shrink from the consequences. But this is terrifying. How in the world does it come about that a man in a position like that . . . ?"

"Salami."

"I beg your pardon?"

"He sliced the salami so thin that nobody noticed. Decided that parents were failing in their responsibility. Little Marja and Natasja, little Roland and Diederik need proper sex education. Parents aren't modern. Little widdle grows into a big nasty Thing. Sweet little pink infolded seashell, big furry cunt. Thought to be traumatic."

"Come on, this is rubbish."

"Of course it is. But there he is, being all pedagogic about what bulls are for, and behold, his own little widdle, which stays so obstinately limp with poor old Zwaantje, starts standing up when he is at ease and comfy with little Anita."

"Van der Valk, do you believe this, because I'm having . . . "

"That I'm telling myself stories? But how else? Obviously we can't have Johnny's dicky touching hers because that's indecent and gives them ideas."

"Commissaire, children have been playing mothers and fathers since the beginning of time."

"Just so, Meneer, and I learned it that way and I dare say so did you, and well I remember too some dirty little sneak running to a schoolmaster yelling Meester, Meester, the boys are taking the girls' knickers down, and how he came pelting hotfoot. This one showed her his own. And I'll just touch yours with mine to show you how it goes. Bonnet was over the windmill then. And he went on slicing salami. Yes, I am mixing the metaphors, aren't I?"

"This is pure hypothesis."

"Sure," wearily. "It could have gone the other way round. Some of these parents are a sight too modern. Little Billy looks to see what's that funny noise and lo, there's Papa giving it to Mama, so he says to Nelly come on Sis, now I'll do that to you. Schrijver finds out, says no no, that's naughty, that's incest, I'll straighten you out."

"The imagination of the press," with nausea, "will be more extravagant even than yours. And as for the public . . . Van der Valk, how many people have knowledge – guilty knowledge?"

"That, Meneer, is going to cut down some tall village cornstalks at a guess. I have only the one name."

"Commissaire, the local inspector is of course to be suspended pending enquiry, but I don't want this bruited abroad. I'd be glad if you could . . . "

"I'm on holiday, Meneer. It was my duty to isolate this man and to bring the matter to your notice. That's as far as I go."

"This man is for me; it's all I ask. And then we say no more, you continue your holiday, and I'll see to it that your conduct becomes the subject of an official commendation." This is referred to as 'pressure' by senior functionaries who would be appalled if you were to tell them bluntly it's blackmail. How else would one entrap, say, a municipal official? 'Look, Joe, this is dodgy but pretty juicy, and we'll see to it that you do all right . . . '

"A detail, Meneer. You'll likely want to impound the man's bank account. Even on a local scale that stuff comes expensive."

"It is well thought of, Commissaris."

The Wilhelminaweg was posh, more than he had expected. Apart from prosperous farms, the wife in gumboots with a wheelbarrow but a shiny big Mercedes outside the door, this had been a poor countryside – but no longer. Here lived owners and chief executives of handy little factories making the cardboard boxes and spare auto parts and plastic thingummys which gave employment, distributed wealth and supported shiny shopfronts or lavish garden centres. Here was not the suburban semidetached, but architect-designed bungalows with terraces and barbecues and expanses of velvet lawn. Quiet assured by a dead-end street where the driving-school did not come to practise three-point turns, and a great many burglar alarms. Fake antique fantasies were in evidence; the thatched roof and the leaded stained glass: the rustic look was in favour but the people inside didn't go shit on any bucket. And this one was quite secretive for Holland, set well back behind tall thuya hedges. Mr Albinga was home from work: a long Audi coupé sat in the driveway. Perhaps he has married money.

The married money opened the door to his discreet ring; a very handsome blonde lady with expensive clothes, a supple figure, too much paint about the eyes and an over-insistent perfume. A smile to match. The voice too, deep and warm. All very hostess.

He raised his hat and murmured something about private business.

"Come in, do." Hallway, with grandfather clocks and either antiques or expensive reproductions. "My man is just in. He's under the shower," laughing at this comic notion. "So I'll put you in here, shall I, and ask you to excuse me – kitchen business," with a wink.

She went lithely off leaving the door open. He could

hear her voice on an interphone, but not enough to catch the words. Some fellow on business, darling, looks civilised enough. He had been back to the hotel to change into the respectable suit, to go with the persona of the Man from the Hague.

The room was in pale pastel colours; if you do drop the peanut-butter sandwich it doesn't matter, we'll get another. A pretty oriental carpet, soft pinks and silvery greys and leather upholstery in a creamy beige going with the curtains. Lots of flowers. Some bits of metallic sculpture, of the sort which bring to mind the line of Chandler dialogue:

'Asta Dial's Spirit of Dawn.'

'I thought it was Klopstein's Two Warts on a Fanny.'

One or two largish abstract pictures, chosen for the bright colouring rather than merit, if any. Jazzing up the décor. A lot of money. Even if he'd married it – what did an engineer in the Rijkswaterstaat earn? Van der Valk had no idea. More than a commissaire of police. A lot more. The room was in decorators' good-taste. It showed no individuality or intelligence but that meant nothing: you don't get this sort of job without plenty of grey matter.

Still, it was a little surprising. This was a world distant from the prim and stuffy bourgeoisdom of the Hortensiastraat.

He turned. A big, fair-haired, smoothfaced man came lounging soft-footed in at the door. Large straight handsome features, good teeth in the same over-warm smile as the wife. An expensive indoor tracksuit in a silvery grey corduroy matching the carpet.

The totally relaxed expression of satisfied comfort, like a pure-bred cat but for the pale shrewd businessman's eyes. Well, we'll see to straighten him out a little.

"Pat Albinga." Patrick in Holland is a snob name.

"Van der Valk," accepting the big smooth paw. "Commissaire, Criminal Investigations." Not a hair turned.

"Hereabouts? Don't think I've had the pleasure before."

47

"No, from the Hague." This usually potent second barrel made no more impact than the first.

"Really? Lots of friends there too. What'll you have to drink?"

"Perhaps not just now."

"Nonsense, man, of course you'll have a drink. You don't look like a man with an ulcer to me. Tequila, Polish vodka, grass or buffalo? I know – there's a good thirty-year-old. Chivas is for the man who comes to read the meter. We don't put ice in this – spoils the flavour."

"An envelope addressed to you came into my possession," nodding thanks for the thick-bottomed tumbler. "Your property?" bringing out the handful of photographs.

Albinga was taken aback properly this time because he gave a casual glance and broke into a huge laugh.

"Don't tell me you've pegged that awful little Schrijver! I told him he was sailing too close to the wind. Bucket of spray in his lap and more in his mouth! Yo ho ho, must drink to that!"

"This is serious."

"Serious for him no doubt – nasty little beast."

"Possession could be serious for you too – grave criminal offence. Have you thought about that?"

"Strikes me that you're the one in possession. No no, I'm joking – drink up then, there's plenty more. I don't mind your trying it on, that's your job. But let's be serious, possession is nothing at all. Looking at photographs isn't even a misdemeanour. You'd have to prove distribution and sale for profit, and that's no skin off my nose."

"And what about debauchery of minors?"

"No no, dear man, I don't figure in any of those elegant nature studies."

"And what about non-denunciation, collusion, and failure to come to the aid of persons in danger or distress?"

"Let's understand each other, Commissaire. By hunting up

the small print in paragraph four subsection thirteen, and going to a lot of trouble, you could no doubt cobble up some miserable little skinnymalink of a charge and drag me into court. Some pinpricking paper, you waste an hour or two of my time, stick me with a magistrate who looks over his glasses and raps my knuckles. That doesn't worry me at all. I ask you seriously, is it worth it to you? You seem to me a man with better things to interest him."

Van der Valk drank some whisky.

"I don't think that coming into court on that sort of charge, and some pretty black tar sticking to you, would do you a great deal of good professionally." And got another roar of laughter.

"Man! I'm a chief engineer in sea-water and sea-bottom conditions – tides, currents, offshore work, anything you like. As things are I'm quite happy. I have freelance consultancy jobs, which in no way infringe the conditions of my employment, with half the oil companies in the North Sea. I don't do badly. But say the word and I could skip tomorrow. Abu Dhabi, Sultanate of Brunei, whatever I want. I ask you again, is it worth it to you? Sure, you could smear me with the press a bit, some nuisance value. Got your little recorder on, have you, in your breast pocket?" Quick fingers and some comic clowning mimed the offer of a comfy little bribe. The nuisance value wouldn't be worth anything spectacular. Ach what . . . say a nice little fortnight with the Club Med? It wasn't the moment to be the constipated little civil servant.

Van der Valk stretched his legs, smiled, drank more whisky.

"I've no recorder. Your offer doesn't interest me. You tell me you feel comfortable in your skin. So do I, and I've no envy of yours. If that stuff's a joke my cock's a kipper."

A grin in recognition of this homely army expression, a dismissive movement of the thick goldbraceleted wrist.

"No need to be tightass, the Japanese hand out this stuff to raise a giggle at the sales conference."

"So much the worse for them," van der Valk bellowed suddenly. "Snigger as you please. That's not for men. That's for the elderly impotent with cancer of the prostate. You like that and I vomit all over you. Here, take your glass. I don't have to frig about with you, you're not worth a penny of my time, I'm on holiday. The Officer of Justice gives this to the press, you'll have the neighbours throwing bricks through your windows. You'll sell this house tomorrow and take a dead loss on it. Now go explain it to your wife."

"Gently gently," said Pat, not taking any offence whatever. "No need to get spiteful. That's all nonsense and you know it very well because if the nastyminded populace caused damage to my property the law would have to make it good. My offer stands, it's a good one, think it over, don't get het up. As for my wife, you caught a glimpse, mm? Call her in, try her out. I won't take any photographs," laughing. "I'll go for a walk, leave you in peace. To echo your army phrase she's hotter than a fortyfive shooting downhill. You'll like it. Cash tomorrow before lunch – tell you what, make it deutschmarks," for all the world like Soames Forsyte at an auction, muttering 'Very well then – guineas.' Go on arguing: perhaps he'll make it Swiss francs.

To van der Valk's mind (certainly he was amused: maybe he was even a little bit seduced) came the classic reply of the nurse, when the fisherman very kindly offers to go to bed with her – 'Not if you were to scrub yourself with soda for a week first.'

The woman had been listening outside the door. She came in without affectation. Didn't sidle, didn't bridle; picked up the decanter and poured herself a drink. Quiet balanced movements which restored calm. She drank half and said, "Pat, whyn't you go look at the football match, hnn?"

She waited until the door shut, took a cigarette from the crystal box on the table, came across for him to light it, thanked him politely, perched on the arm of the sofa, nothing exaggerated. It was as smooth as though rehearsed. There was the soft clonk of the front door, the snick of car door. The motor purled softly. Came the grate of big tyres on gravel, the change to a brick surface, the rising note of acceleration, the sigh of gear change, the fade into silence.

The pendulum of the ornately worked brass clock could be heard ticking. She didn't say anything, didn't change the pleasant, sociable expression. Unhurried, she slipped off the sofa, went over to a writing desk and rummaged in pigeon holes; came back with a cassette, clipped it in, altered the screen angle and said, "This will be nicer than that dirt you boys have been poring over." And while he sat there like a jelly on a dish, there she was on the screen: he didn't recognise the music.

"The point about this is the double image," stubbing her cigarette out, posing beside the screen, slipping into a dance rhythm. "Mm, I'm a really oldfashioned exhibitionist." Starting to unbutton.

Now was it, as promised, the contrast between the artificial triviality of the television screen and the reality next door it? That it was her own livingroom? The amateur, private-show manner? That she was deliberately exciting herself? He wouldn't have looked twice, in a bar, and here it was unexpectedly potent. If blancmange is too soft when turned out upside-down, it will disintegrate; disastrously. He should never have let her begin. How did he go about stopping her, without an unseemly brawl?

Compose the face to a polite indifference. As when the dentist, finding it deeper than expected, suggests a little touch of novocain. A tiny prick inside your mouth. Quite, but it's this other prick which is causing you trouble. Nothing more ridiculous; besides vulnerable.

Van der Valk recalled the other pictures, the cause of his being here. Now that is serious, and this is no occasion for trifling. To no avail: this was no child in front of him. He can also recall that Arlette – when sufficiently tipsy – has sometimes been persuaded into a similar performance, with results ripely comic. It is not so much that this woman is rather better at what she is about, but simply that it's a different woman.

He was suffering from male vanity. Nobody's been castrating you then, have they? You aren't some kind of faggot? No, I thought not.

The best description of this idiotic situation is that left by Chester Himes: how Iris manages to get the cop who has come to arrest her to take off all his clothes and put a paper shopping bag over his head: she cuts holes for his eyes . . .

Maybe you would do well to get your ass out of here. Trouble with that notion is these Jello limbs. And the hard core, there in the middle. It's all too much like that sentimental Hemingway hero who finds himself all alone there at the end of the book with his broken leg and his machinegun.

Now come on out of it. Port main! I'm not going to die in a place like this.

She had got pretty close too, and had nothing left on but her knickers. These were an unexpected help, being a tarty model in black. He got hold of the rope, pulled his best, got his mouth open.

"Can you push the button now to make it go backwards?"

For Arlette has a really perverted habit, of reading crumpled sheets of newspaper in which the vegetables have been wrapped. These are mostly torn from a popular Dutch newspaper which has a nigh-whole damn page of brothel advertisements. The Dutch are completely down to earth about bordels; an institution which flourishes, it seems at times, in every mildmannered suburban street. Competition is thus fierce. The charms promised are advertised with a very Dutch literalness and absence of euphemism, full of waterbeds and leather. Arlette who should be washing the cabbage is instead reading these in a glow of expectancy. The houses don't as a rule attract the notice of the police, and he doesn't know much more than she reads aloud. 'I know about wet sex but what d'you think can be ice-cream sex?'

"Darling," van der Valk is now quite happy, "I'm a bit disappointed. Here was me thinking I was going to get the lesbian mother-and-daughter act" – by now on offer pret'near anywhere. She shrank as though slapped and he got up. That uncomfortable prominence had ceased from embarrassing.

In that steely evening daylight from the big window to the terrace, standing he can see her clearer than from the low armchair and with the light behind her.

She is standing there out of countenance, because her tape has run out and so has she. She is momentarily derailed because she is stark naked and her 'And now' has been switched off and she is vulnerable under the level hard grey sky and eye. He is not sorry for her now when she is just another naked whore with the rings on her skin left by a bra strap and her knicker elastic. Plodding off down the street he will begin to feel sorry just a little . . . a small shred of pity for a wife of thirty-six or seven who thought she'd stay young forever. Lots of sex helps to keep you young, they say. The harsh light shows her a bit soft in the jaw and neck, just a scrap slack-titted, just a hint of bulge between thigh and buttock; just a wee crinkle of lines above the neat pubic triangle. Ach, silly girls, who need to stay forever nineteen and have fewer years than footballers! Even to the heated eye of the traveller seeing only what he wishes to see – only hard boyish little bottoms and elegant proud breasts – they get that jaundiced look so very quickly. All the bordel adverts have little footnotes 'New Girls Wanted'.

4

He had still a job to do and wasn't looking forward to it. The Mimosastraat: ever since the time up in Drenthe – closest he has got to this corner of Holland – it was his name for the little bricky housing estates in grid-pattern. You can see right through them, because of the immense windows front and back, to the identical house in the parallel Dahlia-street; and through there in a vertiginous diminishing perspective to Anemone-street. Here the Dutch live their blameless lives, their conscience as clean as their windows.

The big, the outstanding difference between the Holland of today and yesterday is that the omnipresent calvinist sense of sin has disappeared. Van der Valk thinks of the huge, ominous notices formerly to be seen in railway stations. *Misbruik Zijn Naam Niet*: Take Not His Name In Vain.

He was looking for a symbol of this fundamental change in mentalities. He found it, in the Dutch cigar; then as all-pervading as the Dutch Reformed Church, now practically disappeared. Indeed a lot of people would say that smoking cigars was rather more sinful than fornication.

One saw also a great many windmills (which had pumped the water from the land below sealevel) and unspeakable millions of tulips (a flower which speaking personally he detests). It was all the fault of the Metroland area between Amsterdam and Rotterdam, which is what the tourists see: a land whose drainage had been completed only in the nineteenth century, and whose sandy soil is peculiarly adapted to flowering bulbs.

Come up to the heathland of the Veluwe in central Holland: there isn't a windmill in sight and all the frigging tulips are safely corralled in flowershops. But seven men out of ten would have been smoking a cigar, and the same up here.

Vile cigars for the most part too they had been: of a pale grey inferior smelly tobacco from the colonies. The bourgeoisie had better blends, a bit of South American leaf added to the Sumatra, but the plebs smoked the pungent product universally known as a Stinkstok; holding it – almost universally – in the very centre of the mouth, like a baby's dummy. Which in more ways than one it was.

And Holland stank! This smell pursued one everywhere, even on the street. Oh yes, very much a symbol of macho male domination. While the other, less seen and less smelt, but powerful symbol of the same had been the Calvinist Reformed Church. Particularly here in the north. The war had shaken it. Communications – roads, the telephone, the television set – had diluted and weakened it. And of itself it had dried and withered, so that nowadays you would have to go to the reactionary back-woods of the United States to find the real biblical intolerance in which Ingmar Bergman grew up. Like the stinkstok it had become an anachronism.

Well, you could still smell the cigars here and there. A few obstinate elderly gentlemen maintain the old tradition. And you'd still detect the smell of Calvinism too. Sexy old boys! Greatly given to tumbling the farm girls as well as breeding hordes of children from their unfortunate wives. The female was something to be pushed over, and have its voluminous skirts lifted, as often and as vigorously as time and energy allowed. Which was on average four times a day. This sounded exaggerated since one had also to allow for cigars and heavy meals; but in a sixteen-hour working day they found the time. And work they did!

Your modern Dutch citizen doesn't conform to this folklore. The craggy farmer, adam's apple and brass collar-stud, clasping the pitchfork, smelling strongly of the dungheap, pale blue eyes glaring about, seeing Satan everywhere save under his own greasy waistcoat – this is now a mildmannered clerkly fellow, a bit shortsighted from computer printouts; and not a cigar in sight. His children, probably two, neither in the least interested in farming, sit over their school texts (a bit roundshouldered) and roll themselves a shaggie because factory cigarettes are too damned expensive.

And what, of the Calvinist church, has stuck, still; there unseen, within? Mm, the police psycho would be quick enough to point to the bordels. And since these are quite unconcealed one has to make efforts to add flavour (ah, the cigars had flavour) to the business. The flavour of the forbidden.

The psychologist, in Holland, feels indulgent towards these goings-on, which is why the police interfere very little. Ach, why shouldn't they spend their money on a few childish games? Less dangerous to the health than smoking cigars (all the houses advertise safe-sex), less destructive of domestic peace and content than gambling.

Van der Valk no longer feels quite so sure. These reflections (more properly enclosed in a little balloon labelled 'thinks') had floated above his head during the twenty-minute walk back from the Wilhelminaweg to the centre of the town. He rang the bell in the Mimosastraat. It made – predictably if one had bothered – a set of little chimes.

"Police officer, Mevrouw. Will you allow me to come in?"

Ach the poor, unfortunate woman. Yet one didn't say 'I haven't the heart to give her a bad time.' To give her a bad time was what one had come here for.

He had not predicted the chimes. But he could have, and just about everything else. The house, and a house belongs to the woman, was a textbook of convention. Her hairstyle, her apron, her shoes . . . she'd even wrung her hands. Before answering the door she'd made him identify himself on the intercom. She'd undone many bolts and chains. There'd never

be enough of them to protect her. The police, like the fire
brigade, make more havoc with lives than either burglars or
a fire.

The people of Holland are intoxicated by fashion. They can
be led to change all their household furnishings at the behest
of this god. And do, on average once every four years. This
household had been conservative. The good pieces, inherited,
had been supplemented by assiduous hauntings of the junk dealers who style themselves 'antiquaires'. Not that it makes much
odds. After the cycles of fashion have run through twenty years'
variation upon Modern-Style they always come back again to
the furniture Granny lived with.

She was of course terrorised. The local police had come to
her door, laconically informed her that her man, that pillar of
society, was under arrest and being held at the disposition of
justice, been too prudish to tell her the charges, and the poor
biddy had sat here watching her house disintegrate around her.
Aged six, van der Valk had learned that polished hardwood is
beautiful however debased the design. That Friesian sideboard
– magnificent – dissolving into a heap of dust: the termites have
come.

Pathetically anxious to please. Cups of tea, glasses of gin.
I know a man always likes a cigar! (Three tiny ashtrays with
pictures on them of ladies dressed up like Marie-Antoinette.)

"Tell me, Commissaire, tell me! I must know."

What was he to tell her? That the Zaans clock, swinging,
ticking, was telling the last moments of her life? It is all in a
poem by Jacques Brel, and one line is enough. *Le petit chat
est mort.*

"The present charges are pretty bad. Possession and dis-
semination of pornographic material involving minors. That,
ex facto, is bad since by the nature of his position, in loco
parentis . . ." Stop mumbling shreds of legal Latin like the
witch-doctor. Yes, woman, well may you try to hide your face
behind your hands.

"It will be worse, if evidence comes to light that he was himself engaging in sexual intercourse with girls or boys under age. With this in mind I must recommend you to allow a house search. It's either myself – and I'll show as much discretion and respect for your privacy as the circumstances allow me – or the local police with their warrant duly signed by a magistrate.

"But first of all – thank you, Mevrouw, I prefer my own if you'll permit – I'm bound in law to interrogate you. So that I must ask what knowledge you have of these practices?" And her answers – broken, scattered, rambling, inconsequent and irrelevant – all the '. . .' of typographical convention, since nobody could get it on to a printed page, except the court stenographer who has to. He made one or two feints of writing in his notebook, but all he wanted was the rough sketch, so that he could telephone the Officer of Justice and say 'Here's the picture'. That gentleman would ask all these questions afresh, and a great many more, at much greater length. And have children been coming here to the house, Mrs er – ?

The stuffy sinless atmosphere: he has the feeling that he's getting no oxygen at all. Let me for God's sake get out of here, and go back to rejoin my wife. And breathe please. North Sea air.

So there was nothing but 'to make the most of it'. Arlette grabbed her bag. Mean to say, one storms out in a flounce, thoroughly cross. This is a holiday, is it? What sort of consideration is being paid to me then?

But what then? One can't keep up with a flounce, in solitary state. And there's no going back. Business is business, say the men. Male logic! And utter rubbish. Half of it time-wasting trivialities and the other half a woman could do better. It is always the women who are accused of gossiping on the phone: if they were to listen to themselves for once!

I can see, in all justice, that coming across something perfectly horrible, by sheer bad luck, he should be shocked and disturbed, and has instantly this fatal itch to do something about it. But if the man is not satisfied with the local police, and I do see his problem, with a racket like that existing almost openly (being furtive does not guarantee secrecy; we've just had the proof) – then why not go straight over their heads to the legal authority for the district? Saying the simple truth: 'I have accidentally uncovered a nasty traffic, it's your job to deal with it, here! I wash my hands of the further proceedings. I'm on holiday and my wife's waiting for me outside and the car's on a no-parking zone.'

Instead one is told to run along now, and amuse oneself for the day.

Hm, Groningen. It isn't exactly Paris or New York. Still, it is the capital of the northern province, it has the oldest university in Holland after Leiden, it does have some civilised resources. There would be for example a picture gallery, which might well hold interesting – no, she didn't feel in the least inclined to look at pictures, nor any archaeological museum, nor indeed anything except to make a nuisance of herself. Be egoist! Like King Louis XIII (unattractive character) saying to courtiers 'Come, let's be bored together.'

She could be a good mother, and do some doubtless badly-needed shopping for the children. Without even thinking about it the boys needed new trousers because boys always do, and doesn't Ruth keep saying how short she is of underclothes?

Didn't want to spend a day haggling over boring underclothes. Didn't want to be a good mother.

I look after my children, they are well brought up. So doubtless are most of those unhappy children in the hideous photographs. How many children are happy? Can their happiness be made to depend on a good careful bourgeois upbringing? Probably the chances are about even. Do our well-fed, well-clothed, well-educated, fussed-over children of

Europe have better chances of real happiness than in some notorious centre of child pornography like Bangkok or Manila? Why are we so shocked? We are surrounded here by profoundly unhappy people.

I could, thought Arlette, take a conventional female vengeance. Since I hold the family finance here in my handbag I have plenty of money. I can start by going to have my hair done in leisurely and extravagant manner and then spend a great deal on things for myself I don't really want. And I won't do that because I am a southern woman, a Mediterranean peasant; hardnosed, closefisted, terribly distrustful and very, very economical. I sit for hours, patching the children's jeans, when I could perfectly well go out and buy new.

All true. Arlette was all of these things. As a young student she had flown her independence flag by going to Paris. Being extremely intelligent it had taken her a long time to learn that intelligence is not enough. It is a commonplace. She had learned detachment, which is a rarity.

These women, typically, are tough, durable and hardworking. They are generally faithful, and passionately loyal. As generally, they are ignorant, superstitious, narrow-minded chauvinists. Exactly like the men. Arlette had been very *frondeuse*, a French word dating from the social unrest during the childhood of Louis XIV. A *fronde* is a sling; fires stones harder than you can throw them. The word is used loosely to mean being agin' everything, and especially governments. It is thus highly paradoxical that Arlette should have married a respectable government servant like an officer of police. Especially a Dutch one. It was a frondeur thing to do in the first place, and she's had plenty of trouble coming to terms with it since.

Physically she is not pretty and would never think of herself as anything but plain: she does have some very good features. Might even be proud of her hair. She is looking at it now. It was washed but she has decided to get it cut a bit and that of course means having it washed afresh. It is thick, fine, and that rusty blonde which isn't red and isn't auburn and is generally called venetian. It is also straight, which causes a lot of grief. The eyes that go with this are supposed to be green. Hers are not really green, apart from being too small and too wide apart (more grief). A lot of green eyeshadow is supposed to help and does, she supposes: rightly. The nose is that highbridged kind called phoenician. One sees it in the Marseille area. Very striking, indeed beautiful, and she thinks of it as perfectly hideous. The mouth is wide and a little too thin, the ears are wellshaped (but a bit too big) and there is a lot (too much) of jaw and obstinate chin.

The other excellent feature is her lovely carriage (generations no doubt of Arab women carrying pots on their head): she is straight, supple (the neck is fine) and there is a free, peculiarly graceful walk. The man, a trained observer after all, says that this is a very great rarity indeed. When he saw her first, in a striped cotton frock (Prisunic, not even Marks & Spencer) walking along the Rue de Vaugirard, among the drearier of Paris streets, it was the walk which smote him: he has stayed heavily smitten.

She has never slept with anybody else. Whether he can say the same, subsequent, mm, to marriage, is a fact known only to himself, and probably he's told himself so many lies that he's come finally to believe in them: men are like that.

Arlette's further adventures during the day are not worthy of recall – she enjoyed her solitary day. Since her hairdresser, a very nice, sensitive Dutch homosexual in a lilac smock with an opal ring, had made an unexpectedly good job of her hair she feels – miracle – pretty.

'Yes, I've two children and one adopted.'

'All I can say is that you wear well.'

Yes, there's that to be said for her. Getting a bit lined but it is wearing well. The legs are good, strong-calved and gazelle-ankled; a banality among southern women but one can still be grateful. And there are these unusually long thighbones.

This makes up, even if the fake is obvious, for my breasts being too small and my bottom too big.

She's feeling, in fact, damn sexy. This she supposes is the effect of a) being on holiday; one ought to feel sexy on holiday: and b) a few recent fantasies of the Man: well, why not live up to it a bit?

She has thus given way to selfindulgence. Instead of buying jeans for the boys, and sensible white cotton underpants for Ruth, in the Hema (the Dutch version of the Prisunic, and there's a perfectly good Hema at home in the Hague), she finds herself in front of an exclusive lingerie shop and walks in.

True, the Dutch taste, in Groningen as elsewhere, in dainty underthings is deplorable. The man's taste, formed in furniture by his carpentering father, is austere. It would be no different in Marseille: she rejects utterly the whory horrors. But hallo, the good ladies of Groningen may be inclined to thickness but. The discreetly-corseted vendeuse digs in her bottom drawer, comes up with something extravagant. But they're well made, well cut, will wear well. The man deserves them, and so do I. Never mind the shocking price: he'd pay more than that if he were to start haunting the bordel. White ninon, and quiet as a nun. Though such thoughts, it is to be hoped, do not enter the minds of those holy women.

She did also have an adventure, even if it would have made the police smile tolerantly.

Arlette, rather tired, was walking in the park. The sun had come out, cagily; there were moments of warm sunshine on the bench. She was in her sundayish get-up: the wide-swinging 'good winter coat' and 'the good boots', said to be lizard. The family fortunes are in a crocodile handbag.

Never in a million years would Arlette have worn furs. On this subject, one hundred per cent behind Brigitte Bardot; and one is glad to say, ninetyfive per cent of Dutch women are behind her. So that the crocodile handbag, the partly-lizardy boots, one a Christmas, the other a birthday present from the man, aroused heart-searchings.

She sat on a bench and watched the sun of a northern evening, oblique in a pretty dappled sky: at least she had learned to love the northern light. Beginning to feel chilly she trudged along the path on a vague compass course towards the car. She had seen the boy on the bike but was also vague about this. It is forbidden, to be sure, to ride bicycles inside the park. In a university town one might as well tell people that breathing is forbidden. Awareness increased suddenly and disagreeably when the young man came up abreast of her, reached out and grabbed her bag, and leaned strongly on the pedals.

But this prudent southern woman has her wrist looped in the strap: the leather is tough and so is the wrist. Jerked roughly off her balance she hung on; jerked off her feet and scraping a knee most painfully on the gravel she still hung on; getting the other foot under her and throwing her weight backwards to brake the bicycle she felt vengeful and looked for a weapon. Wrenched sideways and with only one hand the boy could not accelerate, and wobbled. Arlette delivered a ferocious dig in the back with her umbrella. He lurched, the bicycle went sideways and he fell off. Arlette fell all over the bicycle, which was even nastier than the gravel. Not feeling in the least sorry for crocodiles she picked up the umbrella. At least she was on top of the bike, while he was underneath. She hit him a fearful clout on the head, which broke the umbrella. Panting, burning, hurting, looking furiously at her ruined stockings, she got, inelegant, to her feet and felt awful, because the boy was lying under the bicycle with blood coming out of his hair. Females are not logical, and she was being sorry for the crocodile.

"Are you all right?" she asked anxiously.

"Are you all right?" asked an elderly gentleman, panting. He raised his hat, in apology for thus accosting a total stranger. The boy was scrambling to his knees, giddy from the unmerciful thump.

"Vermin. There isn't a policeman to be seen. There never is. I say, you must be hurt." The boy was looking at her with admiration.

"Are you badly hurt?" she asked.

"No, lady." He didn't even say fuck-you. Almost one would say there was liking in the eye but you couldn't tell because there was blood in it.

"Then would you like to get the hell out of here." He picked up the bike, mounted, and rode off. The old gentleman was protesting but afraid to shout.

"We must go at once to the police. I'm a witness."

"Fuck the police," said Arlette with total absence of loyalty.

"Oh I say. You're shocked. You must come to the pharmacy. I insist," with a recovery of male authority. "There's one over there behind those trees. I know the district well. This park's a disgrace. Attacks in broad daylight!" She was looking sorrowfully at her umbrella and searching civic-minded for a litter-bin. "Come, dear lady, we must get you seen to."

The pharmacist's girl looked at her with respect. The pharmacist, bald and pompous, looked at her with respect. A small crowd gathered, regaled by the old gentleman, whose tale lost nothing in the telling.

"Drink this!"

"No. What is it?"

"Sal volatile." Delightfully oldfashioned! Her grandmother when agitated used to take sips of sal volatile. She did drink it and instantly felt better.

"My poor umbrella."

"She caught him a monstrous one round the ear. The lady was most courageous. Little beast. Won't try that again in a hurry, I can tell you that. We must ring the police. And an ambulance."

"Stop fussing," crossly. "There's nothing the matter," submitting to having her knee disinfected. "A few scrapes," looking at her glove, which luckily was old and had been scraped before.

All these dirty old men were being far too attentive. "Thank you very much indeed but I'm perfectly all right. Truly. My car's just around the corner and I want to hear no more about it." Shit, now the police had arrived.

"D'you want to lay charges miss, madam?"

"Waste of time, as you very well know. Look, I just want to go home please."

"We'd like you to co-operate," stiffly.

"I'm the wife of a police officer and I can look after myself." The climate of sympathy was cooling rapidly but they put it down to shock, poor woman. She did manage to get all the busybodies quelled at last. She got into the car in a great rage and some pain. My stockings! My umbrella! Never mind, I still have my lovely underclothes. A fat man in a great fat Japanese car braked frenziedly and cursed, visibly empurpled even through two windows. Arlette, realising belatedly that she'd just gone slap through a red light, slowed in a hurry and read herself a severe sermon. She still wanted to get out of here. Anywhere.

Van der Valk was sitting in the bar, perfectly peaceable and drinking by the look of it gin.

"You seem to have been in the wars."

"I have, rather," now feeling much ashamed of herself for causing scandals. He looked at her amused.

"Go and get into a big deep hot bath." He'd got it right but quite often he did.

In the bath she discovered bruised ribs and a slightly bruised tit – that would be the damn bicycle – and rather a pain there where one is bony under the curve even if nicely padded, just on my fur. The knee is a bit swollen. Nothing very dreadful.

Van der Valk arrived, with more gin, and made polite enquiries.

"Blissful, thanks, but I can't get out. Ow." He helped her out, and dried her. "But sorry, don't get uxorious, I don't want at all to make love and my fan hurts, rather."

"Have you bust the car up?"

"No, I'm glad to say, only my umbrella." She told him: he laughed a lot, with affection and not too much mockery.

"We'll get you a new umbrella. You have struck a blow for justice and so – just for once – have I."

"You aren't still tangled up? Ooh, I'm very hungry."

"I don't think they're quite up to bringing you dinner in bed. Can you manage to hobble? Oh yes, I'll make one or two curt phonecalls in the morning but then I'm free of it. All wrapped up. A few rather pathetic women. They suffer most – quite as usual. I'd just as soon forget about it: it wasn't an exploit."

"Neither was mine. I bought some synthol from a bald apothecary: I'll just dab some in a bit. No, I don't want any help, thank you. I want a great big dinner and lots to drink and then I want to fall straight into bed and snore." She shut him out of the bathroom, because what with bruises and things and she rather suspected a shred or so of residual shock, awfully sorry, but she felt a devouring need to masturbate. Disgusting word for what can be a distinct help, sometimes.

She has hidden the nice new underclothes. Not quite the moment to show him those. The synthol is a sort of modern equivalent for horse liniment. Doesn't smell much, and isn't greasy.

So she sails downstairs, in a skirt well below the knee, and rather a lot of perfume to counteract the synthol. Teeth set, a bit: not going to limp, or wince at twinges (set too in anticipation of another Dutch meal). Pride – for she is a very proud woman. Exacting, of herself and of him. She is proud of him for uncovering a nasty traffic under the nose of the local police (very probably not bribed, but too lazy). And for going through with it even if it meant a boring and unpleasant job bang in the middle of his holiday. He is like that. Nine out of ten would have said they didn't want to know. Integrity is knowing one's job and doing it as best one knows how. Neither the word nor the attitude is much in favour these days. Proud of him, she has to be proud of herself. So suppress a few small discomforts.

He looks up from the menu.

"You look very nice. I feel proud of you. But don't plan on going for a walk after dinner. Not, that is, unless I come with you for protection."

Part Two

Norderney

5

Holland comes to an end up here at the edge of the province of Droningen, because of the Ems estuary. Right in the corner is a little harbour town called Delfzijl, of no great size or importance since the estuary is too silted for deepwater traffic. They ply a trade there with the Baltic ports of the north, bringing in things Holland needs like wood for newsprint pulp, and things Holland doesn't really need, like Volvo cars. Van der Valk wanted to see this place because he ought to have seen all of Holland, and got an agreeable surprise because it is a trim and pleasant little town, with the crocuses out everywhere in sparkling spring sunshine. The water is kept in the basin by locks, and there is a good yacht harbour.

There is also a piece of statuary, in itself of small merit but with an entertaining history, for in the year 1930 the writer Georges Simenon bought a little sailing boat and worked it up this coastline, stopping at night in the harbours for a wash and a meal – and of course to write, with the typewriter perched on an orange-box. And here in Delfzijl he says he began the first of what were to become the Maigret books; and so here by the harbourside, with a very proper feeling of pride, perches Commissaire Maigret in his famous velvet-collared overcoat with his bowler hat and his pipe. Van der Valk examined this, with it has to be said a chill eye, much like that of the seagulls. There have been a good few jokes made about this piece of art, all pretty obvious, and Arlette added another, more obvious still.

"So there was no real need for you to come here," she teases.

"No," sighing deeply. "One does so wish the Dutch police was like this."

"Well, one wishes the French police was like this too." Arlette will, in a future as yet undreamed of, come to know a French police officer named Castang with whom she will become friendly. He will most heartily agree.

Having made his tour of inspection, quite rapid since there is not much to see, he headed south because one must travel some fifty kilometres inland, until the Ems narrows to quite a muddy little river, before one can cross into Germany. But he will remember the bright little town. Indeed it is much like another little town, in the extreme south of Holland – Goes, on the Zeeland coast, where you cross the Scheldt estuary to Belgium.

He has felt a sudden deep fatigue; from the day yesterday, which had held anxiety, and been something of a battering. (And at Goes it had been much the same: he had felt the need to cross the ferry over to Breskens, to go and drink beer and eat mussels in Belgium.) Wouldn't one wish, in these quiet, neat little towns, to be a retired seacaptain, and live in a tiny shiny house, overheated and full of lace curtains, with a birdcage in the window, and look out at the shipping?

And he remembers Jacques Brel's – extremely gloomy – poem about the Ostendaise:

> *Il y a deux sortes de temps*
> *Y a le temps qui attend*
> *Et le temps qui espère.*

('There are two sorts of time: the time which waits and the time which hopes.')

He heaved such an enormous sigh that Arlette, who was driving, said, "What on earth . . . ?"

"Only that Holland is so very small. This goddamn mudbank at one end, the other mudbank at the other – just the same save

72

that the Scheldt stinks worse because more polluted. And in between there are the two big mudbanks of the Rhine and the Maas, and that's all. And in between all these idiotic mudbanks, what a lot does happen!'

She paid no attention whatever to all this introspective aphorising.

"Merde!" she said, stopping at a crossroad and craning to read roadsigns which as always in Holland are on the wrong side of the road. "Where's the frigging frontier? Directions to twenty villages nobody has ever heard of and not a single sign saying Germany! Absolutely typical."

She slammed the car into gear, turned on to what looked like the main road leading nowhere. A kilometre further a sign said *Zoll*, a bored functionary in forest green uniform looked at her with total lack of interest, she gave him a great sexy smile, saying to van der Valk, "Civilisation at last; three resounding cheers."

"Very disloyal and unpatriotic, and of course I totally agree."

"What d'you want to do now?" braking. "I have to tank. Just made it – cheaper of course here, besides so much nicer."

"I want to go to the island of Norderney. Haven't seen any islands yet properly."

"There won't be anything there. Birds, sheep, seagulls."

"No, there's a real seaside town."

"It'll all be shut. Too early in the year. I want to go to Bremen." Arlette pettishly.

"So if it's horrid we'll turn around, and go to Bremen. I want to see something of this East Friesian countryside; not a bit like Holland. Look, the bricks are a different colour, lovely burned orange instead of that awful purple."

"There's a ferry," not looking, deep in the map, "from Norden. Probably once a week."

"So we'll go to Norden, and have lunch, and find out."

"Very well – ooh, look, shitty farmhouse, but such a nice colour."

"Yes," said van der Valk, sighing.

But now, he thinks, we are going to start enjoying our-selves. We should have done this in the first place perhaps: isn't it a mistake to think in terms of holiday, when still in one's own country – and that Holland? It's too small and too populous: this produces a concentrated essence of national flavour, perfectly suffocating. The obstinate certainty of rightness; the sheer bloody-minded complacency of those thin, high, nasal voices, immovably and impermeably anchored in our own self-satisfaction: We Know Better. Tell anybody Dutch that there might be other ways of doing things and the invariable reply will be 'Nee, hoor.' You hear me, and I won't listen, because I've 'eard different.

Large countries are to be preferred because of the patchwork of different countrysides and different peoples who have had to learn to live with one another. The corners get knocked off. However awful the French get, one is consoled by the loose sloppiness, the comfortable incompetence which puts a stop to their nonsense.

Nice Germany. Large. Room to breathe. And now perhaps I will start to be less Dutch, and behave irresponsibly. It will be more enjoyable for my dear wife, too. I will be less inclined to run about meddling with other people's business. I am, alas, a sad prig.

This was a nice countryside because more of it had been left alone, just to sit and be ramshackle. It is East Friesland, which is much like West Friesland, meaning flat, wet, and irrigation ditches. The cows are smaller, less majestic; rather more intelligent.

The weather is nice too. Instead of merely sitting there and raining, because it couldn't think of anything else to do, save maybe snow from time to time out of spite, its April pattern had caught up with them. A bowling northwest wind made the daffodils crouch flat, with their ears laid back. Clouds of every shape, every tint of white and tone of black, with ragged gilt edges, swarmed and scudded. Blinding showers of sleet set the wipers to high speed and Arlette to slowing and dodging behind trucks; and disappeared just as suddenly to leeward of the April sunlight, prismatic in the wet.

Numerous dilapidated villages, made pretty by the German love of tree and flower. And we are the great flower experts! But show a Dutchman a flower and he'll start telling how to have three next year and sell two of them. A German sploshes them about, expecting pleasure, and just as spontaneously, getting it.

"And the French," said Arlette, "prefer artificial flowers because they're so much more economical." He wasn't aware he'd spoken aloud.

Norden is a trim, pretty and prosperous town, where they made a very good lunch, of food tasting strongly of itself, in an alarmingly cosy room with violently patterned wallpaper, but as Arlette says heartfelt, who cares when the lavatories are clean? As the Americans say, Only Germans understand bathrooms. And he could report that the wine was good and so was the beer (having like a careful cop tasted both).

The ferry, it was reported, left from Norddeich, five kilometres down the road. There would be plenty of ferries, no trouble at all. Thus spurred on, they made haste to Norddeich, were rewarded by seeing the sea, reassured by seeing a ferry, and comforted to be told it would be another hour. At this moment it started snowing again so that they bolted for a café. Tea, said Arlette. Ost-Frisian tea? asked the waitress. Certainly. And it turns out to be one of the incidental delights which reward the innocent traveller. Ost-Frisian tea is strong, perfumed, delicious; a corpse-reviver. It comes in a pretty service of its own of excellent and traditional oriental pattern with big red flowers on it. God bless the town of Bremen for having such good taste. Van der Valk, who is Dutch enough to drink tea all day long, feels vengeful towards the brave Dutch firm of Douwe Egbert for selling him sweepings all his life. Only in

Germany, says Arlette with hideous complacency, can one get proper tea.

Thus stimulated – it has the same effect as a whacking shot of pastis does in France – he paces about angrily on the deck of the little ferry which joins the islands of Juist and Norderney to the mainland, telling himself they're sixty seconds overtime in leaving, and why don't those two deckhands wind up their drawbridge instead of lounging there? They're German, aren't they?

Perhaps it is the sort of magic which goes with being rich. At quite literally the last second, unfussed and unhurried, an enormous car slithers up, effortless over the metal hump, settling comfortably into the slot (as though prepared for it) on the car deck; instantly galvanised, the deckhands wind on their winches and the boat goes teuf-teuf-teuf away between the jetties that mark the dredged channel.

Van der Valk studied this big car. He is not interested, and he is not envious. Cars to him are a means of transport rather more stupid than trains, a bit less tiresome than planes, and in general much less civilised than a bicycle. Still, this was quite nice as cars go, being – relatively – unpretentious. Only a Mercedes. Very long yes, very black. They don't come bigger, except for the enormous one made for horizontal African heads-of-state in fancy nightdresses. This is the 500 SE, the coupé model, hardtop with two doors.

Out of it climbed a man who was a match for the car. A big man, tall and broadshouldered; a handsome oval face, dark-tanned by weather as a fisherman's. But more likely just back from a ski holiday since the signs of wealth were evident. He got out springily like someone in good physical condition, and the front of his pullover showed no protuberant belly. He reached into the car for a short furcollared auto coat, shrugged into it, locked the car, looked up, caught van der Valk's eye, and smiled. A warm, winning smile: sapphire-blue eyes were brilliant in the tanned face and the long fine lines

at the temples crinkled up engagingly. His longish black hair
was finetextured, straight, showed no sign of grey. Perhaps it
was touched up at the sides to keep youthful, because it was
an actor's face, mobile and clever. Or a politician's. There was
the indefinable look of poise and assurance that comes upon a
man used to public appearance.

That's reading a lot, for a first impression? But a cop is
trained that way. Add that van der Valk had nothing else to
do. His small sourness melted and he smiled back.

"Cut it a bit fine?"

"I did rather – but I'm in the habit. And they know me – I
live here you see." Another flurry of sleet slashed at them but
the man lifted his face as though relishing it, smiling. Nearer
sixty than fifty. But wearing it very well. "Still, I suppose we'd
better get under cover. A beer would go down nicely – join
me?"

It sounds too as though van der Valk were drinking a great
deal. Almost like another Maigret legend: a case on white
wine, another on calva. This won't do! had said Arlette, and
not just being stubborn: you're getting to be a right piss-artist.
And more especially when hitting middle-age and condemned
now to desk work. Mineral water henceforward, my son!

And noticing a tendency to watery eyes as well as the
distinct beginnings of a belly, he had subjected to discipline. A
scolding voice and a nagging finger pointing at his nose – watch
out for those tiny broken veins! So now that he is on holiday,
he's having a glorious time doing a whole lot of things that are
forbidden: what good is a holiday if one can't be irresponsible?

"Tag, Herr Reich," said the stewardess uncapping two beers
and beaming as they do upon regular customers who make
jokes, give excellent tips and do not pat their bottom.

"Here's to you. On holiday? – you don't look like a man
come for the cure."

"Not a care in the world," agreed van der Valk.

"And Dutch, from your voice. Welcome, landsman; I am

myself, but from so far back I almost forget," putting down his beer and holding out a long fineboned hand. "Jan Rijk. Goes easy into German but just as good in the taal."

"Van der Valk," extending his own paw.

"Heavens, that's fatherlands enough."

"Sure. Native Amsterdammer, that's almost as rare as a real Parisien." *Rijk* = rich, or *rijk* = kingdom; both would suit him well. Business man no doubt. Pushy, exuberant, and when the charm is turned off hard as nails. Where do they learn all this instant palliness – in America? 'Whereabouts you from in the States?' is always their first question. ('Arizona, that's great, I'm New Jersey.') But right now Jan, all-enveloping, is about to sell me life insurance. Still he doesn't mind. This, too, is what holidays are for.

He looked about. Place was full of screaming children, knitting women, card-playing men.

"Lots of people. What goes on, in Norderney?"

"You've never been? Mums and their kids come for the cure." (He hates people who say kids, but no matter.) "Nerves, stress, skin, anything you like. Always been an industry here, massage, seaweed baths, all that. So do a lot of oldies. But ten thousand people live on Norderney and a lot work on the mainland."

"That many? No, me, I'm just blowing where the wind lists, get rid of the dust they call air, back in the Hague. I've a wife too somewhere but she seems to have vanished. I'd an urge to see a Friesian island, before pottering up the coast, 's far's Hamburg maybe."

"Splendid, where are you staying?"

"No idea. I thought there'd be plenty of room, but this crowd's frightening me."

"Och, they come on a discount but it's only midweek, you'll have no trouble. Tell your driver the Vierjahreszeiten, it's comfortable and pleasant and not even dear. What d'you do then, government service? Forgive me though, I'm being personal."

78

"Of course I should be ashamed of it, but there it is. Commissaire of police." He has a rule, not to tell lies until obliged to, and then as few as possible. Also the announcement has an effect, now and then. People are amused, or horrified, and even occasionally frightened. He got an effect, too.

"Now that – really – is – interesting to me. This is something after my own heart. What the cliché calls law-and-order."

"Not much of that, in an administrative rank. Tides of paper shuffle."

"Yes of course. If seven maids with seven mops would sweep for half the year," he said unexpectedly in good English. "But this too is of singular interest. Government is more than a hobby to me – I'm a political-science man. Oh dear, I'm pressing you like a salesman. Now I wonder whether you will allow – hideously importunate but you'll please put it down to a wish to make amends, to show a scrap of hospitality and efface this bad impression – may I beg to offer you and your wife dinner? One doesn't eat badly in your Four Seasons, I'll book a table. Look, here's my card. I say – we're nearly in."

"I better go lasso my wife." One gets things jumped on one, and on-the-spur has no good pretext for refusing. He felt bored – and Arlette might well be amused. So he just mumbled about it's being very kind.

"And I better go pick up my car. Seventhirty okay? Great."

"Blimey," said Arlette. "No, I don't mind; never a dull moment. Why do they need taxis on Norderney?"

"Because the ferry is here and the village is there," said the driver over his shoulder, "but if you want to get out and walk I shan't stop you." And the Four Seasons is comforting and looks very pleasant. And the snow-flurries have blown over, and it looks like a lovely evening.

"Well, why not?" she said. "Shall I take a quick shower

and then we'll go for a walk? No – walk first even if I do look travel-stained. Look, if you feel hemmed in you've only to ring up and say I've a headache; don't feel pushed on my account."

"People with dotty ideas about government service," dubiously, fiddling with the card. It is a personal card, engraved, and it just says *Jan Reich, Schwannallee 4, Norderney, Bundesrepublik Deutschland*, and a phone number. He will have cards saying Drug Dealer, or Armament Sales. Or just Antique Pictures and Fine Furniture. He could be absolutely anything.

But why is he so damn pally?

With a vague idea of being formal, on account of being invited-to-dine, van der Valk put on a suit, changed his shirt, wore a sober tie; this under the approving eye of his wife, who has only glimpsed Herr Reich, been impressed – perhaps too much so by that big black Mercedes – and has made herself rather smart. He is disconcerted to find the restaurant full of a perfect horde of children, piloted by windswept young mums in casual trousers, but the hostess sweeps him off to an alcove table behind a barricade of plants, and says comfortably that the brats will all be off to bed in another few minutes. Herr Reich, punctual to the minute, is himself informal in an expensive après-ski style but gives him an approving look: a senior Dutch civil-servant, realises van der Valk, ought to be a bit formal, in order to be consonant with dignity.

Arlette gets her hand kissed, and the charm turned on.

"It'll be quiet in a quarter of an hour and we can hear ourselves think – three Camparis, my dear, and we'll order in ten minutes – but meanwhile I rather like the thundering herd – doesn't worry you?"

"Heavens, I've three of them."

"How right you are. People gas on about economics and

the balance of payments and who gives a damn? – the children are the only future we've got. No no, Mevrouw, I love that oldfashioned French formality, but Jan is my name; I pray of you." And the two are thick as thieves in no time, leaving van der Valk amused and not the least inclined to glower over the top of his menu.

"If I seem brusque in thus impertinently presuming upon a chance acquaintanceship it's that I detected in your husband an acute and balanced mind." An order for a very good spätlese Johannisberger and a lavish meal with brio accompaniments.

Thus carried upon a pleasant tide van der Valk, content that she should enjoy herself, sits back and says little. Arlette since marriage has been unfairly drowned in Dutch domesticity. Too seldom she gets this sort of stimulus, to knock some of the rust off that earnest (at times humourless) and yet fiercely active mind, belonging to the student he met and married. Raw, yes, indeed decidedly strident before bearing and bringing up children had taught her to give more weight to instincts and emotions, and a bit less to that godalmighty intellect the French are over-inclined to make much of. Remembering that once she was a tremendous revolutionary, if more often on cheap plonk than on this mellow Rheinwein.

Does he stop being a cop? Yes-and-no is the answer to that: he does not lose track of the conversation, despite much merry laughter, and he has the trained cop eye, automatically keeping in practice.

Like around the room: as promised the children have all been whisked off to bed and the restaurant has two-thirds refilled with the second service, taking its time over digestion: minds still preoccupied with business but beginning to drift towards dallying with a bit of fornication: some older and some younger, some winewarmed (he's getting extremely relaxed hizzown self) and some carburating on beer but all benefiting from the cure: Norderney is an island, and where better an atmosphere for banishing cares?

And a couple of odd solitaries: that bald brown smiling man who brings the camera to table with him? A Nikon fanatic: the type which digs itself into a hide and remains there from dawn to dusk hoping to get a shot of the nesting osprey, but right now is making good time with jokes, which are laying snares for a giggling waitress.

Or the tremendously Brit and officers-mess soul over there with his halfbottle of claret and his handkerchief in his sleeve?

He swam back to the present: they were busy with the state of the nation, which seemed to be parlous. As usual. With several other nations, all in extremely bad shape as well. Terribly boring words like 'Vietnam' or 'de Gaulle' came popping up. That dread expression 'Weltanschauung' would surface any second. He woke up a little bit because Arlette, tactless upon occasion, might say something untoward: she has very little use for either states or nations, and has been known to be rude about the General. He woke up a little more with awareness that he was being pumped, and crept his foot out to touch hers.

"The Hague . . . political branch?"

"Not really, no; there's a sort of research study group."

"Aha – Inspectorate?"

"Nor that either." Deprecating, but always tell some of the truth. "We talk about reforming the penal code. We have huddles with magistrates. All very slow, very prudent. The position of women in society, the attitude of churches. The never-ending debate between conservatism and progress – we're a very conservative body," laughing.

"Integrity among persons holding public office."

"Oh yes, decidedly." And it comes to his mind to work up a little anecdotal moral tale about his experiences over the last few days. He suppresses that.

"We are witnessing," said Jan heavily, "a frightening, indeed a fearful decline in ethical standards."

"In traditional Jewish and Christian – " began Arlette. He trod quite heavily upon her foot.

"I'm increasingly preoccupied," began Jan with a preoccupied expression. Van der Valk had a distinct notion that the English gentleman in the thornproof jacket was listening. Well, why shouldn't he listen? There's no rule against it, and Jan's voice is quite loud.

"Take our own country of Holland to which you and I have a strong personal and patriotic attachment – "

"But I'd just as soon we didn't."

"Yes, I see what you mean, you wish to avoid personalities, but we've seen some deplorable examples set, among for instance the royal family itself – but I agree, I agree. Very well, take England, a country in many ways comparable to our own in ethnic population – climate, temperament – a traditionally high standard of behaviour in public life. Why, we can remember a minister being sacked on the spot for accepting a few pathetic gifts – I seem to recall a couple of bananas. Now when you make the contrast with people holding equivalent positions in Latin countries . . . And as for here in Germany . . . but you're quite right, we're in a public place. Now how about some of what the English call pudding?

"The fact is, van der Valk, that it is exceedingly pleasant to me to meet a man such as yourself. Now as you observe, and of course guess, I'm a pretty successful businessman, earn a lot of money fairly easily, am not at all ashamed of that since it depends upon my own efforts, but should feel thoroughly ashamed of devoting capitalist profits uniquely towards furnishing my own comforts. Don't for a second suspect me of socialist sympathies. I believe in natural selection, in economics as well as in biology; the race is to the strong, the rapid and the fit." Van der Valk was nodding away like the toy dogs people put on the back shelf of cars and which movement sets ticking.

"I devote quite a lot of my resources, as do others of our ilk, to a kind of study group something in the nature of your own, and it so happens that I've a fellow staying with me at this moment whom you might be interested to meet. I take exception a good deal to an oily manner but it can be an eye-opening experience. Now I'm diffident about interfering with your holiday movements but if you'd care to come to dinner at my home my wife would be more than delighted and I'd – "

Arlette's turn; her high heel came down painfully upon his instep and he beamed and said he'd be delighted.

"Dear Jesus – I say, let's go out and breathe a bit of fresh air, I've had a lot to drink – but what possessed you? This frightful bore!"

"But it's my job, my dear. The study group isn't really political but we do take an interest in other study groups. As Jan does."

"Hell, we're not in Holland now. I want to enjoy my holiday, which doesn't include listening to some frightful American laying down the law about the iniquitous Kennedys."

"Okay, don't get cross; there are several points and if you'll just be patient. One, if I draw a line around Holland and stay in our tight cosy little family there, life would indeed be boring. Two, Jan is preposterous and I agree appalling: not sinister in any criminal code sense. Is it just the dotty reactionary right wing talking? I should like to find out because it might have a bearing. Three, if I'm to be taken into his confidence I have to compromise myself a little and it starts with an appetite for knowledge."

"But he's completely off his rocker. What's he proposing – that the Dutch invade Flanders? The Flamands loathe the Dutch; flung them out neck and crop in 1850 or whenever."

"Quite so but these over-simplifications may be a sprat to catch a mackerel."

6

Some days are awful. We can generally see them coming, when the alarmclock fails to go off, when we just miss the tram, when the shoelace breaks: we are learning that other hateful pinpricks loom, and are no more than mildly put out when a perfectly good molar suffers abject disintegration at lunchtime while peacefully eating mashed potatoes.

Other days start well and it's generally a good sign. Thus both van der Valk and his loving wife slept well. Going down in the lift there was a helpful message from the management pinned up, saying that the met forecast for this day was warm-and-sunny. Breakfast, in the usual selfservice style of German hotels, was delicious, marked only by his going back for more ham accompanied by a loud crunching noise, caused by tiresome children spilling cornflakes. Everyone is in a good mood, even the waitress wielding dustpan and brush. Arlette, who can be tediously French, has wolfed muesli, yoghurt, rye bread and salami, and three cups of coffee, is discourteous towards croissants (so fetching on the outside, so limp and wet within) or the British bacon-and-egg so lengthily simmered in lukewarm grease.

"Now let's take a very long walk along the beach." For it's all true: the sun in the village resembles Bristol Milk Sherry. Over the dune, on wet sand (the tide is on the way out) it is – she says – that south-american-thing with slices of lime and little saucers of salt. All extremely nice. She is happy, and does childish things like writing her name in the sand with the point of her new umbrella. The sea is quiet. Little wavelets sparkle at one like a Schweppes advertisement.

Van der Valk himself is disposed to be frivolous. At breakfast he has noticed the Camera Man, that incomparably sinister, shaven-headed bronze Lithuanian Buddha; always alone, forever smiling, indefatigable chatter-up of anything and everything female.

"Certainly a spy," he said in a melodramatic hiss.

Oh, that awful literalness of women. "He can't possibly be. I mean he looks so like a spy."

"There is the hideous artfulness. If you wish to hide a letter leave it in full view; known as the Po-poe effect."

"Absolute bullshit; wouldn't take in a baby."

"You'd be surprised. Look, and behave, so obviously like a KGB joke and you disarm all serious enquiry. Where's the other, the Brit with the shapeless tweed hat, who is such a public-school-caricature he can't be anything but CIA?"

Arlette is never more French than when she's being teacherly, preferably on a nice long walk along the strand where you can't get away from her.

"A night's sleep brings counsel," he said. "You are perfectly absurd with your neo-nazi fantasies. Jan Rijk or Reich or whatever he calls himself is no more than the usual business-class sentimentalist who patronises extremes of chauvinism out of vanity."

This was probably very true. Why should she feel obliged to argue?

It's because she's been reading in bed! And what has she picked up, from some railway bookstall? Crude paperback fiction! And instead of throwing it on the floor and turning the light out, she sits up with this tripe underlining things! Still the absolutely humourless student . . .

"Jan is silly, I agree. But he's harmless because imbecile. It obeys no rule of fact or evidence: it's all what you legal people term guilt by association and you ought to know better."

She strides tremendously: in this sort of mood there's no stopping her. Reading of all people John Buchan!

"But you can't take that seriously – wartime propaganda, for the love-of-God, and seventy years old into the bargain."

"Take it seriously! My dear Mann, it's much admired and the proof is it's still read because these people find it worth reprinting. A Fascist handbook! There are three minor villains – a Polish Jew, a Portuguese Jew and an Austrian Jew, in that order. He gives himself away in every line! The hero – as you say around nineteen sixteen – enquires whether the major villain is perhaps 'an International Socialist'? Now we know who assassinated Jean Jaurès – Mr Buchan's friends! You know who he was, this much loved Mr Buchan? One of Milner's young men in South Africa. The crook who deliberately provoked the Boer War! He says, I quote textually – the hero is at a political meeting – 'There was a great buck nigger with a lot to say about Africa for the Africans.' Arriba, arriba!"

"Darling," trying to keep up with large indignant strides, "this was all an eternity ago."

"And Brits are reading it today and drinking it all in. Probably your friend Jan, since he's about that much out of date. It's quite cleverly written, being all moderate and tolerant. Of course I understand the crude propaganda about Huns and Boches, that's common form. But what d'you make of a character, a so-called modern novelist, grossly insulted as a ghastly shit; then all is explained when you're told his name is Aronson! And this is meat and drink to the good ol' boys back in the Travellers Club!"

"But we don't take it seriously."

"You think so? Well, I don't want to condemn people upon their associations, because that is exactly the game they play, and I don't want you to fall into the same trap."

These little North Sea beaches have kept their primitive nature. There is no tamed and civilised seafront promenade such as exists on many Channel and Atlantic resorts, where parasoled and bonneted ladies once strolled in the sunshine, voluminous skirts a-flutter, but with many cosy little nooks if the wind was tiresome, a little tram pottering along the boulevard in case of fatigue, plenty of terraces glassed against draughts where refreshment could be sought, and a clifftop backdrop of balconied villas. Here at the end of the island and seaward of the village there is indeed a bricked path on the top of the seawall, suitable for elderly parties taking a constitutional, but after a mile it comes to an abrupt stop. A blockhouse-like building (closed until Easter) with a desolate flag flapping above it announces a beachfront café, a set of steps leads down to the sand, and thereafter you're on your own with gulls and whoever fancies the more strenuous exercise of a scramble over soft dry sand, and if the tide be out smoother wet sand, which keeps the imprints of ribbed rubber soles where the healthy mind has taken the healthy body out jogging.

Above the beach runs the dune, an irregular wall of piled sand fixed by the matted roots of dune-grass, some four metres high and pierced occasionally by a little passage with steps giving access to the hinterland. Here and there in the dune, guessed rather than seen, are signs of that once-mighty network of bunker and gun-emplacement, Hitler's Atlantic wall, submerged in the wind-driven sand where thousands of slaves had toiled like ants.

"Good, huh?" said Arlette breathing strongly, full of energy. He agrees, with moderation. All very sunny and seabreezy and good for the lungs, and doubtless for his brains too, or whatever may be in that strange bony cavity behind his sinuses. It is good to push his lame leg, make it stump about and stop complaining; but it is beginning to complain loudly.

"I've had about enough, I think."

"We'll turn back," she agreed absently. "Take an inland path if you like, to make a change."

He glanced up towards the dune, beyond which ran certainly some road or path. In the slot had appeared a figure, vaguely male in a raincoat. His eyes tried by the sharpness of sun and wind did not distinguish detail: was there any reason why they should? A jerky arm made a strange sign, at once urgent and furtive, and van der Valk looked around, as one does, to see who the hell – but there was nobody there but Arlette staring tranced out to sea. Along the beach were a few more strolling people, but nobody within range. And when he looked again properly the gesture was repeated: 'the Englishman', he saw. Recognisable by his funny hat.

"I'll just go and see." Perhaps somebody was hurt? It is easy to rick an ankle in that soft sand.

"Call me if the path seems attractive," perching on the sundried stone of a breakwater.

The bony closeshaved face was taut under the hat: eyes glanced sharply round, checking. Nobody was around.

"We aren't overseen or heard here," said the man, speaking good Dutch. "Thought myself lucky, catching sight of you." Calmly, but with a controlled agitation.

"Why?" What was this nonsense now?

"I know you to be a police officer."

"I make no secret of it," resting on his stick, "and I'm on holiday."

"And I need your help." Again that quick look up the uneven paved steps. Would there be thirtynine of them, wondered van der Valk, amused. This is like Arlette's friend Mr Buchan.

"And who," he asked, "may you be?"

"Never mind that now but I have the right," sharp, "to claim your help."

"So speak up," looking down towards Arlette, who was looking the other way.

"Have you noticed a man who is either bald or shaves his head and is forever smiling?" Oho – the spy! "He's a spy."

"You don't say." Keeping his face straight.

"I don't want to lose any more time. This man's been following me, yesterday and today."

"Let him. If he gets annoying, tell him so."

"He was there," pointing up the steps, "and just now he vanished like that."

"Sounds good news."

"Don't play about, Mr van der Valk. I want to go and look, and two are better than one." But this is preposterous.

"Why?" calmly, watching the face which was drawn with a real – or imagined – anxiety. People come here for the cure, and some have neurotic fantasies.

"Because you've been keeping some strange company, Mr van der Valk, and this interests me." The eyes looked straight at him with no sign of neurosis.

"Very well. We'll look for your vanished friend." There were only twentytwo steps – he counted. Beyond, a rough path of self-locking paving led through the dune to the roadway.

An innocent sight. To the left a onesided street of little holiday villas crouched facing the dune. To the right the road rejoined rambling buildings at the outskirts of the little town. Van der Valk's mind was busy. What was this? A trap seemed out of the question: but some kind of test or trial? For what obscure purpose? To whose complicated design? He glanced at his companion. The face was tense and still. But that does not take much talent as an actor.

The little landscape, enclosed behind the houses by more dunes, was peaceful. A woman wheeling a pram walked slowly across, heading back towards the town: upon a path around some municipal shed or garage an elderly gentleman towed a small woolly dog out of sight: an island-hopping aeroplane skimmed in towards the little field: a noticeboard stated that it was forbidden to walk in the dunes without official permission.

"Well?" with some sarcasm. "Your sinister follower could be anywhere."

Lean and brisk in his burberry raincoat the man stayed

still as a pointing dog before leaning forward and carefully not bringing up a finger.

"That second house – there's a shutter open, at the side."

Villa was too pretentious a name for them: smallish one- or two-storey suburban things of uninspired design and a jerrybuilt construction. Of the five or six visible all looked closed, shuttered and unoccupied. Plainly holiday houses, and one bigger than the others had a notice in the window saying *Flatlets to Rent*. And it was perfectly true that the side-shutter of the second – a kitchen or bathroom window – was not quite shut. Van der Valk did not like this. It had a set-up smell.

"I intend to look at that," said the man tightly.

"Just a moment. You will satisfy me of your authority before you go breaking into houses." The man looked around again before diving a hand inside the raincoat and slipping out a plastic folder holding a warrant card of a Dutch government agent.

"You've seen such things before, and you'll forget you've seen it now."

Van der Valk nodded. "Could also be seen across the street." Jealous perhaps of his fine new colleague, but he was liking all this less and less.

"Just so," putting it away and taking out a nine-millimetre pistol. FN, admirable weapon. Belgian government arms factory in Herstal.

"No." Abrupt. "Put that thing away. We're in Germany. Nobody's going to shoot us." He didn't think that kind of card would be all that difficult to fake, either.

"I'm still going in there," said the man. "What d'you propose to do, keep cavé?" with an edge of sarcasm.

"That's right. Not exactly a frequented quarter, this, but if someone calls the cops you're liable to look silly."

The window wasn't above chest height and the man hopped up quite as though he were in the habit.

The street of closed houses, the dune opposite, the electricity sub-station, the path and the ramshackle garages, all dozed in the spring sunshine and there was no movement anywhere. He drew with his stick in the sand. Arlette would start wondering what he was playing at. He wondered himself.

"Van der Valk!" in a cautious whisper, but now the tone was altogether different. "You had better come in. As a witness. He's there, you see."

Bad, bad, bad. But in for a penny in for a pound. His leg made the manoeuvre clumsy, but his wrist was gripped, he got a hoist, a knee on the sill, and never mind the sense of false position – 'he's there' is ambiguous, but not enough so . . .

It was, as one would expect, a bathroom. Beyond was a smell of dust, a smell of damp, the smell of a house that has been closed and empty for several months; very little light. And then another smell too: the firework smell of a discharged gun. But no gun had gone off while he was outside, he'd stake his word on that. The smell had not yet dissipated. The skin was still warm but cooling fast. He could feel no pulse in the lax wrist. In the grey twilight there was little to be seen.

He snapped his lighter for an instant. Scorchmark right over the heart. Very little blood but there isn't much at the entrypoint of this small a calibre. He didn't want to do any handling, and it didn't look as though any handling would do much good. In any case, nothing remotely resembling the big FN pistol he had seen. That thing knocks a hole like a Metro tunnel, and through the brick wall on the far side. Not to speak of the noise, and a bucketful of blood – and blood smells too. The bullet would still be inside him.

Van der Valk straightened up and said, "Out of here as fast as we can." He gave the lighter another instant's flick. The bald bronzed head was still smiling but now you'd call it rictus.

"Professional. Little twentytwo pistol and with a reduced charge so you'd have heard nothing anyhow, but probably

while you were down on the beach. Help me getting out."
There would be footmarks, there would be sand – the handling
marks on the windowsill. This Secret-Service type would have
to swim as best he could; and as for himself . . . But if any
cops were going to arrive they would be here by now. Very
much here.

The man jumped neatly down on the flagged path, pushed
the window shutter to, and laid a warning hand on van der
Valk's sleeve.

"Woman there on the path."

"Yes, it's my wife."

"Of course – sorry." They crossed the road. Arlette's mouth
was open.

"I'll explain later. Well, Mr er – do you call the gallant
boys in green?"

The man had recovered his self-possession.

"Will if we have to. I'd a lot sooner not, but my bona
fides is clear enough if I have to make it so. Those phonecalls
to Bonn, a considerable hullabaloo. They'll take a dim view.
The Hague will have some explaining to do, and they wouldn't
be best pleased either. This is why I needed you as witness –
if the worst comes to the worst. I wasn't prepared for this,"
soberly. "You're a senior officer, I'll defer to your judgment."

Mm, and yes, and why does it happen to me? But just
for now – snap!

"Very well. Then no cops for the moment. Just to see what
happens, for a little. Who set this up, and why? Who wanted to
get you into that house? Maybe you know answers I don't. Get
away from me, and stay away. If you're shopped, call me. And if
I get shopped, then your explanations had better be good ones,
all the way to the Hague, right? Create any diplomatic incidents
and I'll tip you straight down the shitshute. Fair enough. Don't
leave the island. Where you make your reports and how is your
affair and I don't want to know it. I'm bound to stay here too.
Fortyeight hours from now, if there's no kickback, then meet

me on the beach opposite here – eleven o'clock, right? – and we'll take it from there. Somebody else is bound to notice that shutter. Now piss off, back down the beach: we'll go back inland."

"I suppose I mayn't ask questions," said Arlette, "but I better be told something, just so's I don't compromise you if I get asked."

They began to walk. There was still nobody about.

"That fellow!" said van der Valk without sympathy. "Comes the secret agent up to me – knew who I was, too – with a tale of hankypank, and insists on locking me into it."

"But if he was scared and wanted help," taking his arm, for comfort. They looked like any tourist couple, stumping along. Which is exactly what they were. Middle-aged gentleman, slight disability with the leg: middle-aged wife keeping fair looks and quite a trim figure. Conventionally dressed. Nothing to notice about either of them. Turned aside out of curiosity for a day or so on the island, leaving their car on the mainland. Nothing planned, and nobody else knew of it. He felt puzzled.

"Maybe so," he grumbled. "Chap represents himself as a card-carrying government agent, in which case he knows very well he's not supposed to compromise anyone else. Too much mystification, too many complications. These little spystories – a pack of imbeciles thinking they ought to be defending NATO from the Russians. None of my business. Get on perfectly well with Russians and don't give a fuck about NATO." They had reached the hospital, and the outskirts of the village. "I want a beer before lunch. I want to think about all this. I don't like any of it a bit. Haven't come here to play detective, wouldn't think of doing so for a second. German soil, their business. There's a terrace there, looks quite nice. Quiet too.

"Who's to tell what he is in reality?" the grumble went on once the beer was served. "Don't know themselves half the time – the manipulator is manipulated. All out of whatsisname anyhow – the thirtynine steps leading to the sea. Make a cat

94

laugh, only I don't laugh. Fellow shot in that house – not funny."

"Good God!" shocked.

"You may well say. I should go straight to the local commissariat, of course, wouldn't hesitate an instant. We have this idiotic standing instruction that if under any circs we do happen to come across a plainclothes government agent we're supposed to stand mum.

"In order not to compromise activities unbeknownst to us, and which may, I quote, exceed or bypass our professional competence: I never realised until now just how ambiguous that could be. So I stay quiet and do nothing – your turn before and my turn now to have a holiday upset. You now know enough – so forget it. Find me doing anything peculiar, don't look surprised, and play it by ear."

"I know just enough so's I can't forget it," said Arlette.

Going back for a wash at lunchtime there was a message at the desk, written out in a receptionist's careful schoolgirl hand.

'Jan' telephoned. Apologies for short notice but would Herr/Frau v.d.V. very kindly forgive informal suddenness of invit. to dinner Schwannallee 4. around 7 this evening. Signed Reich.

"Phone Herr Reich for me, would you? I haven't his number handy, say we'll be delighted."

Arlette kept the disciplined face of a soldier in the ranks, getting a rocket from the sergeant.

Coming back that evening after much strenuous fresh air, he picked up his key and "Where's the Schwannallee?" he asked the girl.

"Oh it's – you know the square this side of the Kurhaus?

Little theatre on the corner? Turn left past there and it's the street runs along the little park. D'you want a taxi? – well, it's barely five minutes' walk – you're welcome."

"Should we dress up?" asked Arlette in the lift.

"Oh I think so a bit – show politeness, and important local notable. Ho," unlocking their door. Another 'message form' had been slid under it. This was in thin spiky writing done very close, like somebody crowding a whole letter on to a tourist postcard.

A thick local accent phoned Polizei re broken shutter, & stupid tourist stood dripping excitement. Pol went in, left again uninterested after wedging shutter, saying stupid burglary some yobbo, since nothing repeat Nothing worth taking. Interesting, not? & how the hell? This posted 5 pm, if need then in sauna to 6.30, else no. 204. Brownrigg.

"Oh well, fair enough. Quite right to phone."

"Sorry, didn't catch, with the bathwater running."

"Nothing important, just mumbling. Still, that is extra-ordinary. Somebody got it out and not just how but why?"

"Ow! – No, nothing, the water was too hot."

"What a clown though," looking at his watch: it was nearly six. It wasn't very likely anybody had been in since five. Hm, Mr Brownrigg – perfect name for a clown – could sit and stew himself pink in the hotel sauna (not bad, if a meetingplace were needed). Herr Kommissar van der Valk continued most obstinately not wanting to know.

Isn't this one likewise straight out of Alfred Hitchcock, though! You go to look for the body and there is no body. And that needed a piece of sleight-of-hand thought out beforehand, and this was puzzling. Because, well . . .

Herr Kommissar sat on his bed in his underclothes, after getting rid of the evidence. Now this imbecile Brownrigg: so perhaps he *is* a Dutch government agent. It would be like them in a way. Nothing improbable since plenty of Dutch people have an English upbringing and relations, that's okay, but what's the loony doing here?

Narcotics is a likely answer. Holland is brimful of brown stuff and white stuff and everything in between; there is a thriving traffic with Germany. Mm, both Norderney and Delfzijl have yacht harbours.

But apart from the fact that nobody does much yachting in mid March – yes, this is April but it was snowing here yesterday, will quite likely be snowing again tomorrow. Isn't this all too obvious? So you have a double bluff, and the profits are so high that you can risk plenty of losses: while our gallant customs service is busy congratulating itself upon a haul, you slip another bigger one past while they're still preening at the press-conference.

This is all fantasy. Van der Valk knows next to nothing about narcotics since it isn't his branch, and the folk whose branch it is are all highly tightlipped about Smugdruggling.

Perhaps, not having had one this morning, he could do with a shave.

A groaning pinkbottomed naked Arlette – this afternoon's had been a walk almost as long as the Chinese Communist Party's judging by the way she was putting talcum powder on her feet – got out of his way complaining: hotel bathrooms are too small for a couple not actively engaged in fornication.

There are far too many questions, too many wheels within wheels, idiotic complications, and Kriminal-Kommissarissen chasing their own tales. Sorry, tails.

Like Herr Reich, or Rijk: he has lots of money and is maybe investing a bit in narcotics. Why does he invite me to dinner two days running, so hellish friendly of him?

Because I am a Commissaire of Police and said as much: a fact easy to check. He might find that cleverer than sneaking about pretending to be a Brit-birdwatcher like ass-Brownrigg. So he wants to know all about me: well and good, I'm all for it.

And who is the little brown bald man with the grin, unhappily deceased in say-the-least melodramatic circs? Fat Alfie, the great Buddha-idol of the entire French film industry, was so incredibly crude in his plotting. And is the little man perhaps yet another complicated quadruple bluff? Sim Salah Bim, the famous Oriental conjuror, is now about to do his famous escaping trick up his own asshole – and got it wrong. No one ever suspected him of being a narcotics agent of the US Treasury, since he acts the spy so blatantly that even Cary Grant will notice.

So my dear Mr van der Valk, putting cold water on his face to economise on aftershave, do please forget all this nonsense, go and enjoy a good-German-bourgeois-kitchen: as your dear wife says, 'Blow your nose and avoid lechery.'

Arlette, in a fancy petticoat, was putting on a long frock. Nice she does look. Earrings too and everything, it'll be the ivory cigarette-holder next.

In the lift going down was met Mr Brownrigg going up, pink from his sauna, clutching his belongings in an airline shoulder-bag. KLM too, just to prove he isn't Dutch – a pretty touch – but where?

A lovely evening, a bit chill but stars coming out in an evening sky. That's Orion. That very theatrical thing over there is the only other he knows (oh yes, the Great Bear yes, the Cassiopeia) – the evening star, the Good Ship Venus.

Really the Schwannallee was only just around the corner. This fine weather has brought out the daffodils. A real nineteenth-century nouveau-riche villa: fretwork Tyrolean trim to the roof and everything; a splendid example, and Jan met them at the door.

The hall was nice; suspension copper lamp with big glass jewels, shedding lovely red and blue and green and yellow lights on a lot of good, worn turkish rugs which had been put down over some crude Victorian tiles. In the middle of this lay an old white-moustached black Labrador, which growled upon seeing them, red-eyed, but didn't mercifully otherwise react.

"Good doggy," said van der Valk cautiously: any cop has had his ass et-off too many times to be anything else.

"No problem," said Jan cheerfully, "he's like me, too old to be aggressive."

He was glad they'd dressed up a bit. Jan had a velvet smoking jacket, plumcolour, enviable. Beyond loomed Frau Reich, black faille frock, long like Arlette's and failing to conceal thickish ankles, an opulently-powdered, jolly face with some gold teeth. Two very pretty girls. 'My daughters.' Twentyish, one fair, thin, jeans, fuck all this dressing up; the other chestnut-haired, minifrocked, a fancy cut in black and white stripes, long-legged, a round smiling face like her mum's.

And a guest. A big slow gaunt silverhaired type with a television profile, dressed up in a black suit with a string tie like a stage United States senator, and a big slow deep treacly southern accent to match.

A hand like a power shovel reached out to crush van der Valk's: it is not the way to his heart. Arlette thought she was lucky not to be bitten by those white capped teeth.

"My, this makes four pretty ladies, mah luck never misses." She noticed her clothes being taken off by a practised eye.

"The Reverend Margesson is holidaying in Europe," said Jan, "but he has a church in Florida and a following you just wouldn't believe, haven't you, Russ?"

"The Lord has been mighty good," gravely, "and I must repay."

As long as I'm not called upon to contribute, thought van der Valk greatly put out. "Names please," he said to the girls.

"Gisela," said the fair one. She was tall and wore glasses, behind which were appraising, intelligent and beautiful eyes.

"Rohtraut," said the glamorous one.

"Ho," delighted. " 'Wie heisst König Ringling's Töchterlein? Rohtraut, schöne Rohtraut.' " German poem learned at school.

"Right."

"But I seem to remember she was a very naughty girl. Didn't she go hunting with the page, and kissed him?"

"That's me." Gales of giggles. But by all means flirt with the girls, thinks Arlette; anything to get away from this ghastly preacher.

"And I'm Agaethe," says Frau Reich, "and you all must be dying for a drink; do perform then, Jan."

It's a social occasion. Lashings to drink, and a very good dinner. A strange blend of the formal and informal. No stiff German manners – on the contrary, Jan's coarse, easy jollities are very Dutch. Agaethe is not Dutch. But neither is she German, despite her daughters' names. So he asks her straight out, very Dutch himself, and she tells him she is Flamande, which explains the matter.

Dinner is slap-up, in a big diningroom with a Bohemian chandelier and a fine polished table, with lots of silver and served by a uniformed maid. He likes the wife; he likes the girls: their manner towards their father is simple, warm, affectionate. He has found it a pretty good general rule in criminal investigation that where you have a good family atmosphere, there isn't much likely to be wrong. But he is wary. The feeling of being tested is strong. He is still – perturbed? exercised? – by the weird happenings of that morning. He must be careful not to allow misplaced sensitivities . . .

He is suddenly surprised by Agaethe's getting up after the pudding, lifting-the-ladies. Has she been reading some grotesquely oldfashioned book, where one isn't supposed to know about women having a pee? Jan will be saying 'Anyone for the end of the passage?' at this rate. Meantime he is stuck with this frightful Predikant.

"Piet here has some remarkably sound ideas about crime." Jan pouring port, from a nice old decanter.

"Pretty ordinary. Most people have some sort of family life, which gives an anchorage and balance to their world.

A person can be unbalanced; the family copes. Little things like loyalty and affection and commonsense." The Reverend opines gravely with his head. "But if you have two out of kilter the result is a calamity – and crime is a form of calamity. A badly matched couple and each will cripple the other. It's not the sort of thing we have statistics on, in the department."

"But the rise in divorce statistics – "

"I came across an affair quite by accident," in a great hurry to choke it off, "on the way up here. A nasty little outbreak of pornography involving children – "

"Now this is one of the most abominable – "

"Disconcerting because a small town, a tightly knit social structure, traditionally strong on family observance, and here was a man in a position of trust too, local school head – one had to ask oneself what could have gone wrong, what could have created such an unbalance as to leave an honest and conscientious chap so vulnerable – "

"This is a question of which I have very very broad and far-reaching – "

Since plainly a dissertation threatened he said hastily, "Think I'll just have a quick leak before we go back."

"End of the passage," said Jan. "Yes Russ, you were saying?"

He had decided upon a particularly childish trick which sometimes works because so idiotic that nobody would believe . . . he shut the door, and stayed outside it. The worst risk is being caught by the maid, but she won't come to clear until we strike camp. The doors in this old house are solid, and fit closely, but that gravelly American voice and Jan's is loud, carrying.

"Well, what d'you make of our new friend?"

"Acquisition, definitely. As long as you're sure that – " trailing off.

"Perfectly sound in my view – hell, a commissaire of police, it's open, above board, verifiable. A phonecall would . . ."

"Yes, but if it were some kind of provocation?" Mumble

mumble, but for one monosyllable with sibilant and fricative and a hard long vowel sound—". . . spy . . . " And he thought, but wasn't quite sure, ". . . like the other."

This was as far as he could go so sneak quick along the passage, pull the plug noisily, walk back well freighted with food and drink.

"So let's go and have some coffee before the girls get nervous."

"Be joining you in a second," said the Reverend, making for the end of the passage.

"Sinister!" said Arlette. "I should just about say he was. He's the Reverend Elmer Gantry!" This now forgotten book, from the nineteen twenties, written by the tormented talent of Sinclair Lewis (such are the perils of best-sellerdom) had been found by her on a twopenny bookstall on the quays, when she was a young girl, and impressed her vivid imagination with a picture of America that she never shook off. Indeed, all these years later a prophetic quality can be seen in it. Elmer's promise to God on the very last page, to make of these United States a moral nation, isn't at all out of date . . .

"But the girls are awfully nice and so is Agaethe," she burbled on, gushing rather but she had had a lot to drink.

Van der Valk who had had more, to the point of tacking slightly on the pavement, kept counsel, because knowing a little is often too much and not nearly enough.

"Jan invited me to come and look at his boat in the morning if the weather's anywhere what it was today."

"That turns out rather well, because the girls invited me to go swimming with them and to ride, afterwards, so you can go and be all male and knowing over the twelve-cylinder motor without the risk of boring me. Boats don't thrill me much." Like many a Mediterranean peasant Arlette has a horror of the sea.

"Ride?" rather confused. "Ride what – a horse? Have you ever been on a horse?"

"Uh, once or twice. Always time to learn, no?" Courageously. Van der Valk feels about horses much the same as she does about boats. But right now it's sleep which interests him best.

7

What does one ask? 'Permission to come aboard?' He feels himself ridiculous and takes refuge in facetious pleasantry. Not to say waggish.

Jan on a boat is not ridiculous. But still less is he sinister. Boats – unlike cars – bring out the nice side in people. Van der Valk who has a feeling of not having slept easily is ready to believe in nightmares induced by eating too much lobster the night before. Wasn't Herr Reich simply another business man playing at being youthful, who patronises silly political opinions out of vanity? Showing off a bit. It's like the lobster which he had served last night. This is not an animal which flourishes on these flat coasts, sandy and muddy. They like the deeper water under a rocky shoreline, and must have come from as far away as Brittany: there is something ostentatious and nouveau-riche about having them here, packed live in a basket with seaweed. One of the can-do acts rich men are fond of; a swaggering small-boy mode of behaviour.

But the boat is marvellous! Van der Valk walked about, admiring it. This was made easier by its being hauled for the winter on a slipway, shored up with cleverly placed props, so that one can study the hull lines. Local men have worked on the part normally submerged, cleaning off the weed and barnacles, treating the copper sheathing with magic compounds, going over the wood for signs of rot or borers. Jan, who is sitting on the counter in old jeans and a guernsey lettered with yacht-club initials, doing complicated things to a great quantity of new-looking rope, is extremely professional and technical about all this.

"Wood!" said van der Valk. "I thought wooden boats simply didn't exist any more."

"And not just wood but a double skin of teak, I'd have you observe." He's delighted to be didactic about his favourite toy. "Well, you're quite right, they don't, or hardly at all. About the only place you can still get a traditional wooden boat built is Portugal: lovely they are too but not really suitable for this water; they're designed for the deep ocean, the Atlantic – altogether different lines."

"Why does the hull swell out this way?" Mr van der Valk is a landsman; as they say of a farmer, in Holland, 'a peasant who's never seen the sea'.

"Stability," said Jan. "North Sea is shallow water – choppy." And a lot of detail, too technical to follow.

"Wood must be expensive. Troublesome too. Should have thought they'd all be fibreglass by now."

"It's both. But it's worth it. Wood's elastic, and it breathes. First boat I had was steel; a schooner, lovely thing but you were either frozen stiff or boiled like a pig in all that condensation. Come on up, and you'll see."

Van der Valk climbed, stood open-mouthed. Mahogany fittings; a teak chart-table. He was carried away too by this enthusiasm, the boyish pride. Jan Rijk may be a vain and foolish man. And sly; unpredictably a menace. But one likes this open, warm side to him.

"Admiral de Ruyter was not better housed," says Jan, gleeful at the amazement.

"But where did you get this? – it's a museum piece!"

"So she is. Built in eighteen ninetynine. When I found her, after the war, in a boatyard in Harlingen, she hadn't been in the water for forty years. But been so well laid up, with such care, when floated she was as good as new. Look at the spars – Norway fir, and not a shake or a knot. Rigging of course is new. People laugh their heads off when they see this old gaff cutter rig but every single halliard is run back here to the cockpit and I can sail her single-handed like riding a bicycle. What say we take her out tomorrow? The threeday forecast is sunny interludes and windforce three to four, just right – she's a lumbersome old mare of course in light airs, but steady as a rock – your wife like to come too?"

"Hates the sea," laughing.

"Doesn't surprise me at all; Agaethe you couldn't get near this boat, not even roped to two horses pulling her. When they love it women are marvellous, crewing, but the moment they don't, then forget it."

"But don't expect me to crew," alarmed. "I know nothing about it."

"No strain," said Jan. "I'll do all the work. Nice to have company, that's all. Used to be a job, say, bringing her up to a mooring in any sort of seaway. Heavy work, and delicate. So I put in a little motor, Volvo diesel here in back of me. Not to push her along in any real sense – most you'd get is five knots in slack water – but for when it comes to manoeuvring in a confined space, taking her on and off the mooring, beating up a narrow fjord to windward: it's a safety margin really. Was the only thing I did. Motor charges up the batteries for electric light, though I still use the old paraffin lamps in dock, they're so much prettier. Oh yes, and coupled to a bilge pump. She'll take up a bit when we put her in the water this evening. But I get the anchor up by hand still, heave on the winch. Old ways are the best. This," gathering up a coil of the rope he was working on, "all my running rigging – manila hemp. Costs a fortune but stretchy, you see. Like the wood, gives a bit with strain. The less you change with these old boats the better they answer. You know what the ballast is, in this? – solid lead! Like a goldmine under our feet this minute."

"It's a vulgar comment," said van der Valk, "but the whole thing must cost a fearful packet."

"Yes it does," said Rijk simply, "and be as vulgar as you like, I don't mind. I'll tell you two things. The old boy who looks after this is nearly eighty and what will happen when he goes I just don't know myself. Second, I'm a dirty capitalist speculator. What do most people get for their money – five, maybe seven per cent if they're good, ten if they're lucky. Know what I look for? One hundred, and two if I can get it. So I've a flat for business in Frankfurt, and I'm on the road a lot, but summers I spend here, just for this," patting the rifle-stock curve of the lovely weathered wood.

"What's it you do?"

"I buy," with perfect simplicity. "Likely bit of property. Site or a house or a tract. I work out the necessary paper, I cut in my builder, I resell. Dirty, huh? I'm a profiteer, the worst sort. I make lots of juice. And I live pretty simply, this is my one real extravagance. I don't have any glass palace down in Cannes, no fancy swimmingpool. So I use money for ideals – I try to work for altruism. That seem funny to you?"

"No."

"I say, it's nearly time for a beer. You don't mind lunching here, just the two of us? Bread and a tin of tongue or something? Plain, together? And I'll explain."

Arlette van der Valk never had known anyone rich, much. At school or the university there had been a few of those who seem never to be short of money: they had not been important and had made no impact. The world in which she had been brought up – smallscale landowners, growers of not-very-good wine – is, or thinks of itself which comes to the same, the aristocracy of farmers. She had passed her childhood in a Provençal *mas*: the old stonebuilt farmhouses of southern hillsides, often eccentrically altered over the centuries into a sort of beauty. Brought up to independence of mind, certainly, and some contempt

107

for penny-pinching shopkeepers; even more for the corrupt trafficking of local mayors and notaries, deputies and dealers; but herself a peasant.

And while she is married to a man of whom seniority, some intellectual attainment (an oddball reputation), and a sort of distinction have made an important government official, she has not had occasion to frequent the rich.

So that it was more curiosity than anything which led her to accept the invitation to 'come swimming'. And she liked these women who were friendly, simple, and if they had a lot of money did not make a fuss about it. Agaethe, only a few years older than herself, was comfortable: the girls gave her a feeling of youth, as though she were again a student.

She had, however, not taken to Jan Rijk overmuch. That facile charm and overconfident manner . . . and as for that unspeakable American preacher! But she'd liked Agaethe, and this was just a female occasion.

Certainly there was something a bit off. She accepted, however reluctantly, that the Man felt a need to get to the bottom of it, and frequented these people as a tactic. A professional deformation! 'Il avait pris ce pli' (boring old Victor Hugo) 'dans son âge lointain.' He insisted upon getting dragged into affairs that were no business of – but there it is! She could see that he was puzzled. If it were only a simple piece of wrongdoing; like in Holland there – a twentyfour hour job, which any competent cop could follow and resolve. Here it was something which wound about, and led to complications. Not that that would stop him.

So he'd gone off, to look at the ghastly boat, and would likely be pottering about that, nattering, the entire day. But she could go, without any social nonsense, and unwind with these cheerful and agreeable girls. That compromised nobody.

Just so: the maid let her in to the house in the Schwannallee, and pointed the way to the back, which she hadn't seen at night. This was nice! In the old days the house had been built out in a south-facing *serre*: that especial feature of bourgeois houses in northern Europe, a glassed-in verandah or conservatory. And sometimes, as here, they have art-déco wrought-ironwork supporting a glass dome. Now cleared of the Edwardian palms and vines, and converted to a solarium, with the original tiles kept and a little swimming-pool added.

"Even in summer," said Agaethe, "half the time on that damn beach it's too cold and windy." She hadn't brought a bathingsuit. Hadn't thought, in early April!

"Och what!" said Agaethe. "I've got good ones I'm too fat for now, or the girls have half a dozen if you don't mind those skimpy things." She does mind, rather, and was relieved when a faded but classy black and white one-piece was produced which fitted her well enough. She is strongly possessed of the southern sense of modesty, none too keen about showing her bottom in the company of even women, but nobody looked at her. Agaethe, installed on a deckchair in a cotton beach frock, went on reading. The girls, lolling naked on mattresses in a nest of magazines, fiddled with the radio: she settled her straps and felt comfortable.

"Looks nice. You keep slim."

"I'll be one of those stringy grannies," she agreed.

"And I'll be a squashy granny, can't even look at a chocolate éclair without it bursting out all over. Try the water. It's at twentytwo, is that all right? The girls want it warmer but I say then you might as well have a bath. I'm a puritanical northern woman, I like to tingle a bit." Arlette dived, porpoised, turned, floated, wiggled her toes and said "Lovely." Quite true. The sun beating down on the glass might not have much warmth in it but the big radiator saw to that: the air was voluptuous. There was a lot to be said for being rich. She felt refreshed, climbing out.

"Coffee?" asked Gisela, kneeling up to pour out from a vacuum jug.

"Why is German coffee so much nicer than Dutch?"

"Nicer than French too."

"Absolutely true. They overroast it, the pigs, to be economical."

"Whyn't you take off the wet suit? – nicer that way."

"She doesn't want to," said Agaethe indulgently. "You go about naked all day, or would if I let you, but older women aren't that anxious to make an exhibition of themselves. These children are so cheeky," in a hurry lest 'older women' should have sounded tactless.

"But what about your American guest?"

"Packed and gone."

"God be thanked," added Rohtraut.

"Prob'ly perched outside on a tree with a telescope." Gisela moving her feet in time to the music.

"Now now."

"No hypocrisies please, Ma, you couldn't endure him."

"He was rather a lecher."

"Lecher! Fucking murderer is what I'd call him."

"Really, really."

Arlette sat up and pulled off the wet suit, feeling she was on holiday at last and what was there to be selfconscious about?

"I feel on holiday at last," said van der Valk in content.

"That's good," said Jan. Then shifted. "The daily grind is abrasive precisely because it's so damned depressing. You see it – it's encouraging to realise one isn't always isolated, that there are others too who share our ideals and are ready to put their backs into effort. Even a clown like old Russ – yes yes, I know, that earnest humourless manner puts one off, but ridiculous as they are their hearts are in the right place and the funds they bring in are vital to our finance. The weary cynicism one meets everywhere in Europe is one of my great sources of anxiety. The lack of enthusiasm."

Van der Valk, like all cops a professional lacker of enthusiasm, tried to sit up and look keen.

"And we're closer to the front line. People just don't realise. Right here," banging the lovely teak table still littered with the remnants of a piggish male picnic, "one has to be permanently on the alert. Cut through the Kaiser's ship canal to Kiel, and you'll be in the Baltic, swarming with Russian subs. I know: what's the point of an arms' race since they build four to our one? Well, in the meantime I have my eyes and ears, and not just a few electronic safeguards on the house. You haven't by any chance noticed a little fellow hanging about the hotel? Baldheaded chap, brown like a Malay, name of Quijs or that's what he calls himself."

"Yes I have. Hung about with cameras like a Christmas tree."

"That's the one. Quite smart to make it so obvious, to look so blatant as to rouse one's incredulity. People like that went out, you'd say, in a twenties detective story. A bluff doubled and then redoubled in spades, typical Russian trick. He seems to have disappeared. Rather abruptly." With quite a smack of relish in the telling, thought van der Valk. "Ol' Russ went off too, this morning."

Van der Valk, who had felt curious about the Reverend, couldn't help but wonder, is either of these characters as simple-minded as they both appear?

From the Reverend Russ he had had a packet of instructions about Our-struggle-against-the-Commies, so half-baked that no one could have taken them seriously. These dogmas were so simplistic, so crudely Biblebelt that one wanted to pat him on the head: right, my dear man, no doubt of it at all, and William Jennings Bryan . . . A literal interpretation of the Book of Genesis is exactly what we need as safeguard against the bolsheviks.

He had begun now to wonder how much of this the Reverend really believed. Back in the swamps of Florida, one could accept Ponce de Leon thinking he'd found the Fountain of Youth. But back here, isn't it a bit too disingenuous? The crusading myths preached by Heinrich Himmler, when I was a child . . . And Jan Rijk is surely too intelligent to swallow these fairytales of Teutonic Knights?

On Norderney, he can afford to be the ship-based romantic, happy in his beautiful wooden boat. It is the year eighteen ninetynine. The Czar is very much alive. Kaiser Wilhelm, his head ballooning with dreams of his North-Sea-Fleet, is building a delightful monument – it stands to this day in the centre of the village. Not pretty, but funny. It is constructed of stones brought from every city in Greater Germany.

But back in Frankfurt, who is telling me that this sophisticated, hardheaded businessman can swallow such trashy pietism about Our-first-line-of-defence?

Even afloat, one cannot believe in the red menace. In that clear air, looking across to the Gulf of Finland, nobody with their two grains of sense would believe in it. Maybe admirals: if they didn't believe it they'd be out of a job. Out in a boat on the Baltic, you quickly come to realise that drifting condoms are more of a menace than any Russian naval base.

Mr van der Valk is a romantic too, but also hard of head. He does not think it needful to summon Travis McGee to our rescue.

But he does know how schizophrenic people can get. He is indulgent towards the Gantry-fantasy, of making these United States a moral nation. Even the Himmler-fantasy, as held still by a few elderly Germans suffering from prostate troubles. But he finds it hard to accept that Jan can be this far deranged. Jan is a success, a balanced man with a wife and children. If they hear this stuff, Gisela and Rohtraut will simply break out laughing. Like all young Germans he has ever met, they are ashamed of it. But they accept it and are robust about it.

So are there two men here? One a sailor, a sane and balanced man? And the other a hobby-horse-riding lunatic? Feeling friendly towards the first, van der Valk would rather believe the other a figment of his over-ready imagination.

"I've been meaning to ask you, apropos of electronic safe-guards, how do you stand on navigation aids, a boat like this?"

"Ah, that is an interesting point, and very much to the purpose." Eyes gleamed; van der Valk didn't like all of Jan's enthusiasms but he did this one. "Now supposing I'd bought one of these power cruisers, like a Chris, you're with me? Not that I ever would, and I'll tell you why. One, Lucy here is thirtythree feet on the waterline, with her bowsprit say twelve metres overall. She sleeps three in comfort, two here and one forward, since the sail locker occupies the other berth there. For the equivalent space and comfort you'd need a fortyfive-footer, and beam to match; motor-cruisers' lines are much more wasteful.

"Two, they're conspicuous consumers. No good at all in a seaway, helpless as a beached whale, at the mercy of wind and tide: too much freeboard. To keep all that in control takes an enormous amount of power: big twin Mercedes diesels, eating space, huge great fuel tank, auxiliary for the generators, navigation cabin four times the size of mine, because why? – panoramic vision my foot, blind as a bat without radar, sonar, depth indicator, ship-to-shore, you name it and they need it. Big searchlights port and starboard, power winches, power this and that.

"What have I got? You see my cockpit? – I've a binnacle, and a tiller. I've one control for the motor, a hand throttle forward reverse and neutral, full, half and slow. I've a battery charger indicator. In clips I've a bearings compass for coastwise navigation, I can take a three-point fix in under a minute; I've day and night binoculars, and I've a torch. Captain bloody-Slocum went round the world with a lot less.

"What have I here? Chart-locker under the banquette, a shelf of pilot-books. Thermometer, barometer, chronometer, a hundred years old and none the worse, I can assure you. A Grundig Satellit radio for weather and general navigational information, and a transmitter so I can scream Mayday if it should happen and it very quickly can.

"Why do I tell you all this? Because it's a parable, van der Valk, it's the Collect for the Day. Your grand power Hatteras, it's like a modern soundstage, the singer-bugger can't make himself heard without four mikes and ten thousand watts of amplification, can't be seen without that immense battery of floods and coloured whirligigs. A power-boat today can't even cross the Solent from Cowes to Lymington without electronic aids enough to fill a Russian trawler. Take away the power and where is he?

"Now if I were a singer, van der Valk, I could pitch my unaided voice without as much as a pianist to accompany me, I can hit the pillar there at the back of the fourth gallery in the Wiener Oper with the softest note I have: and why? Because I'm trained and because my trust is in God, not the electric fairy."

"Strong argument."

"Take a man such as yourself. It doesn't in fact matter whether you're a police officer or you're gambling in cocoa futures on the commodities exchange. Take away the telephone, the show-up screen and the printout; you might as well be playing Scrabble. Even you – walking down the village street, see a man steal a chicken, you'll still run after him, take him by the neck and Right, mate, you're pegged."

"True," said van der Valk, grinning, thinking of the village in Groningen.

"But the other ninetynine cops in a hundred will go phone up headquarters to ask for instructions."

"Far too true," ruefully.

"This is what binds us together, creates a mutual attraction. If my phone is dead, or of a sudden there's no cocoa, I won't sit there, I'll go out and create a future in secondhand bicycles. Right? This is why I respect a fellow like Russ. Whatever we may think of him personally, there's a man who can exercise magnetism over anything between a hundred and ten thousand people, and he's made that out of nothing.

"Now if you imagine, van der Valk, that people like us who hold together out of sheer ability were also linked by a common collective purpose . . . " Jan's voice trailed off: he was concentrating upon the task in hand, that of splicing a piece of rope with a marlinspike and an enviable manual skill. Or perhaps it had occurred to him that he was going too far, too fast . . .

"Have any finger in the pies of the political police, then, do you?" Now he was whipping the end with something like cobbler's thread rubbed in wax. I haven't seen anyone do that, thought van der Valk, since early childhood.

"No. These spheres of influence are kept carefully separate. They do touch, upon occasion, but it's cut to a minimum, and then at a high level."

"Mm, yes," like a man who needs no telling. "Only ask because there's a fellow straying about, and to me he has the smell of something of the sort. In connection, you know, with this other, the camera artist." Holding the end of the thread to the light, screwing it between thumb and forefinger. "Hanging around acting the goat, with one of those tweed hats – you know, the brim turned down all round."

He decided to lie brazenly and see what came of it. He owed that much to Brownrigg. If they had been seen together, then too bad. The feeling anew of being tested.

"Now that you mention it, yes, but not so's I'd attach any importance to him."

"I've no evidence," said Jan indifferently, "bar that it's the sort they like to use, and that elaborately Brit look – complaining there's garlic in the salad . . . Could just as well be West German government. Or Dutch, come to that."

"Wouldn't mean a thing to me either way. Even if I were on official business, which isn't the case of course, they wouldn't come mumbling their passwords at me. Kripo types and always have been. It's rare to find cops changing over to other branches. We get typecast as a rule, at relatively junior rank. One meets these Stapo people occasionally, on a job, and in general there's friction, and even animosity. They swim in their own pond, and I in mine." This was the truth and Jan nodded.

"Same thing everywhere, pretty well. Still, keep an eye out for him."

Arlette walked, tried a dignified slow canter; fell easily enough into the up-and-down rhythm of a horse trotting. She was enjoying herself.

"Sturdy old riding-school nags," said Agaethe, reassuring. "Know it all by heart and could find their way blindfold. That girth might work loose, looks a bit slack to me. No hurry. Let him out a bit – wooh, here we go." Nor was there any nonsense about boots and breeches. Agaethe it was true wore jodhpurs, of expensive cut, 'because of my large behind', she said with candour. But both girls were wearing jeans, exactly like herself – and basketball shoes.

"Absolutely no need to go clapping in the spurs. When they come to a nice stretch, and are accustomed to gallop, they won't need much encouragement." This caused a small shadow of dread, unfounded, since of course she'd been given an ambling-palfrey. Nags or no, the others were more spirited beasts and urged on with whoops were out of sight in no time. That didn't mean much: the dune trail twisted in and out of the higher ridges, and their voices could be heard no more than a minute ahead. They'd wait. She saw no need to hurry a sedate pace, bumping about and showing huge disgraceful yards of sky between her own behind and the saddle. Oops! What's that?

Startled, she pulled the horse in, and it slowed at once obediently. A strange figure had dodged out of the thin undergrowth almost under her nose. Nothing sinister and only startling because unsuspected: no lurking highwayman but that slightly ridiculous personage who'd been palavering with . . . "There there," patting the horse to gentle it, unnecessarily.

"Thought I might catch you. Quick, here," handing her a piece of paper folded small and instantly adopting the air and gait of a chap out for a nice healthy afternoon hike. Irritated at this repetition of whatever idiotic game-of-espionage had already annoyed, even visibly upset her man, ruffling her in the process, she said nothing, nodded curtly, tucked the schoolboy note in her shirt pocket, shook the reins and kicked Dobbin into his staid canter. There they were, just round the bend.

"Did you stop to tighten the girth?" asked Agaethe kindly. "Jump off and do it for her, Roh – your own too, while you're at it."

"We were just sightseeing," laughing, "and I'm not quite sure how much acceleration I can give my big old Ferrari here."

"Sound kick in the ribs, the lazy old bugger." Hitching the straps a notch the girl gave him a good open-handed slap, to which he did not react beyond a look of mild indignation and a snort to say 'cheek!'

"Try mine – here, I'll give you a leg up. Jawohl – go, Rocket, go." Arlette found herself galloping, jockeying, with her arse in the air and enjoying herself immensely, and forgot all about the silly piece of paper until she was back in the hotel having a shower.

In the middle of this she gave a great jump, said a violent word, and leapt out, leaving rivulets (but it's a tiled floor). She was suddenly extremely conscious of having committed a crime (worse than a crime; an imbecility).

What has happened is that the housewife – cleanly, French, economical – has thrown her jeans on the bedroom floor: she has been invited to ride again next morning, and they'll do very well another day. Her underclothes have been flung in the handbasin with a bit of detergent, because hotel laundries are expensive, slow, and sometimes unreliable. The shirt is dripdry and will do very well on a hanger: it won't be pristine tomorrow morning, but it won't be sweaty either. But alack, she has forgotten the note . . . She fished the piece of paper out of the pocket, propped it on a torn-off tissue, set it to drain on the shelf with toothbrushes, and climbed back under the shower with an uneasy conscience.

Once dry – the things rinsed and hung on the radiator – she could no longer keep the mixture of fear and curiosity at bay.

It was a piece of paper tape from a supermarket check-out; the printed figures were now a pale violet colour but were perfectly readable. Ergo the Secret-Service gentleman, wanting to commit to writing in a hurry, had scrabbled in his pockets: no problem there. Alas, this writing. Not so much the wet as the detergent, which (as they announce with pride) will eliminate stains, including wine, blood, or felt-tip pen. It had only been two minutes, but the message had faded to a pale lilac tint, on the very edge of vanishing altogether. As the paper dried it was getting fainter still. There were eight words in three lines. It began with a capital V – perhaps *Vis* but there was at least one more syllable. *Vis* is Dutch for fish, which didn't help much. The next word, and the second of the line below, was also capped, the same letter, and both, she thought, a *B*. The third line began also with a cap and perhaps it was an *M* but one could no longer be sure. Oh dear, this is bad, and the Man will be cross.

Womanlike, Arlette had already begun to construct defences; was even counterattacking. He was not at home at five in the afternoon: boozing no doubt, on that horrible boat. He should have been home and then she would have remembered. And hadn't he said himself that – what was his name? – was a tiresome, a ridiculous personage, trying to spoil his holiday? The message, delivered in typically absurd fashion, would only be a further source of annoyance, and it was surely quite justifiable to regard it as trivial.

She felt cross and upset. It is feminine to regard that as the man's fault. She felt uncomfortably aware that her thighs, her bottom, and her lower back were stiffened and sore from the pulling of unaccustomed muscles: it would be nice to get the hotel masseuse. She was also hungry from fresh air and exercise. It was nearly six but she didn't dare go and have something to eat, because the Man – oh damn, where was her book? Go have a drink, and a soothing read.

She had finished with John Buchan. Apart from uncomplimentary references to Austrian, Polish and Portuguese Jews, it was utterly ridiculous anyhow (people in Buchan books had also a strong tendency to get given enigmatic notes on little bits of paper – goddamn, she did wish that hadn't happened).

Never mind, he was now expunged, obliterated – not a very happy choice of words, but mean-to-say. Now she had something much more promising, called *The Riddle of the Sands* and the man in the bookshop had laughed. 'You'll enjoy that. It's about Norderney.' Her appetite had been whetted and indeed, it was most exciting. Back in nineteenhundred and three, earlier even than Buchan but much better, a young man in a sailing boat, up along the coast towards Hamburg, had been offered guidance in a gale by a polite but sinister gentleman in a big barge-yacht, well-named the *Medusa*. 'Just follow me – short cut behind the sands into the Elbe estuary' – and the young man alone had been lured into a trap (colossal storm blowing on the sandbanks, with a falling tide) from which he had barely squeaked with a whole skin; and now with a friend to help him he was determined to find out what all this was about. Now Read On.

Hell, at the worst possible moment, both too late and too early, here was the Man; looking anxious too and perturbed. Dropping her book, Arlette let loose a flood of objurgations and accusations all jumbled up with the excuses for her own stupidity, incoherent, so that he had trouble making head or tail of what the hell has been going on. This is known as having

119

a row with one's wife in a public place: deplorable, and there are times one does not manage to avoid it. A real effort was called upon, to keep control of oneself and the voice down.

"Pity," examining the now dry, crinkled, and quite illegible piece of paper. "A silly thing to do."

"So was his a silly thing to do."

"Possible. One doesn't excuse the other. It's also possible that he could genuinely find no better means of conveying information in a hurry. Which means that he judged the information important, which in turn is my horrible luck. Something to do with Fish on Monday – great help."

"Couldn't the police lab recover the writing?"

"Yes, sure, the lab's right here in the village, next to the dry cleaners."

"Well, I'm only trying to help."

"In that case don't fucking hinder, and avoid idiot suggestions." There wasn't much point in squabbling. "Let's go and eat."

8

The gallant Commissaire did not sleep very well. His wife – irritating woman – said he hadn't opened the window wide enough: and/or had forgotten to turn down the thermostat of the radiator. He does not have the objective certainty that he should, about all this. He has examined far too many witnesses in the course of his life to be impressed by their certainties. 'Now to come back to this point, Mr Simpson, you have told me you closed the window a crack, getting up. And you gave the thermostat a turn, by the same token; good. How do you come to be so convinced that this is so?' Simpson falls into a rambling tale, to the effect that an April dawn on the North Sea coast strikes chill, getting up, when you're wearing only thin cotton pyjamas. All perfectly logical, highly circumstantial, and you are quite persuaded that the wretched Simpson is telling the truth – or would be, save that the fingerprint on the thermostat (arising out of that, palmprint on the window lock) are those of the chambermaid: now how d'you account for that? The wretched Simpson, totally overthrown and seeing himself imprisoned for perjury, is still incapable of believing that the entire episode took place in his imagination. It is a police commonplace that your most vivid and detailed eyewitness happened to be standing exactly where there was no clear sightline.

It was quite likely that the brave van der Valk had not even woken up, while telling his wife crossly at breakfast that he hadn't had a wink of sleep between one and halfpast four. Those ridiculous suppositions, milling about in the semi-conscious, produce further symptoms of unsettled malaise, coupled with irrational fears. In the daylight – chilly but sunny, a pleasant sailing breeze, windforce four to five, big white galleon clouds in convoy upon an enormous brilliant sky, looking as unreally blue as the Mediterranean Sea when a mistral is blowing – these phantoms vanish. In theory, anyhow.

He is looking forward to the promised sail, has put on his warmest clothes. He does not want to fall into any more dreams. It is sufficiently chilly, down by the waterside, to keep him thoroughly awake. As promised, the boat was in the water, held on a mooring by fore and aft warps. The tide was up, making ripple noises round the hull.

Jan greeted him with enthusiasm, approved of his hip-length leather auto coat. "That won't take any harm, from a bit of sea-water? We'll get a bit of spray, further out." The diesel started with a rumble. "If you'll just cast off forward? Just coil the warp down, quite roughly, by the anchor-winch." The water went slap-slap, the motor clunk-clunk; the shore receded.

"Right, we'll set a bit of sail. No no, sit where you are. Take the tiller if you like, save me fastening it. Keep her more or less steady in the fairway." Jan went forward, easily balanced to the gentle pitching movement, fiddled with the jib in a leisurely way. Van der Valk became nervous about an approaching ferry.

"That's all right, she's going to Juist, miss us by a hundred yards. Looks closer, on the water. Mainsail up now, and we're away. Put the indicator down to zero and the motor'll stop of itself. You see? – quieter already." He was impressed by the athletic ease Jan showed in hauling up the peak. "Sure she could take a topsail, but we won't bother; it's a lot of work, for a knot of extra speed we don't need. Now we'll go outside the islands, away from all this traffic. You've nothing to do – sit back and enjoy it. Like I told you – simple as riding a bicycle. Wind a point off west-north-west, closehauled we're on a point or two of northwest. Now just the one thing, when we come to tack. Sit back and you're in no trouble, but remember not to stick your head up too far forward, because if we take a beat and the boom jibes you don't want to get knocked overboard, haha, that wouldn't be funny. Right now we're on a nice board, give us a famous slant out."

The boat leaned a little, drove steadily. The islands dwindled to smudges on the horizon. He had the agreeable fantasy, picking up the binoculars, that if he waved, Arlette would wave back. Some sort of rusty old freighter thing was plugging in towards – one presumed – Delfzijl. Another, bigger, was pottering out in (one was vague about compass points) the general direction of Norway. He sincerely hoped it was not brimful of revolting chemical by-products which the Dutch, his dear compatriots, were far too given to dumping out here somewhere, on the admirable principle of out-of-sight-out-of-mind; until, that is, the whole North Sea turns an evil reddish colour and Holland begins to go brown and melt.

"Well," said Jan, slipping a loop over the tiller and tightening it, after a bit of fine adjustment to the mainsheet, "let's go down and make ourselves a cup of coffee."

"Don't we need to keep a lookout?" startled.

"What for? No traffic, this early in the year. She's on automatic pilot: we go and put our feet up." He did the few steps down the companionway into the cabin backwards, holding on. In the silence of the cabin he pinched his ears, wondering where the wind had gone to, and Jan 'put the kettle on' exactly as though they were at home in the front parlour. A newspaper was lying on the chart table.

"I'd forgotten that. Kept for you to see. Interesting item of information, there in the oddjob page." It was the *East Friesland Courier*: a paragraph on the inside page was ringed. "Skimming at breakfast-time that caught my eye; thought it might interest you." Van der Valk read, and was nailed to the leather cushion of the banquette.

The headline read: BIRDWATCHING?

The well-known local restaurateur Herr S., while tra-
velling on the Leer–Cloppenburg main road, was the
involuntary author of an accident with fatal consequences
this afternoon, when a man stepped imprudently on to the
carriageway, with such suddenness that the fatal issue could
not be escaped.

The unhappy victim, subsequently named as Herr B.
of British antecedents, was said following enquiries to be a
keen observer of bird life. His rucksack was found to con-
tain binoculars, a camera, and an observation notebook.
A possible explanation of this fatal gesture, a Road Police
spokesman speculated last night, was a moment of inatten-
tion conceivably due to the sighting of some species rare in
our region. He had come, it was said, from Norderney,
well-known as an observation post for winged fauna.

"Odd coincidence," said van der Valk. His coffee-cup swayed
about when he lifted it, with the swing of the boat. One needed
an elastic wrist, to keep it from spilling.

"What the Polizei says is not always what it thinks," agreed
Jan. "As a police officer yourself you'll know they're pretty
selective in what they tell the press. I've fairish sources there-
abouts and I may be able to hear something. In these so-called
democracies it's often hard to know who's manipulating who,
be it Polizei or Press. Now if we were in Holland you'd be well
placed to get at the truth of a thing like this. One of my chief
ambitions is that we should be structured for quick accurate
information wherever it may be useful."

"A party, really?"

"All that party thinking has always tended to be on nation-
alist lines. The word militia has a bad name, even though it's
only a logical derivation of militancy, which is indispensible.
One doesn't want a lot of self-important oafs strutting about
in uniforms, but sensible and right-thinking people in key

positions. I prefer to think of us as a movement, and fluidly international in our approach."

"But then the aim must surely be to gain control of these key positions you mention, and in any country you name that's bound to – like here in Germany, where any movement of this nature gets a National-Socialist label nailed to it."

"My dear van der Valk, what can you be thinking of? That godless crew whose instincts – many of them good – were perverted by atheism. Look where it led them. We do have to gain strength first in the northern countries – that much we share – because there the corruption is least, and there also the Russian pressure leans heaviest upon us. There too, paradoxically, Protestantism is strongest, which handicaps us in the narrow sense, but the people are basically God-fearing and a unity of Christian belief – " There was a sudden heavy jar or bump, as of a dully thudding impact. The coffee-cups jumped and clattered. Shaken, van der Valk thought for an instant they'd run aground. "What the hell was that?"

Jan seemed unperturbed, but was quick up the companion-way. He gave a sharp turn to the tiller, bringing them into the wind, sails shivering. Van der Valk was staring about at the water but there was nothing to be seen.

"Not that uncommon," said Jan. Their way, checked, had slowed to nothing: the boat wallowed on the water. "Half submerged wreckage. Wood by the sound, a baulk or pile, rolls about waterlogged, you don't see it coming and you don't see it going. Like I told you, her strong build fits her to take anything in reason. But imagine one of those resin-plastic catamarans, skimming along, you'd be a gone goose." Nipping up forward he lowered himself overboard, with no support but the bobstay, came up redfaced but placid.

"No visible damage to the forefoot but under the waterline's a different story. Depends how she hit. Keel's no problem but there could be a plank started, under the sheathing."

"What do we do?"

"Oh we're not going to sink," taking the slanted eyebrow as a landsman's need for reassurance. "Take off the jib," furling and tying it up with adroit fingers, "sail her a bit easy, and if she's making any water we'll learn about it soon enough. If you'll hold her as she is now," closehauled, a stately progress to windward, "watch the mainsail: if it ripples she's starved and give her a scrap more." The wind had died to a light air; the sun shone; Reich was plainly competent. This wasn't the *Titanic*. We have a radio, thought van der Valk, we can go Mayday, Mayday: the flow of adrenalin made this quite an attractive notion. We have an inflatable dinghy lashed on the cabin roof, with lifejackets and things. I don't want to go in the goddamn water – it won't be much above freezing point.

Jan dived acrobatically down the fore-hatch, and could be heard frigging about in the mysterious bowels of the sharp-end: chain-locker, the 'head' – the bits of boat the landsman sees nothing of and prefers not to know about.

"Certainly nothing grave," reappearing. "Maybe some seep-age."

"How do we tell?"

"We rig the handpump," fitting a wooden handle to a metal socket in the side of the cockpit, working it with a to-and-fro movement. "Antique but efficient. First time in the water this year, the wood takes up a little so there's bound to be a bit of loose water. If there's more than that then yes, we're leaking, and I can switch the diesel on, that'll keep anything clear." Van der Valk was impressed with this efficiency. The accident – or incident – had also put a stop to political theorising.

"There," the pumphandle was working easily, with nothing to pull but air. "Clear. Try again in a quarter of an hour, and if there is water there then we know. Head for the barn, while damning logs which lie about. Likely enough a treetrunk from the last autumn gales. Denmark, Norway, anywhere, currents'll do anything hereabouts. Right," retaking his place as steersman, gathering a bight of mainsheet preparatory to uncleating it, "turn her off the wind, won't bother with the jib, let her ride on staysails, nice and easy. Fore-staysail's on a horse," for the amateur, "no need to change the mainsail – shan't let her out overmuch."

"What's a horse?"

"See that rail bolted to the deck? – staysail's on the shackle, runs along it, slaps across on a change of tack. Lazy old fisherman's piece of gear. But the jib or foresheets run right aft here under my hand. What did I tell you? – it's like riding a bicycle. A modern rig you need a crew, and I like to do things single-handed." To be sure.

Ten minutes later it was van der Valk's turn to have a go at the handpump. A tiny bit of bilge and "Nothing but air, Skipper" he could report proudly.

"What did I tell you? Good old girl," slapping the counter as though it were a horse. "Goddamn trimaran'd 've been cut clear in half. I'm a traditionalist, man. Make it south by east," handing the tiller – lovely piece of wood like an axe-helve – back over to van der Valk, "and we'll see the wind under her tail," dodging up forward to reset the big jib.

"Lovely," feeling the bite and kick under his hand. The schoolboy enthusiast! People are like this too, over cars. However bored by didactic exposition of technical detail, van der Valk is enjoying himself too much to think it wearisome. The hardest-headed businessmen are often the most unashamed romantics, at play.

"Got a bigger jib than this, for summer. Lighter canvas. Bigger mainsail too; get the gaff up higher. Topsail's a luxury really. You'd be surprised how these old cutters can travel, then. Who wants a spinnaker? – the Bermuda rig is for cowboys. I'd go round the world, van der Valk, sail her to Valparaiso, nothing I'd like better."

Is this a bad man? That is in any case a rarity, seldom met with by even the police officer of experience; the man who will do evil for evil's sake – in almost every instance recognisably psychopath. More frequent are those, classically of high intelligence and great attractions, of evil omen because so deeply disturbed that they will sacrifice human life to satisfy their needs. In the literature, too little attention has been paid the victims – so often people one is happy to see the back of. There are murders by accident. People with a lot to lose do better to stay away from low balconies high above ground, sleeping pills with a low overdose level, loaded firearms – or loaded egotists. One should recall Marlowe's advice to the dentist who employed the Little Sister as secretary: Don't leave any harpoons lying about the office.

Van der Valk would never know whether anything more than his own forgetfulness, stupidity, or plain euphoria was in question. Getting his first lesson in steering – quite the old salt by now –

"Okay, stand by for the jibe. On the word your tiller hard over, steady up to about west-south-west – ready? Port!" The boom swung over on to what he was learning to call starboard-tack. The mainsheet is hemp because, explained Jan, that is a long fibre, 'stretchy'.

"Ever read *The Riddle of the Sands*?" Jan went on.

"Means nothing to me."

"Not a great reader myself but the story plays round Norderney, good yarn. Two young English chaps, boat much like this, come sailing round here, uncover sort of invasion scheme based on the islands, time of the Kaiser, oh, way even before the Great War. Kaiser widened the Kiel Canal, take big warships, but shallow draught for North Sea work. It's pretty interesting. The engineer planning this has a field headquarters over there," pointing, "on Memmert. And their cover is the usual treasure-hunt story. Around eighteen ten–eleven, Napoleon held Hamburg as solid as Lyon. Best general he had sat there – Marshal Davout, keeping an eye on Sweden. Story goes that he sent a cargo of gold bars back to France in a frigate – *Corinne*. She's supposed to have been caught in a storm, a northeasterly here is something wicked, and gone aground here."

"Sunk?"

"Christ, yes, stick on a sandbank in one of those and you'll break up in five minutes."

"A pity for the local people."

"Exactly. Boxes of gold are very heavy, and this sand is soft. Swallowed up without trace – if there ever was any gold."

"Like the gold of the *Egypt* – or come to that, Captain Flint."

"Ready about, again." Jan had taken over the tiller, to allow him to study these historic features through the binoculars. Now if you sit, in a sailingboat running before the wind, the movement dances you up and down. A horizon viewed this way, through powerful binoculars, is likely to make you feel sick. Van der Valk's mind, ever given to roam, was concerning itself with how the Captain, in the good old days of a clipper bouncing about somewhere (out to hell and gone in the Indian Ocean), standing on his quarterdeck with the eyepiece of his sextant held tight to the cheekbone, managed to shoot a star sight. You had to get it accurate. You barked out 'Time' to Mr Mate standing in the chartroom with *his* eye on the chronometer.

He was practising this. Standing makes it easier because there is more elasticity in your knees than in your bottom (same reason as manila instead of nylon cord for your mainsheet).

There also exists a warning sense, speeding our reaction time before a calamity. Human beings are a lot slower than dogs. Still, this sense must exist, since staring out to sea he could not possibly see the boom coming, and he had heard the 'Ready-about' without registering: but the subconscious does things the conscious is too slow for (one learns about it at police training-school). Undoubtedly he had ducked, or at least bent his knees that much the more.

He rather thought, afterwards, that he had heard the expression used; or read, more likely. To be 'shaved', or 'scalped' by the boom. This is something of a classic. Now he knows why, sitting down, rubbing his head. Jan, with one eye on his sails, the other on marker buoys, for they are running into shallow water, with a tide well out, has noticed nothing, and who shall blame him? The crew had been warned to watch out for a jibing boom. This 'boom' is a spar of Norway-fir like the mast: the diameter of a man's fist. That makes a formidable club, impelled by the leverage of a few square yards of sail, and a spanking breeze. That much more of an arrestor, given purpose behind it.

Purpose? Surely that must be remote in the extreme. But isn't it almost perfect for an 'accidental' homicide?

Consider the facts. 'You know I did warn the silly clown to stay out of the boom's arc. Sitting, there's no risk at all.'

The traditional warning is given verbally. One learns what 'Ready-about' means. This code exists in all trades considered risky. 'Heads' . . . A cook carrying a boiling pot shouts 'Chaud, devant', and the miner, using explosives . . .

With a sailing breeze abaft the boat would be doing what we are learning to call eight to ten knots. Say twentyfive kilometres per hour. You cannot stamp on a sailingboat's brakes: you can't snap it into reverse: you don't make a three-point-turn. It's not a car!

Even out at sea the sharpest pilot would need two to three hundred metres in which to turn and beat back. In these channels among the islands, where the water shoals abruptly, it would be more difficult still. In poor visibility, deprived by cloud and rain of either a star sight or even a two-point coastwise fix, the frigate *Corinne*, finding herself too close on shore, could not find means to claw off. Once a howling gale put square-rigged ships on a lee shore, it also put paid to their chances of survival. This had happened to the invincible armada off Dunkerque.

And if I am stunned by a crisp knock on the head, sweeping me overboard, my chances of survival are very poor indeed. I will drown in three metres of water quite as readily as in sixty. There was no need to plan anything. I am no more than an inconvenient witness.

Rijk, Reich, whatever he called himself, had fallen silent; was piloting with an air at once absent and concentrated, on a road he knew well but which needed watchfulness. That is natural, and he has explained it to me. The boat draws six feet of water, with a fixed keel; giving stability and comfort: 'on a sailing boat this size, a cabin you can actually stand upright in is a luxury.' The reverse of this medal is that among the islands, when the tide is out, you are pretty hemmed in to the dredged channels, such as they are.

He had given way to schoolgirl hysteria, like a blonde in an Alfred Hitchcock movie: imagining things! He is well aware that it is one of his weaknesses.

"You're looking as if you've had enough of it," said Jan in a friendly voice.

"A bit tired, I agree, it's stimulating and exhausting when one isn't used to it."

"Well, we can get in under sail but there's no point, really, in showing oneself clever. I'll start the motor and then take the sails off. There are awkward currents hereabout so keep an eye out. Give a little touch of motor if she seems to drift, while I pack."

Brownrigg had been given a nudge out into the roadway? However farfetched, one could not dismiss the possibility altogether. This inconvenient witness had only been overzealous, or had he really found out something compromising? All of it would be scenario, but for the demise of Herr Quijs. He hadn't imagined that! The little brown man had certainly got close to an awkward fact, and suddenly too. There had been no time or opportunity for any accidents.

He brought the boat back into Norderney harbour. Jan

as pilot, no more than was needed. 'Half ahead. Starboard a trifle.'

"Well now, think we've earned a real Dutch gin, don't you?"

"Weren't you wanting to have her hauled out again on the slip, in case of any damage?"

"Oh tomorrow will do for that, my old boy likes to dig his garden round this time. And the weekend coming up – no good to me alas, I have to be in Frankfurt tomorrow, for some business. What about you – staying on another couple of days? Can't count on this good weather holding alas – April on the North Sea! But with luck we could have another go on Monday. There's no bottom board started or a leak would have shown up."

"I'd like to stay on a day or two. My wife's enjoying herself – thanks to the hospitality of your family. I should really be back in the Hague."

"Ach, give them a ring," comfortably. "Your taking another week won't cause the government to fall."

"Hardly," grinning, drinking gin. Though in the Hague, even senior bureaucrats are frowned upon for starting their weekend at lunchtime on Friday.

Back in the hotel, van der Valk made a phone call. This was to a gentleman in the Hague, who agreed he wasn't going anywhere this Saturday. Still didn't want policemen spoiling his weekend. Van der Valk resorted to bribery. All right, I'll buy you lunch.

And after this he sat in an uncomfortable armchair, smoking too much.

Jan was going to Frankfurt, or so he said. The family was staying on for another week. Or so they said. And Arlette has got quite chummy with them.

Even if an interest is taken in the doings of Herr Kriminal

Kommissar, his popping off for a day will not cause over-excited comment, when Arlette stays here.

Mm, it's no very great distance back to the Hague, if an awkward drive: getting back here the same night might be a squeeze – what time is the last ferry?

Arlette is a guarantee of good behaviour. Put more bluntly, she's a hostage. Not a very pleasant thought. But one could live with it. It would need some tact in explaining. Hamburg, she'd been saying, was calling to her. Didn't want to take root on this goddamn island.

Where is Arlette, anyhow?

And what had that ass Brownrigg been getting up to? Once back on the mainland, had he thought himself free of observation? Shown undue curiosity about, say, the recent activities of Mr Quijs? Since his future didn't amount to much, although his disposal must have caused a problem. Mm, given a boat . . . Perhaps Mr Brownrigg had found out, to warrant his meeting with a nasty accident, that way.

Mm, pretty cute accident, if it weren't to cause complications with the authorities. Damn this island: one is isolated, and blocked from gathering news or information.

He went down to sort out the hotel girl, who was apologetic. Oh but she'd rebooked the room: Frau van der Valk had said you wouldn't be wanting it past Saturday.

"But I'm sure I can find you something" – when Arlette came rolling in all noise and hilarity, with the Reich girl, the fair-haired one.

"Hallo, Gisela, sorry, we've a slight hitch in logistics. Arlette, you've given the room up, but I was counting on staying another couple of days. It's only a stupid piece of business I have, over the weekend."

It was to be hoped she'd catch on. The girl caught on quicker.

"Oh but that's no problem," all friendly warmth. "She'll come and stay with us – won't you? Pa's going too for a couple of days, stupid old Frankfurt, but we've got another week. So we're alone and we'd love to have you. We've been planning a bit of gaiety."

"That's very kind," he said firmly, "and rather handy as it happens." So it was . . .

"Oh, I'm sorry if I've been stupid," hastily making amends. "Of course I want to stay. If you're sure, Gisela – "

"Don't be daft, loads of room. I'll pick you up after breakfast – must dash now, I left the car on the street. Enjoy your weekend," she said to him, politely.

"And now what the hell – ?" not at all politely. "I'm going up to change. I do think you might sometimes have the consideration – " Loud and cross: he hustled her into the lift. One would have to explain. But as little as possible.

9

Arlette felt indeed cross. Bewilderment. And frustration. What sort of nonsense is this now? Police work my foot! We are on holiday, and I don't intend . . .

Once she had simmered down, it wasn't all that bad. Some days later, she would cry a little, in remorse; learning that he had not told her about Mr Brownlgg, hitherto a comic and even a ridiculous figure. Yes – there were times when the less she learned about police work, that squalid business, the better.

Right now, she soothed herself with the thought that a day without the Man might be thought of as rather a relief. Since oh, he could be annoying . . .

By now she was on friendly terms with kind, placid Agaethe. And the girls; vivacious, funny, and she felt at home with them. A day to herself would even be rather nice. Nothing disloyal in that: the Man had a bee in the bonnet about this Rijk: all right, Reich.

The man could well be a crook in one or more of his facets: rich businessmen generally were! But from what she had seen, or heard, these arcane dabblings in political theory were no more than a pastime. On a par with vintage cars, or a sudden passion for hang-gliding. Men were like that.

Her own boys had been bitten by the speleology bug – ropes, helmets with headlights – down horrid potholes. Or the time they could think and talk of nothing but parachuting. Ruth was still madly in love with pop singers!

One must not take it too seriously. The Man had been

upset by that secret-service antic. In her experience Stapo people were humourless pests, whether in the pay of the CIA or the Russians. Politics! With her double nationality she could vote in either country – and never did.

Judging too, and shrewdly enough, by Agaethe and the girls, there were far worse people around than Reich. They wore him lightly. 'Oh Dad – perfect pest with his secret societies, filling the house with all sorts of ghastly people like that unspeakable American preacher. One does so wish he'd take them off on the boat, but that's sacred. Your man's in very high favour, Arlette, people never get invited on the boat unless he's totally subjugated, so I can tell you – compliment!'

Nor were the girls feather-brained misses; plenty of brains and character to make them good company as well as bringing a note of gaiety she missed sometimes in her own life (Ruth would be good company when she grew a bit older). Gisela was reading anthropology, with a notion to a career in archaeological work. There are more interesting things in the world than politics.

"If you're interested in prehistory," Gisela had been telling her only this afternoon, "there are things worth seeing in this countryside. Like the stone circles and the menhirs, which are moon and star observatories and much more sophisticated than they seem, so that one starts to speculate upon religious and philosophical purposes since plainly there's a lot more to it than just a solar calendar for crop-planting or whatever: didn't you say you were going up towards Bremen when you leave here?"

And she'd drawn a little map for Arlette, because just off the Bremen–Osnabrück autoroute there are two remarkable monuments of this sort in the forest: they're called the Bride and the Bridegroom, nobody seems quite to know why. The local village is called Visbek, it's well worth a stop.

As for Rohtraut's pretended sex-bomb act: the girl was in her second year of medicine, so knowing how severe the selection test is after the pre-med year, there's more to her than meets the eye.

Fresh and reposed, van der Valk was driving jauntily across the green and brown countryside of early spring, northern Germany unrolling like wool from a skein, when there used to be skeins; when, one should add, there used to be wool. It gave him a youthful feeling, since Arlette's knitting days belonged to the time when the children were small, and he was pressed into service to hold the skein, in the crook between thumb and forefinger, with enough tension to allow her to wind it off into a ball with great skill and speed – tilting his hands just enough to let the thread turn the corner smoothly. She does still knit sometimes, and the unfinished product sits about for months on end, very female. Mm, rather like official paperwork: never let it be said the word 'female' has any pejorative connotation. The civil service is full of old maids but most of these are male.

Sometimes there was just no means of telling whether one had begun with the right end. The wool hitched and blocked – and sometimes she had to admit defeat, letting the embryo ball slip to the floor while she began again at the other end. But then it would never be the satisfying, even enjoyable job it should be. Hence, dear children, the expression 'a tangled skein', which to you means nothing whatever.

Nowadays the wool isn't even wool. A little label stuck on tells you there are complicated percentages of acrylic. Obscure threads in the yarn. Lose the little label, and you'd need the police lab to analyse what's in it.

Yes, the fine weather has broken, and one does not need Jan Rijk's met forecast to tell one that this is a big northwest wind, with great towering masses of cloud, the odd gleam of oppressively brilliant, and even blinding sunlight, since he was driving almost due south, between Emden and Lingen. Wind within three points of north, since we have learned to be so nautical compass-wise. And it won't take much to turn these violent showers of rain into snow-flurries. This winter can still crack its tail.

Turning off the Münster road towards Oldenzaal – and Holland – the road instantly changed character, into a tangled skein, very, as the pastoral, ample landscape of Germany gave way abruptly to the industrial Dutch northeast; scurrying ants' nest of folk running very fast (why? – where to and what for?) upon purposes known only to themselves, carrying huge burdens with a persistence and obstinacy quite entomologically Dutch: we are an exceedingly weird folk, thought van der Valk.

Somewhere hereabouts there is an autoroute, and when/if found (since the signposting is as usual grotesque) it will whisk him straight across Holland to the Hague. Meantime the phrase 'spaghetti junction' appears to have been invented especially for Enschede and Hengelo and Almelo; damn them all three.

The Dutch road authority is forever building more roads, until the whole country will end as one monstrous pot of spaghetti, and will still never catch up with the explosion of wheeled traffic: oh why can't they stay at home and knit!

This authority is also a great believer in imposing patience upon its people, and makes the traffic lights change with a ponderous weight of decision like a swing bridge: the toll-keeper used to lower a wooden shoe tied to a length of string, to receive the penny due from the chuffing canalboat beneath.

Turning now due west, the wind pressing upon his northern quarter, driving rather too fast but jauntily, with no Arlette to mutter imprecations at that wealth-fattened butcher in the huge Volvo, he spanked along towards Utrecht; a medium-sized anonymous car like a million others.

Monsieur Proust, brooding upon the dance of the spires while the donkey-cart pottered through the Beauce landscape (flat, like Holland) around Illiers, would have been equally intrigued at meeting signposts saying *Utrecht Turn Right*, while three kilometres further is another exactly the same but *Utrecht Turn Left*. And van der Valk, who is at home now, and thoroughly familiar with the psychology, goes unperturbed straight ahead, knowing that he will miss Utrecht by a hair's breadth at the last possible second. And once past Gouda – famous, though there isn't a cow in sight, for those great yellow balls of cheese, the reason why Belgians refer to the entire ilk as CheeseHeads – he knows exactly how and where to disentangle the skein: he is no longer an Amsterdammer but a Hague bureaucrat.

He has a meeting set up with another such: his superior, if not quite his chief; with no direct authority over him but whose good or bad opinion has much impact, far-reaching effect. At first, after his hip wound had brought him a startling promotion – in itself a subtle demotion but such are the ways of administration – he had been very unhappy. Since then, armadillo-like, he has learned to roll himself into a ball, like all the others, presenting a smooth carapace to the world. Kipling's Jaguar, as those of you who read the *Just So Stories* as children will recall, never could quite remember, innocent and a bit dim, what you did to make them uncoil: you dropped them into water? Van der Valk knows better, you drop them into gin. Meaning roughly, you invite them to lunch and make sure it's a good one.

His target is (exactly as in England) much more important than he sounds, owing to the civil-service art of meiosis: litotes if you insist. A deputy adjunct undersecretary in the Ministry of the Interior, whatever it sounds like, is no teadrinking understrapper but one of the most important keys to government.

This one – he prefers to be known as X – looks rather like Robert McNamara, a historic figure who made the mistake of believing in his intellect, which was better than anyone else's. Thus the Ford Motor Company, the United States Government, Vietnam, etc., were dead-easy really: you only had to be bright. Quantify. Be well briefed. Know your statistics. And the older among us remember that Robert got into trouble with all those woolly-minded generals.

Sharp-cut, diamond-faceted of feature as of mind; and some slight physical resemblance in the ferociously disciplined hair, by nature limp and grey, by art gummed, mathematically parted, slicked down hard to the skull: also in the octagonal rimless glasses which catch stray gleams of light, focus them remorselessly, and penetrate, laser-like, the ivory skulls of other civil servants who have the bad luck to be solid bone all the way through from entrance to exit.

X has too his human side, now to be seen in his luxurious home in Voorburg: geometric persian carpets, abstract designs on the walls, a wife to whom van der Valk has to be very polite. And the fact that it's Saturday morning: X is doing his weekend unwind. Over a chess problem? – no no, that becomes caricatural; he may look like a computer but is much less stupid.

"Eat Indonesian?" suggests van der Valk.

"Yes, that would be nice."

"Don't drink too much gin," puts in the wife, simply to underline the fact that she has not been invited.

At this period there was still a restaurant in the Hague where time had been arrested forty years earlier. Holland then 'owned' the immense archipelago of Insulinde. Djakarta was unjokingly called Batavia, and bore a surreal resemblance to a Dutch provincial town. There were canals, gabled houses and civil servants; large, Dutch, and pink.

This restaurant is large and white, with jalousies to filter the blinding light of Java, the floor tiled for coolness against the tropical sun. Here a few years ago could still be seen lizard-like little old men in tropical tussore suits, a leg thrown for coolness over the arm of the rattan armchairs, ordering a gin of the white-saronged, barefoot, brownskinned attendants as perfectly trained in the illusion that Mr Gladstone was still Prime Minister as any waiter in the Garrick Club.

These old men were all eighty then and are all dead now. Instead one finds self-important young men apeing the attitudes (and the same phenomenon can be noticed in clubs in London), warming their bottoms in front of huge fires, talking loudly, flowers in their buttonhole, looking condescendingly at older men who close their eyes and think 'Puppy'.

"Two young gins," said van der Valk. One doesn't drink old gins before a meal. As with martinis, there is much fussy folklore about getting them cold enough, of glasses kept in the deepfreeze and bottles enclosed in cylinders of ice . . . this is Somerset Maugham country. A huge slow fan revolves in the ceiling: the old men used to stare at the jalousie slats as though to see the quick tiny lizard called the chik-chak.

"Two Rice-Tables." The food of Insulinde is in character between that of south China and what the Dutch call with condescension 'that other India', the subcontinent formerly painted pink on maps.

"Two Orangetrees." A longstanding tradition states that the Oranjeboom beer was brewed from a deep well of especially pure water in the secret bowels of the city of Rotterdam.

The two men do not talk business: Rijst-tafel is a serious affair. A row of attendants patter up with oldfashioned copper heaters on which to stand the twentyfive different dishes of fish and shellfish, the many vegetables, the grilled pork on skewers with peanut-butter sauce, the little saucers of soya and sambal with which to flavour one delight after another: it keeps hot and one isn't going to hurry. It is in food and the language that the fragmented memories of Empire seem to be buried. Does the young British soldier still speak of a cup of Cha? He looks the birds over, where his father still might have taken a shufti at the bints. After the first tall misted glass van der Valk switches to cha, from the teapot beside him, because he wants to keep his head clear. His stomach will look after itself; he belches cavernously but there is nothing bad-mannered about this in Indonesia.

A pale imitation of the wonderful dish called Nassi Goreng

is as national as pea soup, and can be bought in cans in every Dutch supermarket.

"Well now," still in no hurry. "This man ·named Rijk, or Reich he calls himself now."

Mr X isn't in a hurry either. This marvellous food, which is not at all heavy, has put him into a good literary mood.

" 'Our interest's on the dangerous edge of things.

The honest thief, the tender murderer, the superstitious atheist.

We watch while these in equilibrium keep

The giddy line midway: one step aside,

They're classed and done with.' "

Van der Valk cocks an interrogative eyebrow.

"Robert Browning. Being Victorian, an interest in metaphysics. Like us. Also much interminable prolixity and some notable obscurities."

"Very like us."

"Now and then the quick, short lyrical pounce. Like a hawk. Pow!"

"Pow," with admiration. "We'd like that to be like us."

" 'Hark, those two in the hazel coppice –

A boy and a girl, if the good fates please,

Making love, say –

The happier they!' "

"That doesn't sound at all like us."

"No, alas. Well, as you say, business. A great pity. We'll have to go back to the office." The waiter was proffering pale, dappled cigars, not Cuban, but still very good. "Walk, shall we?"

Nowadays I suppose Mr X would have a computer terminal at home, but then he was civilised enough to keep things distinct. Not especially wishful to keep PanAmerican Airlines by his bedside; nor even the stock exchange. Interferes with the erectile tissues. Besides, then the office computer belonged to the generation of large metal boxes, which roared and spewed immense masses of print-out into bins.

A word needs saying about van der Valk's job; officially criminology consultancy, overflowing into a lot of (mostly talk about) Modernisation of the Police: stuff that led into unlikely corners of civil defence, the protection of the environment, natural catastrophes (even then nuclear power stations caused worry). This led to links with other departments, like Rijkswaterstaat up in Groningen. Van der Valk's life had recently been shortened by a study of the impact on the population of those damned motorways; some highly hairfine distinctions there between suburban, conurban and merely urban. Come to that, the impact of wayside bordels upon village moralities, which explained the irritating nosy-parker (up in Groningen) just when Arlette was beginning to find herself on holiday.

"Yes, I heard about that," said Mr X. "The press set up something of a squawk about your naughty schoolmaster." To be expected; the Dutch gutter press is quite as avid after sex-scandals as the British counterpart; quite as lurid and nearly as vulgar.

An undersecretary in the Ministry of the Interior has fingers in much more unlikely pies than village turpitudes, such as the Secret Service.

"This Brownrigg, we know about him, I think. We've asked for an enquiry, which will – some months from now – be embodied in a lengthy consular report of a confidential nature. That will all need wringing out of the Lange Voorhout – mm, what's this?" as the machine vomited more paper. "No, sorry, the German police see no reason why this should not be seen as a banal road accident in the absence of – hm, Bundesgrenzschütz in Wiesbaden being tightlipped."

"But he was one of ours, was he? I mean, genuinely so."

"In this building, van der Valk, one of theirs. Your Mr Quijs – I should say the late Mr Quijs – rings no bells here but since people like that have pseudonyms by the dozen, and your description sounds rather like our waiter at lunch, putting a trace through is bound to be more complicated: I'll see tomorrow. However, on your great new friend Herr Reich there's a whole Central Registry full of rubbish, and I'll have to send a clerk for that, which will give the duty gutter-jumper something to do of a Saturday afternoon."

"What about, I wonder?"

"The machine doesn't tell me: isn't supposed to, either. Nothing very startling, probably. Do I detect a note of jealousy in your voice? Your very own destabilising influence, a threat even to the security of the state? It's not very likely. If this material were thought sensitive I'd have to go through complicated procedures before laying eyes on it, and you certainly wouldn't be allowed to feast your gluttonous gaze. Thank you," as a folder got flumped on the table. "We do have a fairly efficient foreign service which drinks a lot of gin but does sometimes work. This tells me," going over the coded indications, "that he's thought worth keeping an eye on, which might explain your Mr Brownrigg.

"Malcontent, of quite a common nature," turning over pages. "Banish the House of Orange, annexe Flemish provinces; frequents a number of reactionary folk, has plenty of money. It all sounds quite amateurish; a dabbler. Gasses on about the threat posed by Turks."

"That's him all right, but could the amateur act be a blind for something a bit more serious? Friend Brownrigg appears to have thought so."

"When young did a hitch with the Legion in Algeria; that's the change of name from Rijk to Reich – one can't really say it sounds interesting."

"I wonder might there be another file?"

Mr X took his glasses off, closed his eyes, smiled and said, "Do you think it possible you might be giving yourself and your discoveries a little more importance than they warrant?"

"Entirely possible, and it would be nice to feel sure."

"You see, if anything of that sort existed, you wouldn't

gain access as readily. We like to keep these things up to date, and we'll have a note made of your conjecture, which we'll circulate to the people interested in Mr Brownrigg. You haven't by any means wasted your time."

"No, but decayed police officer tending to fits of hysteria. Query sign of incipient senility; make a note on the bugger's file."

Merry laughter.

"I shall be in a position to contradict any such unfounded rumour but it's a pity you can't be more concrete."

"No, but this little Mr Quijs had been shot with a small-calibre bullet using a reduced charge, thereafter doing the unaccountable-vanish, which isn't maybe quite as amateur as I'd like. Witness was this Mr Brownrigg who fortyeight hours later chooses such an odd spot to observe the Great Crested Oystercatcher."

"The incipient senility, van der Valk, exists in your imagination – not in mine."

"Damned irritating: assassination attempt upon innocent tourist who unwittingly knows too much is all straight out of some cheesy heroine by Hitchcock. Ye faithful truedog commissaire of police floundering bewildered in bog."

"Have no fear," said Mr X comfortingly. "Shall be seen to. Go finish your holiday in peaceful repose, before Mevrouw divorces you for desertion."

He was not very like a fictional detective. Fiction has to be silent upon the doings of the characters during the in-between bits; when they aren't getting shot at, or heaving about between the black sheets of naked girls, of whom Central Casting has a ready supply. Their lives sound rather dull: they seem to have so few resources.

For consider his situation. If he drove back towards the

islands he would certainly miss the last ferry; find himself in consequence stranded in some unappetising hole. The small towns of Holland or northern Germany are not conspicuous for the quality of entertainment offered. What does the loner, the romantic hero, do in these circs? Play patience on the bed of some grim little room, alone with his beautiful memories? Watch the television, or go to a movie? Hardly, if his mental age is anywhere over eight. Get slowly drunk in some dark bar where, who knows? – as up in Groningen – he might be led into some fascinating intrigue? It's too long to wait, before the blonde comes across to his table.

Of course, there's always Laura's House (new girls in, but more New Girls Wanted). Pay the quite reasonable fee and the first drink's free, there's the live-show, the movie, the waterbeds and whoopee. But the company to be kept here is not inspiring: the girls haven't much conversation either. Not so much the list of the sexually-transmitted-diseases, though they can cast gloom, but like Nina in the song one would rather read a book.

So he stayed in the Hague, even knowing that going home, when one is supposed to be on holiday, is horrible because of the stuffy smell, the dusty feel, the uncanny silence left by the absence-of-wife whom, normally, one should be delighted to be rid of for once. So you go out to friends? He has not all that many friends, and isn't quite sure that any of them will be overwhelmed with joy at his dropping in. He is supposed to be a loner. But the Hague, while not a brilliant capital city, isn't swinging-Scunthorpe either: there is more to do than just go to the chess club. There is a good resident orchestra, there are opera and theatre groups, experimental thisses and thats. One has only to consult the local paper, be cultural for a change, enjoy the light late supper, and go to bed without any more damn thinking. Not very heroic but he slept well.

*

"Nervous!"

Talking to yourself out loud, is it now? A fine thing – you'll be picking your nose next, at the red lights.

"Stressed!" There wasn't any red light. So why are we at a standstill? He gives the wheel a slap, with his palm, and the klaxon squawked. The driver of the car in front scowled at the rearview mirror, turned around to give him a long killing look. Van der Valk returned it with a cheerful wave: instead of making him drop-dead it had renewed his spirits.

"Lousy Dutch drivers." Traffic lurched forward. It occurred to him to turn the radio on, so that he tried that for a minute before switching it off again.

"So we'll have some travelogue. Land's a bit flat, but the entrancing beauty is undeniable. Take notice, there on your right of BioChem's new factory, of an architecture only to be called exquisite. On your left, various Cambodian jungles. Ruins of Angkor Vat just coming up." Mm, roadworks. Widespread sea of mud, in which weighty yellow engines left shining watery trails, like colossal slugs. "And watch out too for the black mambas.

"I don't care what they say back there in Phnom Penh. That little man gets shot, the body disappears, and nobody even notices he's gone? Not even the hotel? And his baggage then?

"Brownrigg tipped the cops off, did he? You'd expect an uproar. Item in the paper, agitated local gossip. Nothing. Should have been. And what does get into the paper? That the birdwatching English gentleman got hit by a car. Not good enough, Nellie!"

He had got stuck behind a big truck. He thought about passing, pulled out halfway and got blown back in again by a fast brother who glared homicidally through the side window, with significant taps on the forehead.

"He's quite right. Ought to be locked up in the bin. Can't drive, and talking to himself.

"But if Jan Rijk should imagine that I'm a total nitwit then he has to have another think coming.

"Oh well, let him. On holiday, aren't I? Why should I bother? And now don't get yourself killed," he added in a mutter.

Skipping a bit – there's nothing in the house to eat so a late luxurious breakfast in an expensive café: a lovely freed-from-responsibility feeling – he got back on Sunday evening having done nothing at all but potter, looking at things he knew perfectly well but had never seen with this unwound sightseer's eye, vastly refreshed and very comfortable with his wifeless day. The happier to find again his wife. She seemed to have had a more exciting weekend.

"Pent, I feel. Not quite distraught but decidedly much pent. Very sex-starved." He thinks, privately, dear me, Arlette being fairly moderate about such things as a general rule: but there, he's a cop and they know there isn't any such thing as a general rule.

"So I'll undress you very slowly."

"Please do. Uh – not all that slowly." What can have been happening?

"Those girls – I say, get something to drink out of the little fridge. The prices are ridiculous but will still be cheaper than room-service. I'm in any case in no condition to be glimpsed by the Zimmer-Mädchen."

"Well then, tell."

"Oh there isn't anything to *tell*."

"How dull it all does sound."

"I had my exciting book, you see. I did some cooking. Their treasure doesn't work weekends."

"So you wielded the dustpan and brush. Don't be under any illusions. I did think of dropping in to Laura's House but somehow never managed it. The Hague Football Club was playing a home game too. Stop keeping me tiptoe astretch this way."

"Don't stop doing that; it's nice."

"Yes, but keep up the running commentary."

"We were planning to play some tennis and it started pouring rain. I wasn't at all averse to sitting there in the solarium eating chocolates but it becomes distracting to have them making love there under your nose. Four feet away while you're trying to read, it's difficult to concentrate. Just a little higher, please."

"Are you telling me the house was full of bawdy young men?"

"Not exactly full but certainly bawdy."

"But what was old Agaethe doing all this time? Or does she share these – "

"Please just concentrate on the matter in hand, or I'll scream."

These restless spirits appeased, provisionally – 'like Adolf Hitler,' said Arlette, 'eating Czechoslovakia just gives one an appetite for more' –

"And now I can resume my narrative without that awful tickle – under the soles of one's feet, you know, unspeakable torment. No, just the two young men, acquired on the tennis court from all I could make out, indulging in immodest performances bang in the room. Agaethe's technique, quite brilliant, is to behave as though they were invisible. She paid no notice whatever."

"Whereas you peeked."

"Peek indeed. When Miss Laura's young ladies are performing on the waterbed together, don't tell me you don't peek – you gaze, with much heavy breathing."

"I am fascinated."

"Yes, rather like King Gyges arranging for the captain of the guard to be hidden behind the curtains."

"I do see; the voyeur element puts an extra dollop of sambal into the rice. I don't think Laura's young ladies are thereby stimulated: rather the contrary if I'm any judge. Their approach to the les show is like eating cold mutton stew when not even hungry. And no suggestions were made that – ?"

"One or two but only out of politeness; halfhearted you know. I'm not their age-group and they're quite uninterested in older women. There isn't any perverse element, you mustn't imagine orgies. There were only two young men and the girls kept them busy."

"Do I detect a wistful note in the mention 'only two'?"

"Don't be absurd, I was there like a nanny, smiling upon the beach games and saying, Put your shirt on dear or you'll catch a chill. Knowing about the pool, I'd bought rather a nice beach frock too. I hope there's some sunshine this summer and it won't be wasted."

"Put it on now for me to see."

"The moment's well chosen since I haven't anything to take off. No, I jumped in the pool now and again when the mixed doubles were on."

"And meantime Agaethe – "

"Deep in *House & Garden* and stuffing herself with chocs and never even raised her eyes except to ask whether anyone would like more tea. But what is she to say? These girls are grown up; is she to point dramatically to the door and say Not Under My Roof?"

"She might even feel some sympathy but loyalty keeps her neutral. Oh yes, that's very nice, makes me wish I had a swimming pool. Must see to get old Jan to offer me some bribes. I turned a good one down last week, not to speak of the very sexy offer from that frightful wife."

"You never told me. Yes, the whole point was that with Pa away on heavy business in Frankfurt the girls do some rollicking about, and I presume Ma keeps her mouth shut or there'd be hell to pay."

"I should think this is fairly consistent. Rijk is exceptionally puritanical. Attitudes to sex much the same as to politics; had our ears pinned back already with his views upon Dissolute Youth. Bright ideas about locking-up-one's-daughters didn't find an echo in Agaethe, who could have suffered from that herself as a girl."

"Um," said Arlette, looking at her nose in the glass. "I liked her." A good touch of Huguenotry in her own upbringing. "There isn't anything to keep you here? I feel I've seen enough of Norderney."

"Tomorrow morning. Bremen? Hamburg perhaps."

"And then Kiel maybe? And up as far as the Danish border? Sonderborg? The boys in the book went up there and it sounded nice."

Part Three

Flensburg

10

A spring day in the north. Showers, but beautiful passages of hot sunshine, brilliant upon the raindrops. The enormous horizon of the north German plain, and great piled white clouds in a big sky. The stinging sun was right in his eyes. He pulled down the visor, fumbled for dark glasses: a glance in the mirror showed the sky behind them to seaward a dramatic purplish black.

"There'll be a right downpour in about five minutes."

"Oo," said Arlette looking backwards. "Lovely." She was studying the roadmap. "Visbek – Ahlhorn. Oy, that's where that monument is that Gisela was telling me about. I'd like to see it."

"I don't fancy plodding through a lot of soaking-wet woods for prehistoric megaliths."

"It isn't out of the way, and the Bremen autoroute's right next door."

"Steer me then," indulgently. After all, why not, if she were interested? The monstrous downpour descended on them, hammered fiercely for ten minutes upon roof and windscreen, went on past leaving a sunshine brighter than before so that curls of steam came off the asphalt. The storm, as sometimes happens, washed the sky. It was going to be a lovely day.

"Wow," she said suddenly. They were travelling through a village – small and as far as he could see of no interest. "D'you know what that was called? Vörderste Thule."

"Mhuh?"

"According to Herodotus that's the end of the known world." A romantic imagination.

Twenty kilometres on she shouted "Hey!" louder still, but he was unstartled, knowing the way her mind went on working.

"The piece of paper. The one the funny little man gave me. That I forgot and put in the wash. *Vis*bek was what it said. Visbek Monday! Today's Monday," in ringing tones of triumph.

"So it is," but in a flattish voice, even discouraging. These flights of fancy do not make much impression upon the police mind. She had joined together two thought associations and imagined an important discovery. But since she was enjoying herself, why pour cold water upon her? There's enough of that outside.

"If we find this monument of yours we can take a look, and I daresay then we can find something to eat in the village pub."

They were coming into a pretty, hobbitty kind of countryside. The Ost-Friesische plain, bare and one-has-to-admit muddy, was behind them. Here there were streaks of better land, wooded, with shallow valleys drained by attractive streams, bordered by old mills, antique patina'd farm buildings. It seemed anyhow a nice place to get out and stretch one's legs. Drowsy sunlight dappled things, patterning the outline of the unfolding leaves. Tender young greens and yellows, ochres and chocolatey browns. Nice, thought van der Valk, pleasantly, almost sleepily relaxed. He had stopped to allow Arlette to ask directions of a local, with whom she was in animated conversation. The farm there reminded him vaguely of something. (Perhaps a painting by Constable seen reproduced on a calendar.)

"Not very easy to understand," climbing back in. "They talk sort of thick. But he knew, all right: I suppose tourists do ask, quite often. You go on about four kilometres and turn right, there's supposed to be a signpost but anyhow a clearing where you can park the car, and yes a pub of sorts from what I can make out, and it's into the woods from there. There are two monuments, one quite close but the other miles away through the woods. The Bride and the Bridegroom. I wonder why there are two and what the significance is."

Obediently he followed. There was indeed a signpost; there was indeed a clearing. There was indeed a pub, seeming closed, and no cars were there. Well, now there would be an anony-mous car with Dutch plates announcing an early-season tourist with on his part a slightly lukewarm enthusiasm for megaliths.

Arlette plunged boldly into a rather wet-looking path. He followed dubiously. The path got better; still a woodland cart-track with little sign of use. She pointed with triumph at a decayed wooden arrow pointing drunkenly at almost any-where, but it did say BRIDE. And ten minutes into the silent woods, but somewhere close by the muted, everlasting thunder of the Bremen autobahn, she gave a sudden small shriek. Twenty metres off the path among the dead leaves there stood a very large stone . . . They clambered across and took it all in slowly. Standing as still as the stone, to let it unfold, gradually, and enclose them.

It seemed fairly neglected; not especially 'tidy' and little visited: young trees growing here and there, and the path obscured by brambles. Not like Stonehenge or Carnac, with notices about the Environment and wire to discourage hooli-gans, and the sad, over-trodden, vandalised look: a turnstile to take money and sell postcards; and a policeman in a con-crete pillbox to make sure you behave, do not drop icecream wrappers, do not scratch *Ted and Sandra were here* upon the stone. For it is a rule. Side by side with the noblest works of man you will find the most base.

This is smaller than the great avenue of Carnac, less striking than the patterned triliths of Stonehenge, and perhaps the more impressive in the sobriety, simplicity, silence.

Van der Valk was standing at the end of a double line of

huge stones in an alignment (as far as he could judge) over a hundred metres long and some eight apart. There were joins, patterns difficult to read where stones have slipped or fallen, or sunk in the sandy, unstable soil. The 'Bridegroom' and the 'Bride' still nine kilometres further (there are several other less imposing megalith assemblages and plainly here is one of those mysterious, puzzling complexes of our prehistory) look much the same: experts have detected subtle variations.

He had suspended breathing, began again, took a long one and said, "Tell."

"I don't know very much. Gisela added a bit. They are about three and a half or four thousand years before Christ. I don't know whether they've been carbon dated. The alignments mark an important point in the sun's passage, an equinox, a solstice, I don't recall. Most of these avenues or circles do that, and where they've been studied by astronomers, mathematicians, one can often observe moon passages, star sights, uncannily accurate. So they're thought to be observatories, calendars. Primitive stone-age peoples would have needed such to measure orbits, calculate planting seasons and so forth.

"Plainly there's much more to it than that. If it were only for sun or star sights, why take such huge stones at what must have been immense effort, and why make such complex patterns? So people call it 'vaguely sacred place' but they can't go further because they don't know. That famous English one, some of it is of huge boulders found locally, called sarsens – but they were worked, shaped. And its other circle is altogether different, bluestone brought from Wales: they think they have the route worked out and roughly the technique but it was long, difficult and highly sophisticated. Why go to all that trouble? Are these local stones? I don't know, but plainly there's a special value and property in the stones themselves. The site is important: people have measured patterns and alterations in the earth currents, the magnetic field and all the stuff I don't understand. But the stones do something else. I wish I knew. I want to try and find out. Some people, sensitive, can feel things in the stones. But that talk about human sacrifices and the like is nonsense."

Arlette stood facing him, some ten metres away, between two of the immense boulders. She put her hand, flat, upon her flat strong pelvic area, covering her womb.

"One feels it here. I'm going to try. It's a woman's thing. Probably you won't feel anything at all. It seems plain that the patterns which are astoundingly accurate even these six thousand years later had a collecting or focussing character. But the stones hold something which we have forgotten and lost."

"A power station? Something to generate energy?"

"We can't tell. Gisela is in a group working on it. I told her she's going the wrong way. I doubt if it could be apprehended through any intellectual process. The likelihood is that it was still dimly known at the beginning of the Christian era, because the early Church took immense pains to obliterate it. Virtually all the churches were built on the exact site of places held to have physical significance. Remember the cathedral at Laon, up there on the rock, towering over the plain. Or Le Puy? – what could that possibly have to do with the Virgin? But they did such a good job of stamping out. The biggest megalith we know, the high one called the Great Menhir at Locmariacquer – it had a complicated mathematical relationship with the Carnac alignments – was knocked down and broken only a couple of hundred years ago by the curé whipping up the local population to combat superstition, meaning put his instead. These places are all palimpsests. But perhaps Heilige Maria didn't make quite as much impact here in northern Germany as she does in Brittany."

Arlette wandered off, leaving him to think. He paced the length of the avenue and back.

No, it meant nothing to him. He was just a cop. Men would have – the first thing thought of! – come digging here eager and zealous for Things. Buried treasures like the gold bars of the *Corinne* sunk deep in the sands off Memmert. Those sands did not readily give up what they had engulfed. Virtually every ship of the monstrous, unwieldy, invincible Armada wrecked, all the way from the sands of Dunkerque; right up the North Sea; around the stormy capes of Scotland; down and around the Irish coast; left its legend of wealth unimaginable to the bitterly-poor peasants of the littoral. From the solid gold-and-heavily-jewelled episcopal cross, invoking God's blessing upon the faithful, to the admiral's solid silver pisspot. And everywhere, down to Galway and Kerry, was the legend of the tall dark handsome man who struggled ashore and lived to father generations of darkly-Spanish children upon the lumpish milkmaids. No no, here were no baronial gold circlets, here were no chieftains' bones; this was as Arlette said: this was a pure place.

There was another smaller group of big stones over there among the trees, which had attracted Arlette no doubt: he felt no inclination to roam, but sat upon a rounded one in the green and gold sunlight, the humming silence, the boom and mutter of the unseen autoroute – the restlessness of one piece of engineering, and the quiet of the other which had been there for five thousand years. He looked at the tiny lichens on the stone. One could make no guess at the purpose. A great, a splendid quiet thing, but a thing. Like the other whose purpose was crude, simplistic: speedy movement.

Surely not! Coarse and blunted as were his sensibilities, he could feel life in these stones, focussed and immensely increased by the interplay between them, whose subtleties he could not even guess at. Helped by the solitude and the stillness one apprehended something of the noble presence: one could imagine some majestic ritual of renewal and dedication; a cleansing and catharsis and some great promise for mankind. A stick cracked somewhere behind him. It would be interesting to hear what she made of it. Women – strange clever creatures, weird sisters, alert and sensitive to so much that we idiots fail in. He could feel the presence of her now a few steps behind him, standing still and relaxed, unwilling to break a spell, anxious not to interrupt a silence which had more to say than any stupid words. He took his stick from between his knees and swung his legs around, leisurely.

Shock waves travel in concentric circles, as one may see from heaving a rock into a still pond. A man had stood behind him, stood now in front of him. However slight the shock, every human being will smile uneasily and say 'You startled me!' Van der Valk was much more startled than that. The shockwaves rippling outward hit him one by one. No mere tourist. Not a man with the same instinct as himself, to walk softly and keep silent in face of a great human work. But a man he knew, and a man who was dead!

There was no mistaking Mr Quijs. The perpetual meaningless smile, the little sharp amused eyes, the cock of the brown shiny – bald or shaven? – head like that of a bird who has just alighted on a branch. All just as on Norderney, down to the greyishblue anorak with the smart fur collar, the hood thrown back. Even to the camera slung by a strap around his neck. The smile was wide, fixed and toothy. In his right hand, held loosely at his side, he was carrying an object of blued metal, but no camera. A pistol.

Van der Valk would remember being struck that it was a Luger pistol – another admirable piece of engineering; an efficiency of shape and balance, a fit in the hand, a flexibility and pointability. This lethal thing has struck the imagination of everyone who has ever seen or handled it, more than any of the other nasty toys designed to the same purpose. The design has altered little since nineteen fourteen: it was so well made. Semi-automatic. A simple, foolproof mechanism. Standard nine-millimetre ammunition. Parabellum meaning 'prepare war', and especially if you wish for peace; cynical Latin saying. The mind flits across a multitude of observations with great rapidity even while a cop-trained body does not move at all. The flow and tingle of released adrenalin goes with training into stillness, recollection, concentration.

"Gave you a fright!" Mm, a touch of sadism?

"Yes. Certainly."

"You shouldn't have come here. You'll be regretting that."

"Weren't you supposed to be dead?" The smile would have got broader if it had room to expand further; stayed unchanged.

"Quite an easy trick when you know about it." Van der Valk without thinking had spoken Dutch. The man did the same, in the voice of a man to whom it comes naturally. "A simple injection of calculated dosage. Some anaesthetics will produce a coma condition superficially indistinguishable. Add a bit of suggestibility, like a shot, a darkened empty house, a few cosmetic effects like blood on the front. Real blood. You jumped to conclusions as you were meant to. A theatrical trick, to smoke you out. As it did eventually. You've been clever, I give you that. Took us all in."

"And the other? He's really dead?"

"Yes. Really dead. So are you." The gun flicked up loosely, pointed at him.

"You won't shoot me with that. Too much noise. Attract attention. Haven't you the other, the little twentytwo with a reduced charge?"

"This'll do. Nobody here. The only car on the parking is yours. Mine too, now. Bury you here – a little further, where it's soft and wet. No trouble. But wait until the boss gets here and he'll decide. Where's your wife?"

"Wandered off in the trees. Interested in these monuments."

"Interesting monuments. Take care of her when she gets back. No hurry."

He could see Arlette now. She was standing about twenty metres away and too much to the side; frozen, openmouthed. If she could get any closer, and to the back, without making too much noise, it might afford them both some small chance. One couldn't put much hope in it. She was a sensible woman. Had much self-control. She stopped and picked up a piece of wood. Quite big, a log of sorts. It wouldn't be much use: it was totally rotted. One had to try and talk, though. And try to move this bad leg. The man watched the leg with amusement.

"You won't try to jump me. That leg won't carry you, and sitting down . . ."

"But you aren't getting far either. Inside of a German jail, and that's it. You've been following me around, so you'll know I went to the Hague this weekend. There's a trace out on you now." The man shook his head.

"I'm dead. And when I come back to life I'll look like ten thousand more. Half Dutch and half Indonesian. Common type. Colonial fun and games, nice little brown girl." Arlette had worked around a bit. But too little. And too slowly. The smallest turn would make her visible, and then it would be all up. He must try to pull the man in closer. A good four paces away, which was too far, even if one could think of anything to try. Which he couldn't.

"You think the German police were satisfied, about Brownrigg?" Smiling nod, of complete certainty.

"And then another unexplained death, in the same district? With what I've already given them? No way at all."

"You shouldn't have come here. Nobody would have worried you, then. Time enough, though, to tell why you came here."

"Brownrigg told me. Help me up, will you? My leg's hurting me. I haven't got any gun."

"I know. No. Get up by yourself." But a half step inward, from the instinct to be watchful, just in case. Not nearly enough, but might barely suffice; if . . .

"Ah!" Cheerful breezy conversational voice. "Here comes my dear wife with two gallant German cops." Pointing off in the wrong direction. With a big helpful out-thrust hand.

Arlette did two things. Gave a colossal shriek, and hurled her log of wood. The man was delayed by looking in two directions at once. The rotted log hit his upflung arm and exploded in a shower of wet dust, moss, woodlice – he might even have been a bit blinded by flying matter, and disconcerted by the fearful scream.

Van der Valk reared up. He had got the good leg under him for leverage. He lunged forward using all the height and reach he had. He didn't try to bring the less-good leg forward, and it wouldn't have borne his weight if he had. So there was nothing to stop him falling, and fall he did like a belly-flopping diver; flat and face-forward on to trodden earth, ground still winter hard: scraping his face on bits of dead stick, knobbly bits of root, a lot of debris you do not pay heed to usually. Man being in general an upright animal.

He had extended his stick to the longest possible prolongation of the straightened lunging arm, launching it from knee height. All this which takes such a time to describe and is in fact quite slow is still speedy enough. I mean that a dive from the edge of the pool seems fast to the onlooker, although to something really fast, like a camera shutter, it is mortally slow and can be arrested in mid-air.

The ferrule of the stick was shod with a brass thimble. This travels through the air slower than a bullet. But sometimes it suffices. Not as wide as a barn door, as Mercutio said crossly, but it will serve, damn it. This projectile, catching someone where he keeps his appendicitis scar, does serve.

Flat upon the floor of the forest with the breath knocked out of him, van der Valk meditates upon these things at some length. It is being cop-trained which makes the difference. Reaction time. The ordinary citizen can study this phenomenon when stopped in a car at a red light, three or four back in the queue. The drivers have all taken a foot off the clutch and accelerated with the other, smartly as they thought, the moment they got the green. Add three reaction times together and the wait will appear as long as honey dripping off a spoon.

Being cop-trained . . . The reader of crime fiction, still more the viewer of crime-television, tends to be supercilious about the ploy of telling the man who is pointing the gun that there's a rattlesnake just behind him. Oh that old gag, we would say dismissively. Our hero ought to think of something new! There isn't anything new and the old ploy is the best: as the sergeant in the police training-school will readily demonstrate to the unbelieving. Reaction-time, again. If the man with the gun has his attention even so little distracted (and he cannot help reacting, it is built-in) he is, however little, flustered. The gun-trained cop takes advantage of this fraction. Very few cops are trained this far, but that's something to be grateful for, really. You can see them on television, but not in the fiction serials. They are the ones who surround the president without seeming to, while he's being jolly with the crowd.

It was possible for van der Valk to take a rest, because Arlette picked up the stick, which he had dropped, and gave the doubled-up brown man a fearful whack with it. Being in a great hurry she did not get him on his bald head, which was what she aimed at, but a good rap on the collarbone is in-ca-pa-ci-ta-ting too.

Taking deep breaths with his mouth open van der Valk scrambled to his feet, ungainly as the burdened camel he resembled. He secured the gun, which had fallen a yard away, looked to see whether pine-needles or dirt had got into the barrel. The weight in the butt told him it was loaded. He snapped the action. A copper-jacketed cartridge spun in the air; he caught it and put it in his pocket. The brown man was sitting on the ground holding his shoulder. Van der Valk took hold of the other wrist, twisted it and said, "Get up."

"You've broken my collarbone," in a tone of indignation.

"We'll get it seen to." He held the brown man's wrist in the small of his back. Even with only one leg he is larger, stronger. But he has only two hands and on this uneven muddy path he needs his stick. The gun is a nuisance and he puts it in his pocket.

Arlette has gone away among the bushes. Modern ladies may perhaps come all over faint less often than in Victorian times, but they are still subject to violent emotions getting the better of them. She reappeared rather white with a little line at the corner of her nose which twitches, even when the rest of her is back under control.

"Can you drive?"

"I'd rather not."

"Very well." They marched in silence, for the quarter of an hour the walk back through the woods took to the clearing and the car. They met nobody.

"Arlette, would you look please in the back of the car?" When Gollum wanted to guess what Bilbo Baggins had in his pocketses he said 'String or nothing' which was unfair but a good guess since elderly gentlemen like Professor Tolkien did often have bits of string economically wound up in their pockets: so did my father, but no longer.

Arlette rummaged in the deposits of filth that most of us have in the back of the car. "That'll do," he said pointing. It was holding a can of oil pinned upright to the side: a length of elastic cable with a hook at each end, called a sandow because it is like the chest-expander used to give you those big weight-lifting muscles, more prosaically as now to secure a heavy package.

Van der Valk made a harness of this behind the man's back to keep the wrist bound, with one hook in the belt and the other in his collar – very uncomfortable but that was his horrible luck, as was explained to him politely. While this was going on he groaned and complained about his shoulder. So van der Valk borrowed a scarf from Arlette to improvise a sling with. Thus accoutred the brown man looked laughable, pathetic, and dejected, in roughly that order. Arlette got a final fit of the cringing shudders and preferred not to look at all.

"Now I'll have to throw it away," meaning the scarf.

Half lying in the back seat Mr Quijs did appear pitiful, but police minds do not work like this. Van der Valk got into the driving seat, examined his scratched face in the reversing mirror, muttered a bit, and became concerned with an administrative problem. All these villages at the other end of nowhere (Vörderste Thule) – where the hell are we to find some real, proper police?

After more muttering, heavy breathing, laborious unfolding-of and invective-at the stupid road map, a town was discovered some twenty kilometres off, one of those bright, dull, modernised German market towns, odd mix of the go-ahead and the sleepy; drowsing in the spring sunshine.

Van der Valk conveyed his prize into port, saying to Arlette through the window, "You had better stay here: I'll try not to be long."

Inside, amid the familiar smell of grey official paint, filing cabinets and Nescafé-plus-disinfectant, he produced papers authenticating him as a Commissaire in the Netherlands State Police, causing the duty law-agent to clear the throat, important.

"What we got here then? – sir," a bit belated.

"I give this man in charge. Possession of forbidden weapon. Threats with same. Assault. That'll do to book him with and hold him on. We'll be having more, in all likelihood. Conspiracy and association of malfactors. Suspicion of homicide – your colleagues in Leer will be interested. All sorts of goings-on, but first we must have the doctor to go over him for damage."

The cop looked at the pistol on the desk as though he'd never seen one before.

"Hit him, did you?"

"Stick," holding it up.

"Cow of a woman," mumbled Mr Quijs.

"That'll do from you. Get the doctor, Gerd," to a colleague

come to see what the excitement was about. "Now then, identity papers."

"Have to make a couple of phonecalls."

"Official business, er, sir? Use inside office. Werner! Right," pointing his ballpoint at Quijs, "let's be having you," exactly as though he were still in the army, lancecorporal hustling the green recruity-yobs.

Official business it has to be now! And what have you done to deserve this?

Mis-ter-van-der-Valk, while in Holland, we agree, you remain a senior grade police official. If you are also a damned busybody, nobody is shocked by that. Even on holiday, seeing something you didn't like and stepping in – that is legitimate. But in Germany you should have learned to shed this self-importance. You didn't, and now you pity yourself.

It is your wife who deserves pity. She merely came here with an innocent idea of enjoying herself.

Arlette was in the car and in tears, a sodden heap of misery.

"I want to go home. Now. At once. Fine holiday I've had, yeow-ow."

"What you need, my girl, is a washroom, and so do I, and what we both need is something to eat. Must be a hotel in this town, I'll ask the Polizei." At the bare mention of which she burst out once more. "Sorry darling, but I cannot just leave all this."

Repaired and refreshed, eating halibut 'to remind us of the seaside', with a small strip of plaster from the car's first-aid box above the left eyebrow (the waitress said kindly 'I hope you haven't had a traffic accident'), drinking nice Palatinate wine in a pleasant sunny room with daffodils on the tables (it was almost like being on holiday) – oh hell, would they never get to Bremen? Why could he never leave well alone? What importance will it ever have to the human race?

Arlette blew her nose and said "I'm sorry" desolately, before adding, "If ever again, which seems dubious, we find ourselves on a beach anywhere will you just please lie down and close your eyes."

Why not, indeed? Because of the all-pervading sense of sin which poor old Toynbee discovered in the human race? What was he to tell her? She spoke first.

"Now going and leaving all this seems to me a sensible conclusion."

"It is."

"I don't want to go back there."

"Then don't."

"I don't want to let you out of my sight either."

"That squirt," said van der Valk patiently, "made a reference to the boss turning up. Who's that, I wonder? Is that by any chance our friend Jan Rijk? Why? What for? To tie me to a stone and take my heart out with a flint knife before eating it? No, because he didn't know I was coming here: that was a fancy of yours. But Brownrigg got an inkling of something due to happen here, and feeling himself under too close a surveillance, took trouble to pass that to you, intending that I should do something about it. An item that he thought or guessed might be of interest to the State of the Netherlands.

"There's no risk, you know. Rijk would disclaim all knowledge of this chap. There's nothing I can prove. Brownrigg could have linked up what happened on Norderney but that's no good to me now. This little man won't talk because if he did he'd risk nastier things happening to him than anything we can do. He'll sit tight and act the idiot with some tale of holding us up for the money in our pockets, and after a few weeks in jail he can look forward to a large bonus. It's unlikely they'll be able to connect him with Brownrigg."

"What do you expect to find?"

"Who knows? Maybe nothing at all. Conceivably Herr Reich taking an interest in ancient monuments, wondering what's happened to the man he set to keep a watch on me, and thinking he's been led up the garden and we've gone on innocently to Bremen. The doubt, you see – had Brownrigg found something out, and had he had the time to pass it on to me?"

It was two in the afternoon when they got back to the clearing. The little rustic Gasthaus was showing signs of activity. Cars were parked in front; more under the trees around; some of them very nice cars. Nothing flashy or obtrusive, like a Porsche or a Jaguar. There was a Rolls-Royce, plain but nice, with Austrian plates: there was also a big black Mercedes coupé they had seen before.

"Ho. A meeting. That's nice."

"What are you going to do?" nervously.

"Oh just walk in saying Hi, and see what happens."

"I can't sit here. I'm too nervous. I'm going to take a little walk by the side of the road. And if you're not back in a quarter of an hour – then I'll be back, with every cop in Schleswig-Holstein in tow." He agreed, grinning.

It was only a country pub, with a terrace for selling icecream and lemonade in summer. A bit of activity round the back, where a clatter of washing-up could be heard, and there was a nice smell of food. The business men were having lunch, and had probably reached the coffeecup stage by now. He opened the door and walked in.

There was the usual little diningroom with six or eight tables but there was nobody there. At the back the usual bar, no one to be seen, but the characteristic noise of someone stowing empties in a case. Hearing his footsteps a big man straightened up, red from stooping, and said politely, "Sorry, we're closed."

"I'm sorrier. Heard a bit of activity. Mm, smells good here."

"I regret," blank-faced, but firm. "The house was reserved for a private party. Open to the public after Easter." The door to the back room opened to allow a waitress to come through with a tray of glasses. She pushed it to with her foot, cutting off a hum of conversation, glancing at him without curiosity. "Just private," said the man.

"Pity. Any chance of a beer?"

"Sorry," with a mild stubbornness. "We're closed."

"Bad luck. Still, saw a car belonging to a friend of mine. Herr Reich. Just have a word with him while I'm here." But before he had taken two steps the man was in front of him holding up a hand.

"Quite private." Very firm this time. The hand was large, beefy: the man as tall as himself and broader. There wasn't going to be any argument.

"No problem," diplomatic retreat. "Tell you what," feeling in his pocket, "I'll write him a line, and you'll be kind enough to give him that. He'll want to know, you see; he's expecting me. I'll be out in the car. Okay?" He tore the half-page out of his notebook. He had written *Better come out & talk – VdV.* The man nodded grudgingly, keeping careful eyes on him. He walked out.

What have they come here for? This isn't just a group of the ol' Freedom-Fighters, singing wartime songs and marking time with beermugs. There are still plenty of those about, if getting old; rather heavy; as the years go by more swimmily sentimental about their good-old-days. A cheap crowd. Reich wouldn't want anything to do with them. The Bonn government knows all about them. They're tolerated in our midst. They are after all Germans, and the less said about them the better. And in return, they are expected to understand realities, and make no noise.

Van der Valk agrees with this policy. It is sensible. It is not hypocrisy. We have all of us things we prefer to see brushed under the carpet. We have turned our page. No, there are better – and much more powerful – freemasonries than that. And with different ideologies. He can remember a few discreet

references on the boat, to the Templars, the Free Companions
. . . hm.

The door of the pub opened. But it wasn't Jan Rijk with
his tanned handsome face, the cowlick of dark hair, the crinkly
smile, the bright vivid eyes.

Arlette had talked about the Reverend Elmer Gantry. And
there he was in person. Or was it his creator? Reaching back,
a long long way, to when he had still been an aspiring trainee
police-officer gaining practical experience in dogsbody work in
every department under the sun, one day in the fifties somebody had pointed to a tall, shambling, broken old man looking
much older and said, 'See that? That's a very famous novelist,
just about the most famous there is. Millionaire! Nobel Prize
winner! The lot!' And he had looked, and thought was there
anything more sad, and more futile, than a once best-selling
writer whom everybody now thought a joke?

The Reverend Russ Margesson had something of the look,
the long chinny staring face, the awkward, poorly-coordinated
movements. But that had been a reddish face, untidy grey
hair – old and worn-out and confused, not even really knowing
whether it was coming or going. This had a sly, mobile, television face; dark hair worn rather long; heavy, clever eyebrows.
A face all masks and public relations: the slow rustic air, the
imitation of an antique Hollywood cowboy looking pathetic and
indecisive and 'Hi, I'm Jimmy Stewart', the thin whiny voice
calling the folks to God – another mask.

"Why, hydee there Pete, mind if I climb in your car?"
There are few things that annoy him more than being called
Pete or Piet – and thank God it isn't Petey – by people he
doesn't know and doesn't want to. But down, dog.

"Got a recorder on in here? Oh, I believe you! Wouldn't
matter if you had. Now you'll excuse my coming instead of Jan.
He's a busy man, and he's busy with a few of these important
European friends of his, people I hardly know, so I got sort of
delegated and designated, you won't mind. We only had that

brief acquaintance back on that wonderful island of Jan's, nice to improve it but I do have to say it, Pete, you're an awful goddamn nuisance, you know it? I told Jan that, I made sure you weren't the right boy for the cause, but he's obstinate, he would have it you were straight goods. But look at you now, you're just a commonplace police finger, aren't you now?"

"Quijs told you?"

"Now who's that?"

"Little brown bald man. Runs errands for Jan."

"No, I haven't the pleasure of his acquaintance but do tell."

"Followed me here. Was a bit naughty, pointing guns and such – you know, aggressive? So I took away the gun and now there's one more reason for the German police forces, several different kinds, to be taking a close interest in you all."

"No Pete, means nothing to this sinner, but if I were you, take a piece of good advice, stop right there. Kind of a Mexican stand-off, you know it? Back at home, we're a rough primitive people, we have this belief in the justice-of-the-people – between the sheriff and the National Rifle Association, life's thread could get cut kind of short; snipped-off, know what I mean? Now here you're very European and urbane and you like to talk about things, sure, great, and no hard feelings, either way. Meaning like you decide you're the three wise monkeys, you know, see, hear and speak no evil; fine. These European people, they're idealists, doing good by stealth, you take my meaning, dislike that blinding light of publicity. Maybe you'll come to understand that, you live long and wise, knowing how to reserve your judgments and keep your counsels.

"Mean to say, just consider the alternatives. Like there're these fanatics around, like we hear, anarchists, people with no scruples.

"Think of living, under like we say close protection, you know, like Bobby Kennedy, and all of a sudden even with cops all round there's this uncontrolled Arab, is he Iran or

Iraq, Syrian or Lebanese or Palestinian, it just doesn't obey any rule of reason. Mean, way outside any control of any rational behaviour, they decide that Joe is an enemy of the revolution, too bad for Joe: sometimes it's bombs and pistolshots close up or sometimes it's this sharpshooter off on the horizon with a target rifle and a telescopic sight."

It's like this all the time back in Uneedarest, Mo., wondered van der Valk, this remorseless diarrhoea?

"Talking doesn't come within the criminal code," he said. "Wishing it did doesn't change that. Even preaching sermons in Fort Lauderdale is an exercise of free speech. Even saying you're going to lead a crusade to kill all the Communists and then kill me. Pretty old tradition of ours, this extreme tolerance. People would mostly say it dates from times when the Spanish political authority showed itself extremely intolerant. That's a while ago but the national-socialist time was a recent reminder that we don't like killing people or putting them in prison for disagreeing with us.

"You're all very rich, of course. Wealthy conservatives are a powerful political lobby. Naturally enough you all think yourselves untouchable. Still, I better say that when we need them we can find articles in the code to fit you. Incitement to crime and apology for crime are both punishable offences. So is conspiracy to subvert government, and even if we aren't in South Africa so is unlawful assembly.

"So I go home and make a report, that's my job, and that'll go on the national security computer where you're all tagged. It's also my job to disregard threats made against me personally.

"You remind me of a village pornographer whom I arrested last week. Can't see any difference now that I think of it. A corrupter of mind and morals, that's the message back to the folks in Tampa, and now get the fuck out of my car."

The Reverend wanted to make another speech but van der Valk had started the motor and put the car in gear, and a pulpit on wheels isn't of much help when there's only one in the audience. He stopped on the edge of the clearing with the corners of the mouth turning down, to take note of the car registration, for what good that might do . . . Odd that they had chosen this place to meet in; a tribute to the power of these old stones. Arlette might very well be right to say that stones have memory, and intelligence. The physicists will tell you it isn't so, but they said that about water, too.

He found Arlette marching along the road with her hands pressed firmly into her jacket pockets. "Next stop Bremen," he said, opening the door.

11

Danger? – yes, there is danger. The fanaticised always are dangerous: they are unpredictable, and they pursue their end, in disregard of risks. Their own, and the risk to those who cross their path. They had killed a man, a government agent, for no more than being over-curious, over-zealous.

It wasn't the same as a village pornographer who offers you a bribe.

The little-brown-man would have killed him, yes and Arlette too. He had been held back only by a fear of exceeding instructions: a mercenary, more than a fanatic. But there had been a touch of the sadist in him, also. Good, the German police would now have a number of awkward questions for that individual.

He had had a glimpse of others just as dangerous. Perhaps not the Reverend; a fanatic, with a large dose of cowardice to help impose prudence. But others – manipulators; the more dangerous since they took no risks: they sat cosy in Switzerland, feeling vengeful, it is to be suspected, towards those who brought embarrassment and especially ridicule upon them. Himself.

They wouldn't come after him with a gun; it wasn't their way. Still, van der Valk feels glad it isn't a wintersport holiday. It doesn't take much courage to start an avalanche.

And Rijk? About Jan he felt puzzlement more than fear. One could like the man, neither a chill watcher of money-markets nor a cheap hired hand. But he would not be happy at looking a fool. He would, though, be cool enough to wait. Danger? The autobahn is also a dangerous place.

And perhaps now, at last! . . . Half an hour of almost complete silence. Arlette pulled down the sun visor on her side of the car, to mend her lipstick in the vanity mirror. Pulling her mouth about, to make it go evenly. Oh dear, it's a worn mouth, a worn face, the eyes are awful. Nasty sharp lines everywhere, one won't look at it. She lit a cigarette, snapped the catch of her handbag as though to lock up the face inside it, glanced sideways at the man.

Another well-worn face, hammered, and a hammered-down look; closed, concentrated, expressionless. This is a face which has seen most human follies and errors and has in consequence few firm beliefs, fewer dogmas, almost no certainties. Still and defensive; defensive because vulnerable, fluid because watchful: the face of the autoroute driver. He dislikes cars but is a good driver; he has the feeling for rhythm, and the antennae one needs all round the car. He cannot just sit on the outside lane. About every sixty to ninety seconds he has a fast-brother coming up behind him in the big Mercedes at a hundred and eighty, and he must know how to tuck himself into a gap.

One needs a bit of cheek, says van der Valk; a bit of brutality. And a bit of humour. He has no consideration for riches, and no concern about morals: neither – he says – has anything to do here upon the autobahn. He will slide out in the path of a Porsche flicking its lights in outrage, as ruthlessly as in upon a retired bank-clerk: they both think the road belongs to them.

The signs which have been saying *Bremen* in smallish letters, along with much other unwanted information, now say it in very large ones; well thank-god-for-that.

It's a nice town, Bremen. Quite small, if you call half a million small, with a pleasant interior old-town behind Vaubanesque fortifications in a zigzag pattern of moat and tower, Wall and Contrescarpe, which is now all parked in a green gentleness of grass and tree. To be sure one has the hideous scuffle of finding somewhere to park, finding a hotel, and making the two coincide, but we've all suffered from that.

Within an hour they were washed, peaceful, and ready to stroll out for a drink before dinner. Nobody goes looking for a glass of wine in the Hansa towns of northern Germany: who wants to drink wine while eating herring? The brick architecture is that of Holland or Flanders combined with the lovely northern baroque. Of course, there isn't a great deal of it left: the good-work done by ardent British bombing in the Hitler time has been all too well completed by the German banks and insurance companies, which exist by the hundred, each uglier than the last.

Arlette stamps her foot and shouts at them in anger, causing her husband to giggle. But she is on holiday at last and happy, and drinks a lot of beer from kind Mr Beck, and eats the local dishes like labskaus. A chap from Liverpool used to be called Scouse, he tells her, wondering whether the etymology is the same. To be sure, Bremen is prettier, but the two towns have the same harsh independence. And the two best football teams in England or in Germany: the fact isn't accidental. The highest unemployment, and a damn-you mentality which catches at her, so that she cries a little, while saying "I am happy, here." Typically, she quarrels with the labskaus recipe. "Better without beetroot, surely? I can do this, at home. Lamb stew smashed with mashed potatoes, and little silver onions, and salt herring, you think, or sour?" Van der Valk, who eats salt herring the way the Dutch do, holding it up above his mouth like a seal in the zoo, smiles upon her; being tolerant towards the dotty French mare.

This town is the right size: one can walk about in it peacefully. It's a long way inland, and the Weser is silted up, so that the big boats stop down in Bremerhaven on the estuary, but it has still a nice fishy flavour, to go with that quickened heartbeat, and when the time comes for Hamburg she is ready for it, and eager.

*

Van der Valk isn't quite so sure that he has seen the last –
or had the last word – of Jan Rijk and Associates, Inc. True,
out of consideration, a bit belated, for his wife he has said no
further word about this-bugger-Jan. He has tried hard to put
it all out of mind. He has done his duty, hasn't he? Even so
conscientious as to run all the way back to the Hague to fill
Mr X in on this stuff which doesn't appear on the computer,
which may or may not have anything to do with the Safety of
the State, but which in his eyes is definitely criminal: people
like Mr Quijs can't just be left at large.

Well, they weren't. He had thrown a loop over that nasty
bit of work; true, more by good luck than good management,
and one would be doubtful whether it wasn't bluff: the fellow
would indeed need to be dotty to have even thought of pulling
the trigger on a police officer, known to be same, just for
showing undue curiosity. Even a Dutch one in Germany.

Wheels would be turning. Back there in the towns of
Cloppenburg and Vechta police commissaires would be asking
questions of Mr Quijs, and of themselves. The Bundesgrenzschütz would be getting into the act, and their big computer.
Ripples would be spreading – as far as the Netherlands Consulate
in Bremen, which he had scrupulously avoided. As far as the
Hague . . . Serious chaps in offices would be wondering why
Mr Reich and his wealthy friends from Liechtenstein had chosen to have lunch and a quiet chat in an obscure country pub
near Visbek. What was the significance of those monuments?
Just another atavistic throwback to Himmleresque fascination
with runes and obscure early-teutonic religious beliefs? But he
wasn't, dammit, proposing to bother his head any further. Not
fair on Arlette. Enjoy your holiday, mate. Was he imagining
things?

A memory kept visiting him, and it had nothing to do

with police work. It had to do with *Lolita*. He had read – like everyone else – Nabokov's book, and there is in this book the gradually growing perception of the Fiend. He wasn't at all sure whether there might not be a fiend loose too in Bremen.

The Fiend showed its presence through Nabokovian jokes, just to tease. He could only remember one of these – the hotel register signed N. Petit, from Larousse, Illinois. Now this hereabouts-fiend – if fiend there were – had none of these flowers which form a daisychain around *Lolita*'s drugstores and tenniscourts. It would not be very literate, and decidedly it would have no humour. It showed itself, if at all, in the guise of a red Volkswagen with a K-registration.

If at all, period: there are a great many red Golfs in the Federal Republic. And the feeling of having a shadow flitting hither-and-yon, while instinctive and thus fairly trustworthy, is not easily demonstrable, if that shadow knows its business. Not in somewhere as small and obvious as the Altstadt of Bremen. In a major city – like Hamburg – a fiend, to keep anything like in touch, would have to work closer up. And would then become more detectable.

"If Paris had a Canebière," says van der Valk, repeating an antique joke, but a good one, "it would be a little Marseille." It is a city where he had once worked.

"And if Marseille had an Alster," says Arlette looking out over the water, feeling abashed, feeling provincial, "it might perhaps struggle towards being a tiny Hamburg."

On the one side is the art gallery; a prim grey and yellow palace in nineteenth-century classical. Not really ugly but totally undistinguished. Still, holding its own, definitely; it stares, across the railroad tracks, with a justifiable arrogance, even legitimate self-satisfaction, at a monstrous cube, apparently constructed of expanded polystyrene, in a depressing grey and without a window: called Horta or Herter, nobody will ever for a single second remember what. I am civilisation, says the Kunstmuseum: you are merely barbarism. Nobody noticed your coming, and nobody will regret your going. Which will be soon, we trust.

Hamburg was of course fearfully bombed, and the insurance companies sit there in block after block built of small print, their mean windows squinting introspective upon squalid works. They glare at the Alster, hating it, for daring to take up so much good office space. The Jungfernstieg has a confused, dumb appearance, as of having been translated overnight from De Kalb, North Dakota. There are a few beautiful buildings left in Hamburg. There used to be a tree in the Sahara: the Tree of Ténéré. Then one day a big truck sort of lurched into it. So they built a metal one instead, so that people wouldn't miss the landmark.

Arlette ate Aalsuppe, which would be exactly like eating bouillabaisse in Marseille: getting a real one is a rarity. Legend says that the tourists kept complaining there was no Eel in it, so that they started putting in eel too: why not? There's nothing better anywhere. Van der Valk, of course, displaying heavy Dutch humour (coarse; worse, crass), is with difficulty restrained from asking for hamburger. He'd have got it too, without that appalling bun: the real one has just onions. And to this day, in Hollywood, they imagine that double chicken consommé was invented by Louis B. Mayer.

But what did they do, asked Arlette, with the *first* chicken? They didn't just throw it away?

Seriously, she says, the Aalsuppe would not be easy to make at home. You'd want a special Hamburg granny, and she'd be busily occupied. Ginger root, and cinnamon stick, and pepper, and mace – perhaps you can buy it here blended specially, in a little magic bag. Like tea-bags with jasmine in, suggests van der Valk, and gets a dirty look.

She would like to go on a boat, upon the Alster, but though the sunshine is bright the wind is too cold: they took the ferry instead, where one can sit sheltered. Wondering about the Fiend, he studied his fellow passengers. There was a quiet, heavily-built chap with too much indifference to his surroundings; a broad heavy face with thick eyebrows and dark rings under the eyes which looked at nothing; a big shaved jaw which chewed gum. Retired early from the Hamburg Police perhaps, and still in good shape.

He thought of a number of simple ploys, the simplest being to get off the boat and get back on again at the second it cast off. Arlette would say, "What on earth are you playing at?" A good question. This was all paranoia. What possible use could it be to anyone to follow him about? He had made it as clear as could be that he had no continuing interest in sects with self-imposed missions for changing the face of the world. Most of them are fraudulent as hell, anyway, but are set up as religious institutes, making it impossible to peg them for extortion of funds. Charity or cultural foundations: you can't even get them on income-tax evasion. There isn't any law against setting up political studies groups. They can preach subversion quite openly, and until you can bring proof of an act of violence, committed or sponsored, no legal authority will do anything but shrug.

He was in a false position, damn it. He had made Reich look ridiculous, he had spoken phrases of open contempt and derision to the preacher, and it was possible that they might decide to make his life a misery out of pure spitefulness. Walking about here with his wife, he was vulnerable, if anyone chose to make him so.

Every cop in a criminal-investigation branch – even in Holland – has been threatened with vendettas, since he has been instrumental in sending people to prison. He is a professional, doing his job, and he doesn't take threats very seriously. He is grateful, though, not to be in the Royal Ulster Constabulary and have to go through that drill, every damned day, of ensuring that the car in which your wife proposes to go shopping has no explosive device attached to it: even if you yourself are known as a decent, fair-minded and unprejudiced cop, you're still a filthy Protestant.

The French, the Italian, the Spanish police forces lose twenty or thirty men a year through assassination, and they accept this risk as part of their job. And I am Dutch, and such things have never been known in Holland. It is absurd. He wanted to say Look, I am taking a stroll, purely for my wife's amusement, in this fancy shopping district on the Upper West Side which they call Pöseldorf. *Pöseln* meaning to potter, and that's just what I'm doing.

The man who might have been an ex-cop got off at the Rabenstrasse and walked away through the park without even looking at him.

Do outrageous, idiotic, tourist things. Get rather drunk.

Arlette remembers that evening in a splendidly beery, fishy restaurant (huge model sailingships hanging over all the tables, very nice), eating thoroughly volks-Hamburg things, fried plaice Finkenwerder style, with rashers of bacon and potato salad. In a good mood of wit and irony, 'one of his glooms' came upon him. He is given now and then to the *vin triste*, a depression after three or four glasses of schnapps (served very cold: she has tried it but disliked the taste).

He hasn't had any. He has had a few beers, which would be enough to make him pleasantly loose and lazy, drawl a bit, become good company.

"I'm a stupid old cop. And an old cop is an old bastard."

"What awful nonsense." He is some five years off his pension. Sure; with his disability (the rifle bullet in his pelvis) he could take his pension any time.

"Yes. Seniority means pen-pushing, and that's all I'm good for now; collecting meaningless statistics and telling juniors how to do the work they're much better at than me. Not street-wise any more. Stupid!"

"That's preposterous. A sergeant of thirty, yes, he's doing

183

the street work; that's what he's for. But for responsibility, experience or understanding, he has to turn to his senior officer and that's you."

"He doesn't, you know. He can do it better, and knows it. And why? Because when you get old you lose sensitivity. You don't hear bats any more, you have lost your sense of touch. Do you remember being young, in summer, on the beach? How wonderful it was being naked, feeling the air on your skin, the feel of the water, the current of the whole world around you. You can't do that now. You'd just feel cold."

"But that is a platitude, a truism, si la vieillesse pouvait et si la jeunesse savait; you lose in ways and you gain in others. I often feel I'm only now beginning to learn, to see things."

"No. If I hadn't been a pompous, interfering, righteous old cunt I'd never have got involved there in Holland last week."

"You did what had to be done."

"No. A week or so more and that fellow would have fallen of his own momentum. He was trapped in his own web: inevitably a parent would have found out and denounced him."

"And meanwhile you have maybe saved another two or three children from corruption."

"And then I would not have thought myself clever fiddle-fucking around with Jan Rijk. There are hundreds, thousands just like him, earnest, humourless, self-righteous, telling us what's wrong with politics or economics or theologics, because they feel obscure guilts about the way they make their money, whereas we know perfectly well that it all comes out in the wash. I'm sick of this boring place – let's pay and clear out. All I've done is spoil your holiday."

There wasn't any point in arguing.

"Now I want to go to the Reeperbahn," Arlette tells him, out on the street.

"What on earth for?"

"I want to see the girls."

"Far's I know there aren't any. All phone numbers now in blameless bourgeois districts. Let's see, whereabouts are we?"

Somewhere in the harbour quarter. The night was cold, clear. A brisk walk was indicated. This would do one a lot of good. The way is through the park. Up rather a steep hill. Halfway up Arlette clung to him in acute alarm.

"Oh God, what's that?" A great enormous stone-age Giant. On examination it turns out to be Bismarck, looking out upon St Pauli with puritan disapproval.

In direct contrast to her expectations (she is thinking of the alleyways in Amsterdam's old quarter) the Reeperbahn is a broad and handsome boulevard with trees in the middle and a large police station, rather nice; art-déco brick of the twenties. The only sign of vice is a large crowd of American matrons outside the Hotel Monopol, hawkeyed for prostitutes and cross because there aren't any. On one side is a squalid row of slotmachines and penny peepshows for the maladjusted young. Arlette is much frustrated.

"There's one saying Live Show," dragging him forward.

"Very well but watch out for the price of the drinks." Indulgently, but there's a scrap left of street-wisdom.

As suspected it's too dark to see anything, but the law says there has to be a bar list: *caveat emptor* but these places are careful, because they'd better. So he smiles benignly upon the bar girl and flicks his lighter to read the back 'The ordering of drinks constitutes a civil contract and under article 318b of the Code any refreshment called for and whether or not consumed must be paid for.' Sighing deeply because this means fifty marks for a whisky he lit Arlette's cigarette and turned his attention to the girls.

This softened the blow: they are quite lovely. She isn't expected to do anything but have a beautiful body and show it. This work is not hard but the hours are long, so that though quite well paid she goes about it with languor: she sails on wearing knickers, takes them off after about ten minutes and dances for another ten while naked. The rule is very simple; she must be unblemished and absolutely normal. She does nothing whatever obscene, vulgar, or even provocative. Her stint is immediately replaced by another, identical: a natural blonde, body-painted to a golden tan.

Too often I have been told that it's a great handicap to a police officer, to have imagination, van der Valk reminds himself. Too often indeed I've had it proved, to my grief and sometimes to my danger. I've had it proved over the whole of this last week. Stimulated by the delightful island, by Arlette's tales of sands and spies and sailingboats; by Jan Rijk's political fantasies, by the perverse (indeed obscene) theatre of that horrid little Quijs, by the exaggerated self-importance of that poor wretch Brownrigg, calamitous attractor of unwanted and unneeded dramas . . . I too started imagining things.

And at last I had to come to this ridiculous place, which has been living on a borrowed reputation since 1940, when the deep contralto voice of Lale Andersen went round Europe singing 'Unter die roten Laterne von Sant Pauli' – catchy tune it had – and here of all places, at last my imagination has paid off, and instead of a bored naked Hamburg bargirl it shows me a glorious shining-muscled Amazon, like this one. Hippolyta naked.

Suddenly intensely happy he slid off the bar stool and muttered, "Seen enough?"

"God yes, I'm bored stiff. I thought it would be Laura's House in the Hague, with the waterbeds and the lesbians and the mother-and-daughter act."

"Old and medieval as I am, I haven't been in a joy-house for twenty years, but d'you know, darling, I rather doubt it."

Newcomers were being shown in by a bustling little man with a feeble little torch. And as this flitted along the three or four rows of the tiny theatre, van der Valk saw the Fiend.

Or thought he did: with his hangdog countenance and his dirty mind and his knees sticking out? The torch had flickered too fast and too feebly in the gloom accentuated by the bright light on the little stage (a dark girl now, with rather a ripe behind). He couldn't be sure and he *wouldn't* be sure, but might that have been the Reverend Elmer Gantry? Who could surely have seen far greater obscenities in Fort Lauderdale – but there, the far-off hills are greener. Apart from the risk of being recognised by one of the faithful.

Then if not the Fiend, quite a good imitation. Or am I again entrapped by my failing eyes, my dulled ears, the brightly-lit vision of a female body plastic enough to be modelled by Rodin even in its halfhearted gyration in front of a mirror? The fishbowl act – but it's myself inside the fishbowl.

"Such a deception," Arlette had taken his arm, now quite sober, and they were tripping along the pavement towards the U-Bahn station, "but I do have to admit, I was a bit pissed, and I did ask for it, and you did warn me, and I'm sorry to have cost you a hundred marks just for three sets of pubic hair and that terrible old porn video on the television screens: oh well, who knows, perhaps it's a stimulus."

She does indeed her best. She sometimes does buy extravagant silk underclothes. One can always get soppy disco dance music on a bedside radio.

"The principal problem," she says with great seriousness, "is that only the most expensive hotel rooms are big enough to dance in. And there's no bar girl to pull the string of my knickers when the customers get impatient. We ought to have booked in to the Atlantic."

"Three hundred marks a night, thanks very much."

"How discouraging you are. Still, I come free."

12

They spend three days in Hamburg. The detail will have importance, later.

Arlette is very serious, next day, about Art. You see, Hamburg is like other war-damaged cities. One notices the art because there is so little left. The Sandtor harbour, the only example left remaining of late nineteenth-century mercantile warehousing, will probably not be there much longer, judging by the greedy eyes upon the splendid site. Arlette, faithful as John Betjeman to crocketed gothic skylines, is torn between her wish to stay and revel in this delectable town and that – just as burning – to push on and look at the Baltic fjords before the roily flood of industrial effluents destroys the OstSee altogether.

First fjord on the Baltic side of the Schleswig coast is Kiel, and here she lost her temper altogether, because the entire centre of this prosperous town, marvellously sited on the hills above the estuary, has been utterly given over to the ignoble structures of commercial squalor at its nadir: she stamps her foot and yells. Dear God, there isn't even a pub, and they lunched on Chinese food of the worst sort and beer brewed 'judging by the taste in South Korea'.

"But if one were to move out further down the fjord – "

"No, no, and no, it's all exactly like Southampton." The car is turned resolutely north, Arlette driving it in a flow of vengeful mutter against other road users. Van der Valk has something of an eye out for fiends, notably red Volkswagens with a K-registration, but no fiends are in view. Perhaps they got left behind in Hamburg. One would see them from afar rather better in this pastoral landscape.

For Schleswig is pretty. He studies it, while she threads the traffic. Not at all like Holland – hilly and wooded, with cows in green valleys, red houses, steep-roofed and as though awaiting the arrival of storks and swallows from the south.

"Any moment now," says Arlette, who is cheering up perceptibly.

And far, mercifully, emptier than Holland. Only the northern sky, huge and ever-changing, is the same. But this of course is Denmark – this is the province which Bismarck's Germany annexed by conquest in eighteen sixty, tilting the country into the long unhappy century of lunacy. On their right was the sparkle of water now and then; the long narrow serpent of Eckernfjord thrusting into the heart of the peninsula. Tantalising glimpses of wooded shores sloping down to tiny beaches, minute harbours filled with the needle masts of little pleasure boats; for this is the paradise of small-yacht sailing: the tideless and almost stormless Baltic.

"All very nice around here," he says wistfully, but she shakes her head, being masterful, drives on impenitent past the spires and markets of Schleswig town: agricultural flavour of tractors met upon the road and a fine windborne waft of farmyard manure.

In fact she has a bee in her bonnet; good English phrase if worn down to cliché: since reading *The Riddle of the Sands* in Norderney she has seen the whole casual, unplanned take-it-as-it-comes holiday trip as a pattern, which she must see out to the end. Up here was where it began. Here in the harbour of Flensburg was where – halfway through a September at the turn of the century – the conceited young man from the Foreign Office caught his first sight of the *Dulcibella*. So that here is where she insists upon going. This is the frontier. Flensburg is the last town on the German side: the northern shore of the fjord is Danish.

"Peaceful folk, Danes."

He spoke with approval. Germans have been warlike for too many years of the last century, so that even today people feel suspicious of them: is there something sinister about their refusal to behave belligerently? It is so easy to forget that every European people has behaved this way at one time or another.

"Danes used to be perfect terrors."

Even Arlette is looking about her in some surprise, as though expecting the people to be wearing horned helmets. Berserk warriors with matted beards, blood-boltered battleaxes.

Van der Valk feels a need for alertness, to keep his wits about him. There is no need to be neurotic. There is no sign of a red Volkswagen with Karlsruhe plates. There is nothing at all which in any way suggests the presence of a fiend. But the very placidity of this countryside is telling him to underestimate no one, and especially not Jan Rijk.

As they reached the town the sky, which had been sunny, cloudy, windy and delightfully fickle-April, blackened in the most ominous fashion and they were greeted by a drenching cloudburst of cold westerly rain, causing the struggle to find one's raincoat sleeves while still sitting in the car. He was out of sorts now; feeling fatigue, feeling too the burden of uncertainty that is edged with anxiety: like the sky.

But she was in fine fettle, belted into a trenchcoat and with a funny hat, disregarding grumbles – this, at last, is what she has come to find. Even if she's had to go all the way to the Danish border for it. The little towns of northern Holland, in the sixteenth and seventeenth centuries still important seaports with an impressive wealth and maritime arrogance, grown from trade to the furthest orient known, have withered altogether from the silting of the estuaries. Around the hump of the Groningen peninsula, the Ems and Jade never gave access to more than tidal inlets. In Bremen she had seen something of what she wanted, but like Bruges it is too far inland. There's no sea there. Hamburg, yes, of course. But it is too big, too masterful, too vulgarly obsessed with financial puissance. Flensburg is exactly what her imagination told her must exist but which she has so far sought in vain: a real port but small, simple, and unspoilt. The odd English bomber, driven off course by the winds of the Nordsee and blinded by rain, sloppy navigation and a good shot of fatalistic halfheartedness, did drop a few under the vague impression that it might be Kiel or Lübeck. Without conviction.

The head of the Flensburg fjord is a straight, narrowish passage of some three or four kilometres, between steep banks. The wooded northern shore is the expected bourgeois quarter of shipowners' villas and the convents of holy-mother-Church: the town is to the south, in a long ribbon between quay and hill, with the original fishing village at the tip between. There is a Danish flavour with names in -og and -øg. There are many small charming houses in a simple curving northern baroque of the seventeenth and eighteenth centuries, and many more much larger in the pompous italianate-classical of the eighteen-forties. This is all very little spoilt. Nothing here became big or pretentious, and little coasting steamers with trade to the islands and Stockholm or Rostock still feel at home. In the landlocked Baltic the hysterical empire-building mentality is lacking: one feels as far from Hamburg as from Shanghai.

Arlette is greatly content, full of plans to explore the Danish side of the fjord – Sonderborg sounded nice – and the North Sea coast of Schleswig . . . she pulled herself up with the remark that her husband appeared distracted; melancholy.

"Not still distraught, surely? About that stupid man Reich?"

"Just perhaps a little sad." A sadness, he was thinking, of having the choice between reason and folly and knowing that one will always choose the folly.

"Oh dear, and I was just thinking this was a good base and a nice hotel – have a look out at our view over the fjord."

"I don't think you need worry particularly. I've no intention of getting flustered, but we haven't seen the end of Master Jan.

Captain Jan, perhaps," looking out at the pretty harbour. "I've been recollecting the phrase of an English admiral. During the Napoleonic times. 'I do not say the enemy cannot come,' he said. 'I only say he cannot come by sea.' Which was nicely put and I'd rather like to say the same."

"You're tired. I'll change my shoes, okay? They got a bit wet. We'll go out for a beer and decide upon somewhere to eat."

The rainstorm had passed and peaceful twilight was coming down upon the scene. There was a nice alleyway down to the quay through the courtyard where they'd left the car. Arlette looked about her as though upon the shores of the Mediterranean where Algerian corsairs might suddenly disembark. Jan Rijk thinking himself a Viking?

"Oh yes, we've been followed." There was no point in trying to put it off longer. "One gets an instinct for these things."

She stopped dead in the street, facing him, her fine eyes alight.

"You mean there's another lunatic. Like that horrible little man in the forest. They'll try to shoot you? You must tell me. I won't have anything concealed. I had thought that was all over, once you'd seen the German police."

"No no, there won't be anything like that," laughing heartily. "But Rijk was left humiliated and ridiculed. He'll see that as a defeat. He's not the man to swallow that – he'll want to try and restore the balance, at the least. Here's a place; what d'you make of this?"

"Scholle," said Arlette studying the menu posted outside. "Scholle, scholle, eel, salmon – I refuse to eat salmon in a place like this. Seems clean and pleasant," peeking between the curtains, "harpoons and things pinned up. There should be clam chowder like in Nantucket. Come on."

Sitting in front of a beer, but still disquietened, she pursued.

"But what was this about coming by sea — that seems highly absurd and artificial."

"Is it? I'm not that sure. I've been thinking about Jan. Put it very crudely, there are two, Rijk and Reich; you agree?"

Arlette tasted her beer and nodded, meaning yes; also that the beer was good, and not too cold.

"There's two of everyone, no? Look at you, all cold and reasoning just when everyone's thinking you sleepy and dreamy, and just when they're expecting you to act the cop being precise and logical, you do silly things from instinct." At which naively expressed argument he had to laugh, but with affection. She was a stout support, in all his worlds.

"There are perhaps half a dozen of you, and mostly awful: cliché that. Same of any woman that's worth salt. But let's keep to our very simple statement, because we don't know much more about friend Jan anyhow." Breaking off to order their dinner, decide against wine, stick to beer. 'Scholle' is only plaice but the unpretentious will always be the best, and the freshest.

"Perhaps — it might not even be true, but for a start — Rijk is your hardheaded Hollander, businessman through and through. Reich is abstract where the other is concrete, threaded through with ideologies, poetic notions, woolly political theories. It's the one we've seen most of, the one who keeps a boat on Norderney, dreams about reuniting Holland and Belgium, throwing out all the blacks, putting the drug-users in a work camp on a preferably nasty island. All the whores on another island? — we'll start running short of islands but no matter, this dotty side saw me as a potential ally. Whereas if I'd been selling scrap metal he'd have seen through me inside three winks.

"People are far too complex to predict, but my instinct says it's Reich we have to contend with because that's who we met on Norderney. After the fiasco there at Visbek — that Quijs was plainly round the bend in the pipe and they'll throw him to the wolves, for the local police to chew on – what was friend Reich's reaction?

"Rijk would go straight back to Frankfurt, with a shrug, saying forget it. What's a Dutch police officer when all is said? What could such a one prove? Nothing! What could he do? Put our boy on the computer as a potential ju-ju man? He must know he's there already, along with tenthousand other freemasonries, sects, movements, quasi-religious, the computer's full of this shit and nobody takes it seriously. That would be the sensible thing. But Reich – he might be feeling me under his skin, see it as a personal thing, an account that has to be settled."

"But that might be dangerous," sitting bolt upright and looking frightened again. "He employs people like Quijs, a cheap sadist maybe, but there are more dotties like that."

Van der Valk shook his head, fishing a bone out of a mouth full of fried plaice and potato salad and shrimps.

"I daresay," with difficulty, "he does have some kind of network all along these coasts and some of them nasty bits of work. But he can't possibly risk anything open, certainly no overt violence. A senior civil servant, and a cop into the bargain! I thought in Hamburg he might try and drag me into some blackmail situation – you know, arrange to find me with a screw of white powder in my pocket. But up here he'll think he's got me bottled, and what could easily go wrong in Hamburg could look simpler here. But I've got him bottled too, which he might be too vain to realise. I have to seek means to winkle him out."

"But what was this about by sea?"

He finished his beer and signalled for another. "Say he went straight back to Norderney. He has his boat there, and on his boat Reich feels at his best, his purest, his strongest. He learns I'm in Hamburg, he has an easy sail to the Elbe. I made no secret of our intention to potter up in this direction. While we were revelling in the St Pauli fleshpots he had plenty of time to bring the boat through the canal to Kiel. He could be here this minute," putting his knife and fork together and belching with Dutch satisfaction, "in any one of about a hundred little harbours or marinas round here. It's odds on he knows this coast very well, it's a yachting paradise . . . I want to find a lonely spot, better than this, tempt him out, isolate him, and provoke an encounter. Now, what about Schlei Fjord?"

Arlette looked at him, with her eyes enormous. She turned suddenly, burrowed in her shopping-bag, in which she keeps improbable quantities of cardigans, hairpins, spare shoes and tourist literature, stray cosmetics, aspirin, and sticking-plaster.

"I bought a tourist map of Schleswig. I know all about Schlei Fjord. It's where *The Riddle of the Sands* begins. It has nothing to do with the story but it sets the atmosphere, and I made sure because I wanted to see it. It's just south of here, it's thirty kilometres long, goes right up to Schleswig town, and the entrance is only eighty metres wide, and that won't have changed since nineteen hundred and three, whatever else. Quite near the mouth it narrows again and there's a little town called Kappeln."

"We'll go there tomorrow," said van der Valk. Fish doesn't get in one's teeth the way horrible meat does, but he was looking round instinctively for a pub toothpick. There ought to be duck quills, in hygienic little paper wrappings, in an apéritif glass on the table, between the ashtray and the salt-shaker. There always are in Holland and he missed them. What is Germany coming to? "It's known as pegging out the goat. The bleating of the goat attracts the leopard."

"I have faith," said Arlette, brave after two beers.

A pottering sort of road connects Flensburg to Kappeln. Impatient Mercedes cars get hung up behind trundling agricultural machinery.

Thirty kilometres along, the village clings steep and huddled to the hillside, corkscrewing downward to the waterside. The fisher houses have been turned into smart little bourgeois residences. Schlei Fjord narrows here to a bottleneck, crossed by a bridge before broadening again, and there are tiny coasters moored to minute quays, bringing farm produce to Hamburg just as the galliots did in nineteen-hundred. Everything here appears child-size, as though it were all designed to be a wonderful toy. Ferries no bigger than the launches on the Alster trundle the passenger out to the narrow opening of Schleimünde, and in to the great real world of Flensburg Fjord; across to Sonderborg and the Danish islands: a mild and pretty waterscape for the summer tourists to dip their fingers in.

Only do not look too closely. Above all, do not begin asking questions about the tonnage of artificial fertiliser leaking into the fragile, gentle, uncomplaining Baltic: a polite and silent violence that police officers ignore. A stately procession and impeccably legal; like gangsters at a Mafia funeral.

A handsbreadth further, the quay is grassgrown and the railway line furred with rust. A score of yachts lies moored to a wooden jetty, and one or two owners have been stirred by the sunlight of a spring anticyclone, into taking the tarpaulins off cabin roofs and putting the cushions out to air. One will think tomorrow about those corroded shroud screws, but enjoy meantime a lazy cup of coffee, a languid exchange of gossip. Shoreside there is a low comfortable building labelled Yacht Club. It is bright with flowers and clean curtains, and rows of pennants from every other yacht-club in Europe. A delight, and a polite young man told Arlette that of course they could have a drink, and lunch too; as long as they didn't mind it simple.

However German the coffee (for which one may be thankful), the hamburger, simply called hack-steak, or the beer, anyone English would have found the scene irresistibly, nostalgically Edwardian: Ratty and Moly bent over a decayed dinghy (Toad liable to arrive any moment with his horrible great new Chris-craft). Still more – the Potwell Inn, where Mr Polly served Omlets and Uncle Jim disturbed the peace armed with a dead eel. Reality need not intrude for an hour or so. At another – decrepit – landingstage a hundred metres further, three or four old wooden craft of the galliot era sat gently decaying in the company of an antiquated dredger with nothing but the rust holding it together, and here van der Valk went peacefully to sleep while Arlette (bored by boats, even hating them slightly) pottered off to the village with a vague mutter about postcards. In the light air of the outer fjord three or four small boys careered upon sail planks, clinging heroic to the wishbone.

When woken by a timid touch on the shoulder he thought it was Arlette, opened a lazy eye. An urchin of twelve or thirteen was grinning at him.

"Herr vun der Vulk?"

"That's right."

"Message for you. He says," screwing up his eyes under the mop of wetted sundried spiky hair, in the effort to concentrate upon a memorised phrase, "he says, he'll be at Maasholm at six, if you wish to talk with him. That's all," scurrying off abruptly. Van der Valk sat up, just as abruptly. It had worked! That was Uncle Jim all right, dead eel and all. (What was it the tourist told Mr Polly? – 'He appears to have brought you a present of fish.') He had better assemble his dull wits. It was only four, but the sun was westering fast and casting shadows. April in the north, the twilight comes down fast.

Where is Maasholm? Arlette has the map.

"Oh, there you are. What a time you've been. Work to do," interrupting explanations, rambling and complicated, "where's Maasholm?" It was a tiny village, the other side of the estuary near the fjord's inlet. Nothing to notice about it save that the ferry made a call there. To be reached by turning off the road back to Flensburg, some fifteen kilometres along. No hurry, and one would have time to sniff about. Arlette of course became instantly crossgrained, raising a cloud of fears and objections.

"You won't go. It's a trick, an obvious trap. Spies all over the place: how did this nasty child know how to find you?"

"Don't be ridiculous, the car's parked in the obvious place there by the bridge, Dutch plates, sticks out like a thumb, he'd only to follow his nose, small boys see and know everything." Becoming authoritarian, "You will please not interfere. Just drive the car, park it there wherever, sit there and wait for me. Read or knit or what you like, I won't be over half an hour. Make no melodrama – if that's what Jan wants, the thing is to deflate it."

The twilight was coming down fast. The evening star sat enormous and obsessive on the horizon. Seems mostly to be called Morgenstern, in German. There was a poet called Christian Morgenstern with an acid sense of humour and van der Valk recollects a ridiculous rhyme.

> *Ein Wiesel*
> *sass auf einem Kiesel*
> *inmitten Bachgeriesel.*
> *Wisst ihr,*
> *weshalb?*

A weasel sat upon a rounded stone in the middle of the brook. Had he any idea why? The poem, which is very short or he would never have remembered it, concludes laconically 'Sophisticated beast. He was doing it for the sake of the rhymes.'

It was only a potty village of tiny, crouching fishers' houses. It went out to a little point, along a muddy foreshore where punts (there would be wild duck here in winter) were hauled up in graves in the reeds. Beyond there was a 'hard' and the usual cluster of sailingboats at moorings. One or two bigger boats lay at anchor, a little way out, but there was not light enough to see whether one was Jan's. The 'Mondkalb', the full moon which showed the weasel to the poet, was missing. Stars, large and bright in the clean air, gave uncertain light.

Beyond the point, the shore hollowed into a harbour with the ferry stage, a pavement for unloading herring, a pub, a wooden hut selling fish – what more would you want. A few loiterers awaited the arrival of the ferry: it could hardly be called activity but Jan would avoid the gaze of the curious. Van der Valk retraced steps to the hard, sloping seaward so that a small boat can be hauled, shored upright, and have its hull cleaned of weed and barnacles. There wasn't a soul there. Against the small light of the evening star the needles of masts performed their gentle mazy dance: water lapped softly on the greasy concrete. He lit a small cigar and waited.

"I could kill you now," said Jan's voice. "I could have had you killed a dozen times. In Hamburg, anywhere along the road."

"Bullshit," said van der Valk. But despite everything his flesh crawled, his blood raced. He couldn't help but remember the fake, in Norderney; a fake which had taken him in. A reduced-charge .22 fired from a pistol which can be bought anywhere. At a distance of two metres kills you as stony-dead as any great big thirtyeight police positive. The noise of a piece of firewood snapped in two.

"Look at me." He looked, and was afraid.

"And supposing you did." His voice came out brittle and dry as a dead stick, in winter. "Even deafened and blinded by vanity you hardly imagine that would pass unnoticed. You followed me. Do you really think the police have not got people capable of following you? There's a man out there this minute. Colt Python, threefiftyseven with the long barrel, magnum charge, the evening star's shining right there on the foresight. Go through you like a bulldozer. Snap half those masts off, going out to sea." A giggle swelled and broke out as a big laugh.

"Man. I talk too much when I'm frightened too."

"Very well then. Come on out into the light. Let's have a talk, then. Both learn some truths."

The shadow detached itself from the shadow of a boat. A boat hauled out on dry land looks bigger than it does in the water. Jan looks bigger too, in a bib-overall and canvas deck shoes. Taller, wider, hair longer and more curly, jaw squarer and smile broader, the eyes further apart and glinting with regalement of a good joke. He looked piratical, but he also looked dangerous.

"How did I know you were in Kappeln?" enjoying it. "How did I get a message to you? There'd be a dozen witnesses to show that I'd never left Sonderborg, and all the cops in the province couldn't tell it different. Assuming they tried." And it might very well be true.

"No no Jan, that won't do. You're a sharp enough business-man to realise I'd be much more dangerous to you dead. Alive I'm just a bureaucrat who has you on a file. But dead – you know the Dutch. Tenacious. Rancorous. They wouldn't let go. These petty kingdoms of yours, here or in Norderney, or Frank-furt either, aren't worth anything. People as a whole have too much common sense to take you seriously for long. The only grip you have is fear. To scare people with little stories. Just like the Swedes finding Russian submarines in Malmö harbour."

"Ah. Fear . . . I can arrange, my good Commissaris, to give you some lessons. You are afraid now. And it may not be over, not now or ever, not if I don't want it to be. Remember that. You can learn to feel the fear every time you close a door, every time you cross a road. Your wife can learn to feel it, too, and your children . . ."

"I'm not altogether with you in this, Jan. It's true perhaps that you looked an ass in front of your friends, when I walked into that secret conclave of yours in Visbek. Some embarrassed explaining was needed there, hm? How did I happen to find out about that? Still, you've plenty of time to cook up more of these little conspiracies: I haven't done you that much damage. Put a dent in your vanity, but you'll get over it soon enough.

"And I laid violent hands on your henchman Quijs. But then he wanted to do the same to me. And when you think of it you ought to be grateful. He was getting ideas above his station; he'd have finished by getting you in much hotter water than that. I don't really know why you feel the need to get excited."

But this speech, designed to cool Rijk down, had the opposite effect.

It was dark by now, and the stars blazed. The whole Schleswig firmament full of the lovely things. Van der Valk's eyesight had had time to get attuned to this light. He could see Rijk's face. And so, of course, could Rijk see his own. A pleasant social smile, he hoped, like a man at a party who has had two drinks and is looking around for a third. While Rijk's face looked set, the eyes glaring.

"Yes." A stiff, cold voice. "How *did* you know that I would be in Visbek?" And seeing a psychological advantage to be gained, van der Valk thought it time to play his ace. Arlette would be growing anxious. He wasn't going to mention the garbled message from Brownrigg, so belatedly grasped.

"Your daughter told me." It was true too, in a way. Gisela, the anthropology student, had aroused Arlette's curiosity (in no doubt perfect innocence) about that interesting prehistoric structure in the woods south of Dremon . . .

But Reich's reaction was violent and very nasty. His hand went to the bib of his overall and pulled out a knife. As fast and as practised a gesture opened it one-handed. A sailor – a sailing-ship sailor – is never without a knife. Has learned to use it, and in emergency quickly.

The blade was pointed towards him. Reich had made a step forward. A nasty twitch was showing in the big jovial jaw.

Van der Valk didn't like this. On such slippery greasy cobbles his leg was worth even less than on level ground. His opponent was big, active, wearing deck shoes, and he has already seen him cat-quick. A stick is not worth much against a knife. What the hell have I said?

"Yes," slowly. "My daughter." The voice was even. A mad voice, saying mad things, in lunatic storybook clichés.

"I have learned, in this context, of your activities. You went to the Hague, for the weekend, upon your meddlesome activities. You came back early, upon the Sunday. You took advantage of hospitality offered. You took advantage of my absence to debauch and assault my daughter. Don't attempt to lie to me, you scum, I had it from her own lips. You made her drunk and seduced her. You took your pleasure with an innocent girl. You will pay for that now, with a knife in your belly. It'll take you an hour to die, you filth. And not a man here but will applaud."

There is no deus ex machina. Nor dea, awander in the woods wondering about stones. I do not understand. I can see that I might have a tiny, a remote scrap of chance, to trip him with the stick and to pray that the cut is deflected just enough not to be mortal – but keep talking, keep talking.

"Do you wish to learn the truth, Jan? If you cut me you never will. This will be something you'll regret all your days. For the reasons I've mentioned, and much more, now you've got a big personal reason of your own. You won't find out the truth, unless you give me time." Starlight shone on the used, practised blade. It shook a little, but not enough. If he makes up his mind to one jump he's got me; I'm finished.

"Listen to me Jan, do that at least, give me this much; she lied to you, I don't know why, but it's so. I wasn't there. Arlette was but I didn't get back and that's readily proved. I don't know your daughter at all apart from seeing her in your house and I was kidding you when I said she'd told me about Visbek; it was my wife she told and quite innocently when they were out riding together. There was no treachery, it's a plain coincidence." Gabble, and keep gabbling. He drew breath fast.

"Christ Jan, stop and think. Why should she say such a thing? I don't know, I'll take a hack at it, just give your mind a chance to look at my guess – quick litmus-paper, true-or-false. My wife while in your house heard one sentiment repeated by your wife and both your daughters, and that's that they didn't like the Reverend Russ one little bit, because behind that pious façade he's nothing but a coarse lecher, and the most innocent girl can see that where a man mightn't."

He could now make out a path; terrified as he was he must keep the gabble going.

"What he doesn't dare in Miami, for fear of being black-mailed, he'll do in Hamburg; furtive, cheap, and in anyone else just pathetic. Do you know where I saw him? In a tourist trap, working up his courage to go round the corner and give the whores a christening. How I came to be there? Because my wife too has led an innocent life, and just like all the tourist ladies in the Hotel Monopol she wanted to see what a Reeperbahn come-on girl looks like. You and I know that she looks like any other. Girls are the same everywhere and a whore behind the fishmarket has just the same fanny as Princess Soraya, and my wife is just the same as your daughters, but they might have found out a harder way." He drew another breath.

"Just think about it, Jan. Think too that you tend to make the same mistake as a lot of smart businessmen. You behave to your enemies as though they were friends, and your friends as though they were enemies."

The knife, held in the fist that was clenched too tight, shook. Rijk said nothing but his face shone. Sweat? So does mine. I could be peeing in my trousers and I'd never even notice. Do not be proud, van der Valk, don't ever be proud. The man had you there at knife-point and you stood there yacking, and you damn near lost control over your own bowels.

"I'll think about it," said Rijk harshly. "I won't just think about it. I'll find out. Peg this one good in your mind, van der Valk. If you have lied to me, tell yourself this: you'll never draw another breath again in peace and ease. You'll spend every minute counting off the days left you."

Van der Valk felt himself tremble. He did not see Reich go. He heard nothing either. Maybe the man had a dinghy and pushed it out and put sculls into the rowlocks – one can hear oar-strokes a long way off, at night, going off to an anchored boat. Or maybe he was telling the truth and had left his boat in Sonderborg, and would take the little motorlaunch ferry back across the fjord. What did it matter? He had heard and seen nothing.

After what seemed a long time he had pulled himself together enough to trudge back the two hundred metres to the square outside Maasholm village where Arlette had parked the car and sat in it for surely a very long time. You did not look good at all, Mr van der Valk. You weren't good. You were ignoble. You acted ignobly – you were ready to do anything to save your miserable skin. Be not proud.

Arlette with the rooflight turned on was reading the guide-book to all the Hamburg restaurants, for lack of anything better: anything to keep her nerves quietened. She looked up at his slow, shuffling approach, keeping herself under strict control, showing it only in the violent, thrusting bang of the pamphlet into the glove compartment – "You have been an eternity."

He climbed into the car, lame and laborious, and sat back limply. "Eternity is what I'm just back from."

She said nothing, turned the ignition key roughly, accelerated crudely. He felt the sweat soaking his shirt, his cotton vest, his underpants, his woolly socks.

"Boy!" she said, once back on the main road, "do you stink!"

Epilogue

There were three or four days of holiday left but they passed uneventfully and nobody wrote in a diary what Sonderborg had been like, or Sylt. Nor that Arlette caught her foot in a bramble bush, neglected it, and the scratch festered: nor that van der Valk, attempting to make love to his wife, made a fiasco instead and wasn't proud: now if, like a Tom Sharpe hero, he had caught his kok in the bramblebush – that, he remarked at the time, might have been something to write about. The only consequence was that he told the story to Arlette. One didn't need to be Dr Freud, to fit two or three bits of fact together. She had been witness to rogering antics over the weekend in Norderney.

"Rijk – or is it Reich? – uptight about upbringings of young girls, and his daughters more than any. In another context they might have been contented to stay home and play Scrabble. As things were – it explains Agaethe's odd passive role. Sympathising with the girls, ready even to put up alibis for them, but felt the conflict too, loyalties to her husband. The noticing nothing, the not even being there, was her way of handling a difficult situation. Rijk and Reich both, perhaps. That tough authoritarian sort of business man, accustomed to unquestioning obedience and servility from secretaries and underlings, will often have a violent clash with student-age daughters. How did he come to think I had? Found some compromising evidence perhaps, and the girl said the first thing that came into her head. She doesn't have to be the

Jewish-Austrian girl on her way in the train to the white hotel, in order to have fantasies."

And his own delightful and virtuous wife, thought van der Valk. She felt no yen to be rogered by the students; she's one of the – if one says monogamous can one also say monoandrous? And perhaps hence, a day or two later, a virtuous and rather lovable envy of a Hamburg go-go girl? Who can tell? He dislikes questions which begin with 'How d'you account for . . . ?' He's an old and experienced enough cop never to account for anything.

At home in the Hague, the weather completely broken up, rain and wind rattling the windows, his chief problem is being three or four kilos overweight; it's all that German beer, and he isn't any good for the squash court any longer, not with that gammy leg. He'd better do some bicycling, like a good Dutch citizen.

His own role throughout having been dubious he has not made official reports (ludicrous things do happen, on holidays), but an unofficial chat with Mr X is in order.

Who has this awful Dutch sense of humour and rolls about laughing.

"You aren't going to ask me to put protection on you?"

"Good God – heaven forbid."

"Just as well, guards are terribly expensive, it's all we can do to keep gorillas stumbling after the Secretary of NATO or the Common Market. The Brits have so much Special Branch kept running after the IRA there's hardly a cop left over for ordinary street duty. Let's say" – arranging his pen-set and desk-blotter to be tidy – "I upgrade that file a bit, sort of flesh it out a little. They were disturbed about the man Brownrigg, and there were suggestions about trying to extradite your little Mr Quijs, but he turned out to have acquired German nationality so that's not on. They'll manage to tuck him away for a spell. You fulfilled the main object, which was to bring Rijk out into the open, thereby rendering him harmless. So quieten your nerves and soldier on with the paperwork, laddy."

So that it might have been towards the end of May? Not in the diary, but the neighbours (civil servant, wife something professorial) were on holiday in the south; before it gets-too-hot and the hooligans arrive. Van der Valk, having had his holiday, was not much interested but Arlette had been pressed into service in a neighbourly Dutch fashion to water the good lady's house plants. She had reciprocated earlier. The balconies of these flats ran the width of the block, and there were only canvas screens between, easily unlaced. It didn't make for much privacy, but then there never is much privacy in Holland.

And then it was a nasty day; grey but hot and humid, with sudden gusts of wind, just the sort which blows pots of geraniums off the balconies to the detriment of those below, and Arlette had gone fussing to see that all the bloody-pots were well anchored – and a nervous glance above: several inhabitants in this rather grand block were away. The sliding windows were open. Van der Valk sat tieless with his feet on a chair, reading. And Arlette with her plastic watering-can was pottering – potting? what was the right word? – when there was suddenly a terrific yell. Also a crash. Convinced that a pot had gone over, cursing, trying to remember whether the clause in the insurance cover . . . getting to his feet with resignation he stepped out, pushed through the flapping canvas, and was greeted by . . .

Arlette stood in one corner of the balcony, rather white but holding on to her watering-can with great determination. A few steps away stood a man, seeming quite elderly but the face was distorted by rage, or fear, or maybe pain, because another man stood just behind him, holding his wrist wrenched and forced up into the small of the back. This second man looked to be about sixteen but seemed to know what he was doing. The round boyish face was vaguely familiar.

"Who d'you catch there then, son, Spiderman? Little bit

of housebreaking?" The older man tried to lunge, and to spit, but both fell short. Fog cleared; behind the dishevelled hair and twisted face he recognised the Reverend Russ Whosit. And dammit, that little boy is a plainclothes cop. "Woho," said van der Valk cheerfully.

"Come and have a drink," said Mr X's comfortable-sounding, pre-lunch, telephone voice. The hotel lobby was full of potted palms, leather armchairs, businessmen drinking whisky. X was in a dark suit and highly spry, raising hell about the sherry.

"I do not want lukewarm British sherry out of some damn Waterford decanter which hasn't been dusted. I do not want American sherry served me with iceblocks in. I want a simple glass of Spanish sherry served me out of a simple Spanish bottle which has been properly chilled like any other white wine and you have the cheek to tell me there isn't any. Oh there you are, van der Valk, I do *not* recommend the sherry.

"Your dear friend the Reverend. Comes sailing across the frontier like a tourist. Rather intent upon bodily injury, he has a highly confused tale about your other great new friend accusing him of filthy designs upon his daughter and this was somehow all your fault. Good, we can peg the bastard from here to kingdom-come with breaking-and-entering, possession of unauthorised weapon – these people making free, thinking themselves still in Florida. Great big gun he had! However, I've talked to the Minister. He's not at all keen on upsetting the Americans right now, so I'm thinking of simply having this misery conducted, with the utmost ignominy, to the frontier, handcuffed on the station platform to two really big loutish smelly policemen, and a great black stamp put on his passport saying Expelled. Come on man, make up your mind, what are you having to drink?"

The book that van der Valk had been reading when interrupted was *Brideshead Revisited*. Sometimes comic and sometimes tragic, and there might be passages flawed, or one felt a bit uneasy with, but so damned well written. He'd finished it last night in bed. Arlette too had liked its firm view of what married women can and cannot do. Then at the end there is an epilogue: the soldiers are billeted in this splendid country house, and the adjutant picks up the narrator on the way to the 'anteroom' for a pre-lunch drink like here, and says something like 'You're looking unusually cheerful this morning.' And the bugler is sounding 'Pick 'em up, pick 'em up, hot potatoes'.

Very, very appropriate. But think if a bugle call were suddenly to ring out in this pompous establishment, like that.

All the businessmen would choke and fall off their chairs with the sudden fright.

Pick them up just the same, the hot potatoes. That is your job.

MORE MYSTERIOUS PLEASURES

HAROLD ADAMS
The Carl Wilcox mystery series
MURDER   #501 $3.95
PAINT THE TOWN RED   #601 $3.95
THE MISSING MOON   #602 $3.95
THE NAKED LIAR   #420 $3.95
THE FOURTH WIDOW   #502 $3.50
THE BARBED WIRE NOOSE   #603 $3.95
THE MAN WHO MET THE TRAIN   #801 $3.95

TED ALLBEURY
THE SEEDS OF TREASON   #604 $3.95
THE JUDAS FACTOR   #802 $4.50
THE STALKING ANGEL   #803 $3.95

ERIC AMBLER
HERE LIES: AN AUTOBIOGRAPHY   #701 $8.95

ROBERT BARNARD
A TALENT TO DECEIVE: AN APPRECIATION
OF AGATHA CHRISTIE   #702 $8.95

EARL DERR BIGGERS
The Charlie Chan mystery series
THE HOUSE WITHOUT A KEY   #421 $3.95
THE CHINESE PARROT   #503 $3.95
BEHIND THAT CURTAIN   #504 $3.95
THE BLACK CAMEL   #505 $3.95
CHARLIE CHAN CARRIES ON   #506 $3.95
KEEPER OF THE KEYS   #605 $3.95

JAMES M. CAIN
THE ENCHANTED ISLE   #415 $3.95
CLOUD NINE   #507 $3.95

ROBERT CAMPBELL
IN LA-LA LAND WE TRUST   #508 $3.95

RAYMOND CHANDLER
RAYMOND CHANDLER'S UNKNOWN THRILLER:
   THE SCREENPLAY OF "PLAYBACK"   #703 $9.95

GEORGE C. CHESBRO
The Veil Kendry suspense series
VEIL   #509 $3.95
JUNGLE OF STEEL AND STONE   #606 $3.95

EDWARD CLINE
FIRST PRIZE   #804 $4.95

K.C. CONSTANTINE
The Mario Balzic mystery series
JOEY'S CASE   #805 $4.50

MATTHEW HEALD COOPER
DOG EATS DOG   #607 $4.95

CARROLL JOHN DALY
THE ADVENTURES OF SATAN HALL   #704 $8.95
THE ADVENTURES OF RACE WILLIAMS   #723 $9.95

NORBERT DAVIS
THE ADVENTURES OF MAX LATIN   #705 $8.95

MARK DAWIDZIAK
THE COLUMBO PHILE: A CASEBOOK   #726 $14.95

WILLIAM L. DeANDREA
The Cronus espionage series
SNARK   #510 $3.95
AZRAEL   #608 $4.50
The Matt Cobb mystery series
KILLED IN THE ACT   #511 $3.50
KILLED WITH A PASSION   #512 $3.50
KILLED ON THE ICE   #513 $3.50
KILLED IN PARADISE   #806 $3.95

LEN DEIGHTON
ONLY WHEN I LAUGH   #609 $4.95

AARON ELKINS
The Professor Gideon Oliver mystery series
OLD BONES   #610 $3.95

JAMES ELLROY
THE BLACK DAHLIA   #611 $4.95
THE BIG NOWHERE   #807 $4.95
SUICIDE HILL   #514 $4.50

PAUL ENGLEMAN
The Mark Renzler mystery series
CATCH A FALLEN ANGEL   #515 $3.50
MURDER-IN-LAW   #612 $3.95

LOREN D. ESTLEMAN
The Peter Macklin suspense series
ROSES ARE DEAD   #516 $3.95
ANY MAN'S DEATH   #517 $3.95

ANNE FINE
THE KILLJOY   #613 $3.95

DICK FRANCIS
THE SPORT OF QUEENS   #410 $4.95

JOHN GARDNER
THE GARDEN OF WEAPONS   #103 $4.50

BRIAN GARFIELD
DEATH WISH   #301 $3.95
DEATH SENTENCE   #302 $3.95
TRIPWIRE   #303 $3.95
FEAR IN A HANDFUL OF DUST   #304 $3.95

THOMAS GODFREY, ED.
MURDER FOR CHRISTMAS   #614 $3.95
MURDER FOR CHRISTMAS II   #615 $3.95

JOE GORES
COME MORNING   #518 $3.95

JOSEPH HANSEN
The Dave Brandstetter mystery series
EARLY GRAVES   #643 $3.95
OBEDIENCE   #809 $4.95

NAT HENTOFF
THE MAN FROM INTERNAL AFFAIRS   #409 $3.95

PATRICIA HIGHSMITH
THE ANIMAL-LOVER'S BOOK OF
   BEASTLY MURDER   #706 $8.95
LITTLE TALES OF MISOGYNY   #707 $8.95
SLOWLY, SLOWLY IN THE WIND   #708 $8.95
THE BLACK HOUSE   #724 $9.95

DOUG HORNIG
WATERMAN   #616 $3.95
The Loren Swift mystery series
THE DARK SIDE   #519 $3.95
DEEP DIVE   #810 $4.50

JANE HORNING
THE MYSTERY LOVERS' BOOK
   OF QUOTATIONS   #709 $12.95

PETER ISRAEL
The Charles Camelot mystery series
I'LL CRY WHEN I KILL YOU   #811 $3.95

P.D. JAMES/T.A. CRITCHLEY
THE MAUL AND THE PEAR TREE   #520 $3.95

STUART M. KAMINSKY
The Toby Peters mystery series
HE DONE HER WRONG   #105 $3.95
HIGH MIDNIGHT   #106 $3.95
NEVER CROSS A VAMPIRE   #107 $3.95
BULLET FOR A STAR   #308 $3.95
THE FALA FACTOR   #309 $3.95

JOSEPH KOENIG
FLOATER   #521 $3.50

ELMORE LEONARD
THE HUNTED   #401 $3.95
MR. MAJESTYK   #402 $3.95
THE BIG BOUNCE   #403 $3.95

ELSA LEWIN
I, ANNA   #522 $3.50

PETER LOVESEY
ROUGH CIDER   #617 $3.95
BUTCHERS AND OTHER STORIES OF CRIME   #710 $9.95
BERTIE AND THE TINMAN   #812 $3.95

JOHN LUTZ
SHADOWTOWN   #813 $3.95

ARTHUR LYONS
SATAN WANTS YOU: THE CULT OF
   DEVIL WORSHIP   #814 $4.50
The Jacob Asch mystery series
FAST FADE   #618 $3.95

ED McBAIN
ANOTHER PART OF THE CITY   #524 $3.95
McBAIN'S LADIES: THE WOMEN OF
   THE 87TH PRECINCT   #815 $4.95
The Matthew Hope mystery series
SNOW WHITE AND ROSE RED   #414 $3.95
CINDERELLA   #525 $3.95
PUSS IN BOOTS   #629 $3.95
THE HOUSE THAT JACK BUILT   #816 $3.95

VINCENT McCONNOR
LIMBO   #630 $3.95

GREGORY MCDONALD, ED.
LAST LAUGHS: THE 1986 MYSTERY
   WRITERS OF AMERICA ANTHOLOGY   #711 $8.95

JAMES McLURE
IMAGO   #817 $4.50

CHARLOTTE MacLEOD
The Professor Peter Shandy mystery series
THE CORPSE IN OOZAK'S POND   #627 $3.95
The Sarah Kelling mystery series
THE RECYCLED CITIZEN   #818 $3.95
THE SILVER GHOST   #819 $4.50

WILLIAM MARSHALL
The Yellowthread Street mystery series
YELLOWTHREAD STREET   #619 $3.50
THE HATCHET MAN   #620 $3.50
GELIGNITE   #621 $3.50
THIN AIR   #622 $3.95
THE FAR AWAY MAN   #623 $3.50
ROADSHOW   #624 $3.95
HEAD FIRST   #625 $3.50
FROGMOUTH   #626 $3.50
WAR MACHINE   #820 $3.95
OUT OF NOWHERE   #821 $3.95

THOMAS MAXWELL
KISS ME ONCE   #523 $4.95
THE SABERDENE VARIATIONS   #628 $4.95
KISS ME TWICE   #822 $4.95

RIC MEYERS
MURDER ON THE AIR: TELEVISION'S GREAT
   MYSTERY SERIES   #725 $12.95

MARCIA MULLER
The Sharon McCone mystery series
EYE OF THE STORM .... #823 $3.95

FREDERICK NEBEL
THE ADVENTURES OF CARDIGAN .... #712 $9.95

WILLIAM F. NOLAN
THE BLACK MASK BOYS: MASTERS IN
   THE HARD-BOILED SCHOOL
   OF DETECTIVE FICTION .... #713 $8.95

PETER O'DONNELL
The Modesty Blaise suspense series
DEAD MAN'S HANDLE .... #526 $3.95

SUSAN OLEKSIW
A READER'S GUIDE TO THE CLASSIC
   BRITISH MYSTERY .... #728 $19.95

ELIZABETH PETERS
The Amelia Peabody mystery series
CROCODILE ON THE SANDBANK .... #209 $3.95
THE CURSE OF THE PHARAOHS .... #210 $3.95
The Jacqueline Kirby mystery series
THE SEVENTH SINNER .... #411 $3.95
THE MURDERS OF RICHARD III .... #412 $3.95

ELLIS PETERS
The Brother Cadfael mystery series
THE HERMIT OF EYTON FOREST .... #824 $3.95
THE CONFESSION OF BROTHER HALUIN ... #808 $3.95

ANTHONY PRICE
The Doctor David Audley espionage series
THE LABYRINTH MAKERS .... #404 $3.95
THE ALAMUT AMBUSH .... #405 $3.95
COLONEL BUTLER'S WOLF .... #527 $3.95
OCTOBER MEN .... #529 $3.95
OTHER PATHS TO GLORY .... #530 $3.95
OUR MAN IN CAMELOT .... #631 $3.95
WAR GAME .... #632 $3.95
THE '44 VINTAGE .... #633 $3.95
TOMORROW'S GHOST .... #634 $3.95
SOLDIER NO MORE .... #825 $4.95
THE OLD *VENGEFUL* .... #826 $4.95
GUNNER KELLY .... #827 $4.95
SION CROSSING .... #406 $3.95
HERE BE MONSTERS .... #528 $3.95
FOR THE GOOD OF THE STATE .... #635 $3.95
A NEW KIND OF WAR .... #828 $4.95

BILL PRONZINI
GUN IN CHEEK   #714 $8.95
SON OF GUN IN CHEEK   #715 $9.95

BILL PRONZINI AND JOHN LUTZ
THE EYE   #408 $3.95

ROBERT J. RANDISI, ED.
THE EYES HAVE IT: THE FIRST PRIVATE EYE
  WRITERS OF AMERICA ANTHOLOGY   #716 $8.95
MEAN STREETS: THE SECOND PRIVATE EYE
  WRITERS OF AMERICA ANTHOLOGY   #717 $8.95
AN EYE FOR JUSTICE: THE THIRD PRIVATE EYE
  WRITERS OF AMERICA ANTHOLOGY   #729 $9.95

PATRICK RUELL
RED CHRISTMAS   #531 $3.50
DEATH TAKES THE LOW ROAD   #532 $3.50
DEATH OF A DORMOUSE   #636 $3.95

HANK SEARLS
THE ADVENTURES OF MIKE BLAIR   #718 $8.95

DELL SHANNON
The Lt. Luis Mendoza mystery series
CASE PENDING   #211 $3.95
THE ACE OF SPADES   #212 $3.95
EXTRA KILL   #213 $3.95
KNAVE OF HEARTS   #214 $3.95
DEATH OF A BUSYBODY   #315 $3.95
DOUBLE BLUFF   #316 $3.95
MARK OF MURDER   #417 $3.95
ROOT OF ALL EVIL   #418 $3.95

RALPH B. SIPPER, ED.
ROSS MACDONALD'S INWARD JOURNEY   #719 $8.95

JULIE SMITH
The Paul McDonald mystery series
TRUE-LIFE ADVENTURE   #407 $3.95
HUCKLEBERRY FIEND   #637 $3.95
The Rebecca Schwartz mystery series
TOURIST TRAP   #533 $3.95

ROSS H. SPENCER
THE MISSING BISHOP   #416 $3.50
MONASTERY NIGHTMARE   #534 $3.50

VINCENT STARRETT
THE PRIVATE LIFE OF SHERLOCK HOLMES   #720 $8.95

DAVID STOUT
CAROLINA SKELETONS   #829 $4.95

REX STOUT
UNDER THE ANDES   #419 $3.50

REMAR SUTTON
LONG LINES   #830 $3.95

JULIAN SYMONS
CONAN DOYLE: PORTRAIT OF AN ARTIST   #721 $9.95

ROSS THOMAS
CAST A YELLOW SHADOW   #535 $3.95
THE SINGAPORE WINK   #536 $3.95
THE FOOLS IN TOWN ARE
   ON OUR SIDE   #537 $3.95
CHINAMAN'S CHANCE   #638 $4.50
THE EIGHTH DWARF   #639 $4.50
OUT ON THE RIM   #640 $4.95

JIM THOMPSON
THE KILL-OFF   #538 $3.95
THE NOTHING MAN   #641 $3.95
BAD BOY   #642 $3.95
ROUGHNECK   #643 $3.95
THE GOLDEN GIZMO   #831 $3.95
THE RIP-OFF   #832 $3.95
FIREWORKS: THE LOST WRITINGS   #833 $4.50

COLIN WATSON
SNOBBERY WITH VIOLENCE: CRIME
   STORIES AND THEIR AUDIENCES   #722 $8.95

DONALD E. WESTLAKE
THE BUSY BODY   #541 $3.95
THE SPY IN THE OINTMENT   #542 $3.95
GOD SAVE THE MARK   #543 $3.95
DANCING AZTECS   #834 $4.95
TWO MUCH!   #835 $4.95
HELP I AM BEING HELD PRISONER   #836 $4.50
TRUST ME ON THIS   #837 $4.50
The Dortmunder caper series
THE HOT ROCK   #539 $3.95
BANK SHOT   #540 $3.95
JIMMY THE KID   #838 $3.95
NOBODY'S PERFECT   #839 $3.95

TERI WHITE
TIGHTROPE   #544 $3.95
MAX TRUEBLOOD AND
   THE JERSEY DESPERADO   #644 $3.95
FAULT LINES   #840 $4.50

PHYLLIS A. WHITNEY
THE RED CARNELIAN   #841 $4.50

COLIN WILCOX
The Lt. Frank Hastings mystery series
VICTIMS   #413 $3.95
NIGHT GAMES   #545 $3.95
THE PARIAH   #842 $4.95

DAVID WILLIAMS
The Mark Treasure mystery series
UNHOLY WRIT   #112 $3.95
TREASURE BY DEGREES   #113 $3.95

GAHAN WILSON
EVERYBODY'S FAVORITE DUCK   #843 $4.95

CHRIS WILTZ
The Neal Rafferty mystery series
A DIAMOND BEFORE YOU DIE   #645 $3.95

CORNELL WOOLRICH/LAWRENCE BLOCK
INTO THE NIGHT   #646 $3.95

AVAILABLE AT YOUR BOOKSTORE OR DIRECT FROM THE PUBLISHER

Mysterious Press Mail Order
129 West 56th Street
New York, NY 10019

Please send me the MYSTERIOUS PRESS titles I have circled below:

103 105 106 107 112 113 209 210 211 212 213 214 301 302
303 304 308 309 315 316 401 402 403 404 405 406 407 408
409 410 411 412 413 414 415 416 417 418 419 420 421 501
502 503 504 505 506 507 508 509 510 511 512 513 514 515
516 517 518 519 520 521 522 523 524 525 526 527 528 529
530 531 532 533 534 535 536 537 538 539 540 541 542 543
544 545 601 602 603 604 605 606 607 608 609 610 611 612
613 614 615 616 617 618 619 620 621 622 623 624 625 626
627 628 629 630 631 632 633 634 635 636 637 638 639 640
641 642 643 644 645 646 701 702 703 704 705 706 707 708
709 710 711 712 713 714 715 716 717 718 719 720 721 722
723 724 725 726 727 728 729 801 802 803 804 805 806 807
808 809 810 811 812 813 814 815 816 817 818 819 820 821
822 823 824 825 826 827 828 829 830 831 832 833 834 835
836 837 838 839 840 841 842 843

I am enclosing $_____ (please add $3.00 postage and handling
for the first book, and 50¢ for each additional book). Send check or
money order only—no cash or C.O.D.'s please. Allow at least 4 weeks
for delivery.

_____

_____

_____ STATE _____ ZIP CODE _____
State residents please add appropriate sales tax.